A CIA-manufactured plague, bioengineered to attack coca plants and eliminate cocaine production, mutates. It destroys food plants worldwide. Governments collapse, and billions die. Michael Paine Martin, the son of a mercenary leader, tries to protect himself and his family from the ravages of anarchy.

J. B. Durbin

Time of Anarchy
Book One
World of Paine Series

J. B. Durbin

J. B. Durbin

Copyright ©2019 by John Brian Durbin
ISBN - 9781090597878
Volume One
1st Edition
Printed in the United States of America
Kindle Direct Publishing
Author photograph © Debra Durbin

DEDICATION

I want to say a special thank you to my wife, Debra, for reading, editing and supporting my writing over the past few years. She is my anchor and I couldn't have done this without her help and love.

This book is dedicated to the memory of George Kaniwec, my father-in-law. As he would have wished, proceeds will be donated to help wounded warriors.

Prologue - The Plague

Mitais wiped the sweat from his brow. The tops of the branches were swaying above him, but he couldn't feel the breeze because of the netting. Stretching, he went back to work. Picking a leaf, he stared at it as it crumbled in his hand. He saw the plants were sickly near the end of the carefully planted row.

He called out to the guard. "Santiago, please come look at this."

Santiago un-slung his AK-47 and walked over to the worker.

"What seems to be the problem?"

"These plants, they're all sickly looking. See how the leaves are turning brown? I do not think they're going to live long." the worker held a crumbling leaf in his hand.

"Don't worry, Mitais. Those gringos are at it again. They think they can kill a few plants and claim they are winning the fight against drugs." The guard slipped the sling over his head and took out a small digital camera. As he walked down the row of plants, he snapped photos, planning to have them delivered to his CIA contact as proof that the drug eradication program worked. *This will stop the attacks for a while.* Satisfied that he had enough images, he packed up the camera and walked back to his post.

Matias plucked a few more leaves from the infected plants. They disintegrated in his hands. He took a deep breath, wondering if he should mention it to Santiago. "Jefe, please come back here."

"You son of a donkey." Santiago stomped back to the last row. "This had better be good, or you won't be walking well after I finish with you."

"Please take out the camera again. It looks like these plants have changed."

The guard viewed the pictures and compared them to the infected plants. In the five minutes he had been filming, twelve more had wilted. He could see them changing. It looked as if a giant blowtorch slowly moving down the line of plants at a walking pace, crisped the leaves. He crossed himself and sent the pictures.

*****

Jasper Walkins pulled another can of beans off the shelf in the storage room of the bunker. "We got all we need right here."

"You might want to lay off them beans before you kill us all with your gas." His brother Ritt laughed as he put the AR-15 he'd cleaned back into the rack. "If we run out, this will help us more than anything else."

"Yup. People with guns can do whatever they want to." Jasper heard static coming from the living area. "Dammit, woman. I told you to leave that thing off. I don't care what's going on out there."

"You'd better come listen to this." His wife, Suzanne, turned up the radio. An announcement came over the speakers.

.... a three-megaton device in the Amazon River Valley to stop the spread. The Brazilian Government reported that the blast destroyed the infected areas. They've requested that the United Nations resume humanitarian relief operations .... ssss .... contamination is over. On the domestic front, the White House denied developing the plague ... ssss .... evacuated today .... ssss .... demonstrators set fire to the building .... sssssss.... moved to secret bunkers.... sssssss ....government offices being ransacked.....military unable to cope..... desertion rates... ssssss.

The radio went silent.

"See, I told you the shit would hit the fan someday."

Chapter 1 - Corvis Foundation

The room temperature remained exactly seventy degrees. A faint smell of lavender permeated the air. Gloved staff members wiped condensation from the glasses of ice water until Sarah Moore, Steven Corvis' personal assistant, waved them out. The room slowly filled up with executives.

"The CEO will be here in one minute." Sarah positioned the oversized chair precisely twelve inches from the highly polished table. "Remember not to stand when he arrives."

The buzz of conversation died as the door opened.

Steven entered the room. His short stature bothered him. To even the playing field, he sat in a custom-made chair that made him appear to be larger. It dwarfed the others around the table.

"First order of business." His slightly higher than average voice came out softly, so people would have to strain to hear his words. "How are our food supplies?"

"We have sufficient provisions for our factory personnel and our security forces, thanks to your planning, sir." The logistics manager put the food consumption data on the display. "Current projections show that our supplies will last for another seven months."

Looking up from the information displayed on the screen, Steven ordered, "Cut the rations by one-third. That way we can make it until the government gets their shit together."

"Sir?"

"The New United States accounting office called to ask for our help." Steven Corvis stood on the specially built dais, towering over the assembled executives. "They've wasted billions on research into the feasibility of sending platforms into low-earth orbit." He turned on the projector. An artist's rendition of a plasteel globe, floating in space, appeared. "The plan is simple. Put farming platforms into orbit and ship the food back to earth. In typical bureaucratic fashion, they spent a ton of money and came up with nothing better than improved solid booster rockets. The rockets have insufficient lift. They can't put up platforms of adequate size."

"What does that have to do with us?" Sandra Smolenski, his COO, asked, curious what Steven had planned.

"On my orders, the Corvis Foundation converted all its research efforts from software to propulsion systems three months ago. We came up with a prototype plasma engine." Steven ignored the shocked looks of his staff and brought up the schematic. "The engine is very simple in design and has a high lift capability. It is easy to assemble and operates on liquid hydrogen." The picture changed once more.

The next few slides were of assembly lines in Corvis factories located in Northern California and Oregon. "In exchange for a tax-exempt status for the next 100 years, I offered its design to the New United States Government, which ordered us to begin production."

"That won't help us today," Sandra replied. "We need more than a tax break."

"Give me some credit," Steven gave her an evil smile. "They would have stolen the engine design if I hadn't given it to them. They could have nationalized the foundation." He moved to his chair at the head of the table. "I kept the patents to the software needed to operate the engines. We have the manufacturing plants they need to build the engines. The platforms are under our control."

A new slide appeared. "The government will also provide the food and electricity needed to run this operation. The NUS Army will provide protection for our facilities. Of course, they allowed me to have my personal protection force. We need to recruit more officers. I want to make sure all of us are safe." Steven sat down, leaned back in his chair, and put his feet on the polished tabletop. "Without me, nothing works. I just became the most powerful man in the world."

"Rumor has it that Poland and Ukraine are successfully growing a plague-resistant wheat." The head of R&D cringed at the look he got from his boss, but doggedly continued. "If they can get the crops to grow, we won't need farms in space."

"The plague destroyed almost all the plant life on the surface. If it did it once, it can do it again. The platforms are our insurance policy." Steven glared at the scientist. "There could be another plague."

4

The executives around the table shuddered thinking about another apocalyptic event like the Coca Plague of 2029. The CIA's bacteria stopped the influx of drugs. When it mutated, it attacked green leafy plants. Billions of people died from malnutrition. Plant life slowly began recovering, but people still starved.

"Let's hope that never happens."

"If it does happen, I want to be able to control it. That's what I hired you people to do." Steven looked at his desk top. "Make sure the press talks about the possibility of another plague. The more people fear that it could happen, the more money we'll make." Steven changed the monitor once more. An ugly nanobot appeared on the screen. "Next order of business. I expect a report on the new nanoprobe development within ten days. If you can't get it done, I'll find someone who can."

Everyone at the table squirmed in their seats. The last person who missed a deadline disappeared the compound, never to be seen again.

Steven sneered at the frightened faces. *Weaklings,* he thought. Many of his family members were present, but he didn't trust his sons as far as he could throw them. He looked directly at his eldest. "Peter, stay for a moment. The rest of you can leave, now."

He watched as the others quickly gathered their things and scurried out of the room.

Trying hard not to scowl, Steven looked at the large, paunchy man sitting at the end of the table. His eldest son Peter shifted in his seat. *He's probably got some whore's sweat all over him.* He knew about Peter's debauchery. Steven could use that against him, should the need arise.

"NUS is supposed to protect us, but I don't trust them anymore than I do you." Steven watched as Peter's face turned crimson. "I have spies everywhere, so I know about your 'harem' and the way you steal from the food supplies."

"Father, that's just…"

Cutting his son off with a wave of the hand, Steven snarled, "I don't want you to speak. Just listen. I'm planning to end the ideocracy we've been living under for millennia. The United Nations and the governments of the world are completely useless at maintaining order. I want to create a world government that will be efficient and effective." He paused for a moment. "All it will take is food and money. We've got plenty of capital, and now that we control the space platforms we have food."

"Not to mention the control of software planet-wide."

Crossing his arms, Steven stared at his eldest son for a full minute. He watched Peter squirm in his seat. When he finally spoke, he made his voice as chilling as possible. "Open your mouth one more time without being told to speak and you'll never talk again."

He saw sweat stains appear on his son's shirt.

Peter opened his mouth, then slammed it shut so hard Steven could hear his son's teeth click together.

"Before you interrupted me, I was talking about control." Steven glared at Peter once more, then looked at the notes on his tabletop display. "I want you to take charge of the nanoprobe development project. Build me probes that I can manipulate. Wealthy and powerful people depend on them for everything." He looked down at his son. "You may respond now."

"I'll get right on it." Swallowing twice, Peter licked his lips to keep them from sticking together. "What's my budget?"

"Use whatever you need. Just get it done." Steven glared at Peter, watching him begin to squirm again. "You can divert a portion for your own uses, but if you dip too deep, I'll cut you off."

"I'll get right on it." Peter stood, assuming he'd been dismissed.

"One more thing. We need our own military force. I want you to begin recruiting soldiers. I estimate we'll need at least five thousand to protect ourselves if the NUS fails." Steven looked down at his notepad. It showed a list of mercenary groups that were operating within the old United States. "Find me a good soldier-for-hire. I'll need someone competent to run the military after we gain control. There are lots of opportunists out there, some might be hungry enough to do anything we ask of them." He tapped a few keys and the list appeared on Peter's screen. "Start with this one."

Peter looked down and read, "Kentucky Regulars. Two thousand members. Josh Martin, commander."

Chapter 2 – Spartan Life

The heat and humidity were nearly unbearable. Following his father across the parade ground, seven-year-old Paine gawked at the interior of the starkly furnished barracks. He flinched when the charge-of-quarters yelled, "Attention" at the top of her voice.

"Carry on, I'll be in the area all day." Josh reached behind him, grabbing Paine's arm, and dragging him down the hall to his new home.

The overwhelming loneliness Paine felt threatened to break him down. He knew if he cried, his father would punish him. Taking a deep breath to stop the tears on the verge of breaking out, he thought about what happened to his brother. *Father took Adam away when he turned seven. He sent him to the soldier's barracks. Now it's my turn.*

"I can't have you being coddled by your mother anymore. It is time for you to grow up." Josh pushed Paine into Adam's room. "You'll live with your brother from now on."

Seeing the look in Adam's eyes, Paine felt a sinking feeling in the pit of his stomach.

"You have three minutes to be in the center of the parade ground." Josh stormed out of the room.

"Do whatever he says. He won't kill us," Adam whispered. "I hope."

Standing in the middle of the old Mammoth Cave parking lot, the boys sweated under the hot summer sun.

"Time to get used to obeying orders." Paine could feel his father pacing back and forth behind him and Adam. "Don't move unless I give you permission. Do you understand?"

"Yes, sir," Adam yelled. Paine looked over at his older brother. He didn't see the slap coming from his father.

"What did I tell you?" Josh hissed into Paine's reddening ear. "Don't move."

Light-headed from the slap, Paine could feel himself swaying slightly. He tried to keep still.

"You boys need to be tougher than anyone else in my unit. You represent me. Show no fear, complete every task, and either succeed or die. Do you understand?" Josh stopped pacing.

Feeling his father directly behind him, Paine answered immediately. "Yes, sir."

"Adam, you are my heir. I need you to be as ruthless and merciless as I am. It's the only way you can survive." Paine felt Josh move close to him. "And you are his backup. You're responsible for keeping him safe. As far as I am concerned, boy, you are expendable."

Flushing, Paine stayed quiet. He waited for his father to continue.

"Face each other."

The two youngsters turned inward, only a foot apart.

"Adam, punch him in the gut."

Without hesitation, Adam buried his fist in Paine's midsection. Paine doubled over, trying to catch his breath.

"I told you not to move." Josh grabbed Paine's shoulder and jerked him to a standing position. "Adam. Hit him again."

The second punch took Paine's breath away again, but he stayed upright. Tears were streaming down his face as he fought to maintain control of his shaking body.

"Kick his left shin," Josh yelled.

Adam's boot contacted Paine's shin. He almost lost his balance, but once again stood straight.

"You stop those tears, or so help me, I'll start in on you. You have five minutes to get yourself under control." Josh walked away, yelling over his shoulder. "Don't move until I return. And no talking."

Once Josh went into the main building, Adam opened his mouth slightly and spoke without moving his lips. "I'm sorry, Paine. You know neither one of us has a choice."

Seeing the tears forming in his older brother's eyes, Paine could not keep his own from flowing freely down his face.

"Stop that, right now," Adam whispered. "If Father sees you crying, he'll have me beat you half to death. You know it hurts me to do this, but I'll do whatever he says. If I'm hitting you, he isn't."

Taking a deep breath, Paine eased the lump in his throat. He kept gasping for air as he thought about what Adam had done. The first punch had been nowhere near as hard as it could have been, it just caught him by surprise. He'd been ready for the second one and realized that Adam pulled it just before contact. The kick hurt but could have been much worse.

Knowing his body blocked his father's view of his left hand, Paine used it to sign, *"Thanks, brother. Love you."*

*****

The room went dark at lights out. Paine closed his eyes, wishing his mother could be there to wipe away his tears. Hugging his pillow to his chest, he pictured her face. It helped him drift off to sleep.

Adam pulled the stolen flashlight from between the mattress and the bed slats. He crawled out of bed and climbed into the top bunk. He reached out for his brother's face.

Feeling a hand over his mouth, Paine reacted by trying to slap it away.

"Stop," he heard Adam whisper, "I have something I want to show you."

They slid off the bed. Still groggy and breathing hard from the rush of adrenaline that surged through his body, Paine followed Adam out of the room and down the hallway. The narrow beam projecting from the flashlight Adam carried lit the way. They stopped in front of the laundry room.

Careful to make no noise, Adam slowly pushed open the door. He grabbed Paine's hand and led him through the maze of laundry bins until they reached the back of the room. Widening the beam of his flashlight, Adam pointed it at the non-descript uniforms hanging on the rack.

"Watch what happens when I do this." He pulled a jacket from its hanger and reached inside the right front pocket.

"What the heck just happened?" Paine exclaimed as the jacket seemed to disappear.

"Pretty cool, huh?" Adam touched a hidden switch and the uniform reappeared. "I found this by accident. Father put me on laundry duty for not standing still enough. My sergeant had me washing these clothes. She told me not to lose them, then laughed when I accidentally touched the switch." He grinned. "I thought father would beat me for losing something, but she just chuckled and showed me how to turn it off again."

"What are these things?" Paine reached out to touch the fabric. He felt for the switch, brushing the hard button. To his amazement,

9

the jacket disappeared again. He could feel the jacket in his hand. He glared at Adam, shaking with suppressed laughter.

"These are phototrophic uniforms. They're from before the plague. Something called MIT made them for the old USA Army." Adam took the uniform back and put it on the hanger. "She told me only a handful were ever produced. Father somehow got his hands on them. He gives them to soldiers for special missions."

"Can we use them to hide from father?" Paine hoped he could somehow get away from Josh.

"No, but I do have a better use for them," Adam pulled the smallest jacket from the rack. "I use them to steal food. Follow me."

Silently, they crept down the hall. Paine wondered why they were going back to the barracks room they shared.

Once the door closed, Adam sat on the lower bunk and patted the empty space beside him. "Sit down little brother. What I'm about to tell you has to be kept secret."

Nodding, Paine waited for Adam to continue.

"Once father leaves on a mission, I plan to visit mother. I'm going to get all of us out of here, away from him."

"How are you going to do that?" Paine worried that his brother would be harshly punished if Josh ever found out.

"I can't tell you, not yet. Just let me work out the details with mother. Once we figure out how to escape, we'll let you know." Adam began to tear up. He put his arm around Paine and hugged him. "If Father finds out, he may do something really bad to mother and me. I don't want you to be hurt, too. Can you wait until we finalize our plans?"

Not able to speak, Paine simply nodded his head.

"Good. Now you go to sleep." Adam pulled the jacket on and vanished. Only his head and his feet protruding from the bottom of the jacket were visible. He grinned. "I'm going to go steal us some food."

Paine watched him pulling the hood over his head.

"Stay here. Get some sleep. Father will try to break you down tomorrow, so you need to be well-rested."

The door opened, seemingly by itself. It swung shut, the latch clicking. Paine thought, *Thanks, Brother. Be safe out there.*

Chapter 3 – Ashley's Story

Noise and smells assaulted Ashley's senses as she entered the packed dining facility. Soldiers, fresh from physical fitness training, sat sweating in the warmth of the room. Most of the conversations centered around the rotten food, and how far past the expiration date most of the Meals Ready to Eat (MREs) were. Some of the soldiers tried to negotiate trades for better tasting meals.

Ashley could hear all kinds of offers, from trading duties to sexual favors, being discussed. She blocked it out as she scanned the room. She saw her son in the center of the facility, all alone, eating his meager ration. It broke her heart to see him by himself in the crowded room. No one wanted to be seen with the commander's son. Worse than that, today he turned eleven. Ashley wanted so badly to talk to him.

The sergeant detailed to guard her stood by the mess hall entrance, talking to a young female soldier. Ashley went to the server's station and collected her ration pack. She took a chance and walked over, sitting with her back to her oldest son. Sure the din in the mess hall would cover their conversation, she said, "Same old stuff. MREs for breakfast, lunch, and dinner."

"Why can't we get some decent food?" he replied, not looking up from his package of chicken pesto pasta. "The famine is over. I hear the space platforms are producing food year-round."

"The Ukrainians and Poles are growing wheat again, so you'd think we'd be getting some fresh bread." Ashley put a spoonful of pasty food into her mouth. She spoke with her mouth full. "Keep a look out for that, it may come soon." She hoped Adam would get her message to watch for her guard.

"No bread in sight," Adam replied.

"That's too bad. If we had some good food, maybe we could survive a long trek. Somewhere other than here." Ashley moved her head to the right, looking down the empty table. "I miss you, son. Happy birthday."

"Can't get any bread right now, but it's available. I promise some will come your way soon," she heard Adam say. She felt him brush against her back as he walked away from the table.

Slipping the desert pack off the table top, she put it under her uniform jacket and into her pants. *Soon we'll have enough food to get out of here.* A surge of fear ran through her as her guard appeared. "Time to go back to your room, ma'am."

Making no attempt to look for her son, Ashley got to her feet. "We need to go to the camp office. Colonel Martin wants me to do some research on the cave system. He told me to find a way to move equipment inside to protect it from these incessant attacks we've been getting."

"I didn't get those instructions."

"Then you'll have to explain to him why the information isn't on his desk tomorrow morning," Ashley looked at the sergeant. "I'm sure he'll understand." She could see the fear in the guard's eyes.

"Follow me." The guard led Ashley out of the dining hall. "I'll take you there right now."

*****

Shortly after midnight, a soft tapping at her door woke her. Ashley knew Josh would just open it and barge in like he always did. He did it to disturb her.

Bracing herself for another visit from Josh, Ashley stood next to the door, waiting for something to happen. Light shone in from the hallway as it opened, but no one entered. Putting her foot in the open doorway, she stopped it from closing. Ashley looked up and down the hallway. Empty. Thinking about trying to make an escape attempt, she ripped a piece of cloth from the hem of her nightgown and stuffed it into the bolt hole. The door closed but did not lock.

Wondering what new, torturous trick Josh had planned for her, she sat down on the edge of the bed to think about her next move. She drew in a sharp breath as Adam's head appeared in front of her.

"You scared me near to death," Ashley whispered. "If I hadn't blocked the lock, you'd be stuck here until Josh or one of my guards showed up. The door only opens from the outside."

"It's okay, mother." Adam put his arms around her and hugged her close. "I would have just stayed invisible until someone came to let you out."

"What exactly is going on?" Ashley felt phantom arms around her.

"I borrowed a phototrophic uniform from the laundry. I've been using it to steal food for me and Paine." Adam shoved a napkin wrapped parcel at his mother. "You were right about the food. There's real bread in the dining facility, but it's only for soldiers who go out on missions. I got some for you."

"I don't want it." Tears streamed down Ashley's face as she waved her hand at her son. "You take it. Give it to Michael. He needs it much more than I do."

Adam's laugh surprised her. "Don't worry, mother. I've got plenty for little brother. Besides, he doesn't like to be called Michael anymore. Since father moved him into the barracks, he's going by his middle name." He pressed the stale loaf into her hand. "How did he get that name, anyway?"

Taking a small bite of the first bread she'd had in nine years, Ashley savored the taste for a full minute before answering.

"I named him Michael after my father. Paine is my mother's maiden name. Your father said I could name him anything I wanted." She couldn't keep the bitterness out of her voice. "He told me Michael is just an insurance policy, in case you die."

"How did I get my name?' Adam removed the uniform and sat across from his mother on the bed

"Your father named you. Adam. The first man, and you were the first man born to him." Ashley fought to keep her voice steady. "You had an older sister."

"Had?" Adam looked at the anguish in his mother's eyes.

"Josh, your father, took her from me. He told me she died from SIDS, and that he put her into the compost heap." Sorrow rose up into Ashley's throat. "I'm sure he killed her."

"I can't believe Father could be so evil." Adam took his mother's hand. "Could he?"

"He's done a lot of things you wouldn't believe."

"Like what?"

She saw the inquiring look in Adam's eyes and decided to tell him everything she'd kept hidden all these years.

"I think you're old enough to know the truth. Your father worked with the CIA. They sent him to find me and bring me to justice." She held up her hand as Adam opened his mouth. "We don't have much time, so let me tell the story. If Josh catches you here, with me, you'll end up on the garbage pile, too."

Adam stared at his mother. He waited for her to continue.

"I worked as a junior scientist on the project that developed the plague." Ashley looked directly at her son. "It was only supposed to attack coca plants, the plants they made drugs from. The US government commissioned the project. My team made the breakthrough, we created a bacterium that killed the plants." She clasped her hands together, bringing them up to her mouth. "Then it mutated and started attacking anything with chlorophyll in it. It destroyed most of the world's vegetation, leading to the famine."

"You're responsible for all those deaths?"

"I guess you could say yes. There were plenty of other scientists on the project. My best friend, Amy Pace, and I tried to get them to stop the production of the weapons-grade bacteria. No one would listen. Amy quit before the plague started, but I stayed on, working on a different project, and hoping we were worrying about nothing."

"So how does father come into this?"

"My boss gave Amy some plants from the control group that had been part of the study, as a parting gift. She didn't want them, so she gave them to me." Ashley closed her eyes, seeing the leaves of the plants crumbling before her eyes. "They'd been infected. I knew that once it mutated it wouldn't stop, so I quit my job, sold everything, and tried to run. Your father caught me in New York. While taking me to Langley, I confessed. I told him what I'd done."

"Is that why he formed the Regulars?"

"That happened later. He killed a woman he'd been working with and turned her body in as mine. He slashed my wrist to get blood for the DNA test, cut off my hair and put it in the body bag." She pulled the sleeve of her nightgown up and showed Adam the scar. "The government thought he killed me."

"What's that?" Adam pointed to a small tattoo on her arm.

14

Laughing softly, Ashley remembered the night. Amy had a serious amount to drink. She'd dragged Ashley to a tattoo parlor, insisting they both get matching tattoos.

"Just something I got before Amy left for parts unknown," Ashley ran her fingers over the butterfly. "A remembrance of better times." She shook her head and continued, "Anyway, your father brought me here. When the government collapsed he got the local National Guardsmen to join him. He had his own little army and stolen food supplies. We survived. Millions didn't."

"But I thought you two were married?" Adam looked confused.

"That never happened. He does whatever he wants, including some very bad things." She drew in a shuddering breath. "He's been raping me ever since I've been here. You, your brother and sister were born because he decided he wanted children. I've had no choice." Ashley couldn't stop the tears as she looked at her oldest son. "I'm glad I have you. I love you and Michael with all my heart, but I can't stand the way Josh treats you. We have to get out of here, away from him."

"How? He keeps a watch on you, and he never lets me and Paine out of his sight, except when we're sleeping."

"I have a plan." Ashley pulled the hand-drawn copy of the cave map out from under her bed. "Let me show you."

Chapter 4 – Caught in the Act

The digital clock on the bedside table flashed as the time changed.

"It's 0300. You'd better get back."

"I don't want to go." Adam grabbed his mother's hand. "But I know Father will hurt you if he finds me here."

"You can visit me any time you want." Ashley tapped on the table, a simple code using her name and the boy's names as the password. "Sneak out and come to my room if you're scared or want to talk. Just remember to prop the door open, or we'll be locked inside. Your father will hurt us both if he ever finds out." She had him repeat the code.

"Can I bring Paine next time?" Adam slipped the phototrophic jacket back on. "Maybe he can help us with the plan."

"Planning is going along fine without him. Just keep him well-fed. He needs to be strong for the escape attempt, so don't save any of your own food. I've been keeping small portions of my MREs. I think I'll have enough for the three of us in another six months." A deep aching sensation welled up in Ashley's heart as she thought about her younger son. "The less Michael knows about this, the better for him. If Josh finds out what we have planned…" A shudder ran through her body. "Let's keep him out of it until it's time to run."

"OK, mother, but remember, he wants to be called Paine now." Ashley felt invisible arms encircle her waist one more time, then Adam disappeared. The door opened and closed. Alone once more, Ashley finally allowed herself to cry.

*****

"Sir, there must be a problem with the power cells in the phototrophic uniforms." The tech sweating as he explained what he'd discovered on his last systems check for the special equipment.

Josh stared at the report, then raised his cold eyes to the tech. "You have all the manuals. Do they say anything about intermittent power drain?" He noticed a twitch in the tech's right cheek. *Good. Everyone fears me.*

"We only have the user's manual, sir. It says, 'In the event of power drain, contact depot-level maintenance.' I'm afraid to try to fix the problem."

"Why?" Josh sneered. "Isn't that what I pay you for?"

"Yes, sir." The tech gulped. "But I figured you'd throw me out of the compound if I ruined one of the uniforms. I don't think I can fix it and didn't want to try without your permission."

"You figured right." Leaning back in his chair, Josh let the tech squirm for a few seconds. "You need to find out why the power cells are draining."

"I can put them all on the diagnostic console for forty-eight hours and see if there is any indication of what's causing the drain."

"Why didn't you do that before bothering me with this problem?" Josh began working on the reports littering his desk. After a few moments of silence, he looked up at the trembling tech. "Get out. Give me an answer in three days."

*****

The sound of Adam's stomach growling broke Paine's concentration. He looked up from studying the first aid manual.

"I have to go get us some more food." Adam rubbed his gurgling gut. "Otherwise, if we're attacked, the enemy will be able to locate me by the noise." He threw a light punch at Paine's shoulder.

Deftly avoiding Adam's fist, Paine put the book on the bed. "I'm good. Sergeant Williams taught me how to eat ants. That's all he lived on for six months when the plague first started." Paine made a face and mimicked throwing up at his brother.

"Ants?"

"They're a bit crunchy, but once you roast them, they aren't bad. I usually sprinkle them on my MREs." Paine laughed. "They add a spicy flavor to the most disgusting meal."

"The dreaded cheese and vegetable omelet," Adam shivered. "Good thing the ants are already dead or that crap would kill them." He marveled at how quickly Paine adjusted to the life of a soldier. His little brother spent all his time working on mastering every task the sergeants gave them. "You stay here and study. Maybe someday you'll be as good as me."

He heard a snicker cove from the top bunk. "I'm already better than you are, Adam. I maxed my last test, and you got a slap from the old man."

It wasn't the first time Adam got punished for coming in second place. Paine had been doing better, he tried to be the best in so many ways. Adam never told his brother that he intentionally failed some tasks. He hated watching Paine suffer at the hands of their father.

"Well, you'd better work harder. I've noticed a few things you're doing wrong." Adam smiled at the intense look he got from Paine.

"What things?"

"You think I'm going to tell you? You'll find out tomorrow during testing. I don't want to lose to you again." Adam knew that Paine would stay put, and work on not failing. He didn't want his brother to ask to come along on the food mission. He had to go see his mother.

When he got to the laundry, the uniforms were gone. *Damn. Must be out on a mission. I know Father is off the compound. I need to see Mother.*

Adam checked the hallway before leaving the laundry room. *Empty.* He quickly walked toward Ashley's room. They were so close to determining the route they would take through the caves. Adam had already scouted the first leg of the journey and marked the place where the escape route deviated from the old paths used for cave tours. Thinking about the next step and freedom, he froze as he felt a hard hand grasp his shoulder.

"What are you doing here after light's out?"

Careful not to show any fear, Adam turned and looked down an empty hallway. *Damn! Now I know where the phototrophs are.* Acting surprised, he blurted out, "Is anyone there?"

He flinched as Josh's head appeared, then assumed a rigid position of attention.

"I'll only ask you once more, what are you doing?"

"I'm stealing food for Paine and me, sir." Adam quickly responded. "We don't get enough. I've been raiding the kitchen. It helps make us stronger, sir."

He saw his father's eye narrow. Sweating in the cool hallway, Adam waited for a response. He felt like his father could see into his soul, seeing the escape plans he and his mother were making.

"Stealing food is punishable by death in most places. There are people out there eating rats and bugs to stay alive." Adam felt his father's menacing glare. "Some have even eaten their own young."

"Sir, I only did what I thought you would do."

The chuckle that escaped his father's mouth surprised Adam. "You're right, I would probably do that. But you get no food tonight." Adam let the breath stuck in his throat out slowly. "Or for the next three days. You and the boy are on water rations as of now. Get back to the barracks."

Adam assumed his father returned the salute, even though he couldn't see it. He double-timed down back to his room. Feeling relieved, he thought *three days with no food is a hell of a lot better than being caught in mother's room.*

*****

We are nowhere near the dining facility. Josh thought as he followed his eldest son down the hall. *And he had no food with him.*

Chapter 5 – Telling Lies

Sweat drenched his body as Adam jerked awake. The nightmare ended with him lying in a pool of blood. He vividly remembered his father laughing as he gasped for breath.

"You okay, brother?"

"I'm all right, Paine. Just having a bad dream."

"Afraid of coming in second again?"

"Yeah. Something like that. Go back to sleep."

The alert siren suddenly screamed in the air.

Both boys jumped into action, gearing up and running to the armory. Adam had a sinking feeling in the pit of his stomach. Careful not to let his anguish show, he grabbed an assault rifle. "Hurry up, Paine. We have to get to our defensive positions now."

Not waiting for his brother, he sprinted out the door and ran into the compound. Mortar fire and rockets slammed into the parking lot, sending shrapnel everywhere. He staggered as several fragments struck his vest. The body armor he wore kept him from being wounded.

Feeling rather than seeing movement behind him, he assumed Paine followed him. He hit the ground hard as someone tackled him from behind.

Rolling forward, he kicked at the hands grasping his legs. He knew Paine wouldn't do such a thing. His rifle lay just out of reach, so he pulled his knife, stabbing his attacker in the neck. He felt the warm blood flowing over his hand.

He saw Paine struggling with another marauder. The undersized Paine fought to get free. Adam scrambled over to his rifle. *Please don't let me hit Paine.* He shot the man in the head.

"Come on, Paine. We gotta move." Adam yelled as he got to his feet. He looked back to see his blood-covered brother stagger from a bullet strike. "Paine!" he screamed as he headed back to give first aid.

Two more men jumped on Adam's back. They crashed into the ground. One punched Adam in the side of the head. Stunned, Adam could only look up as one of the attackers pinned him to the ground. The other pointed his rifle at Adam's head.

Automatic rifle fire ripped through the standing man. The second screamed as Paine fired parallel to the ground, into the body of the attacker holding Adam down. He felt the bullets hitting his tactical vest as they passed through the dead man. One passed through a gap in the armor and lodged in his chest.

"I'm hit." Gasping for air, the memory of his nightmare flashed through his brain. "I don't think I'm going to make it."

He watched Paine get to his feet and stagger toward him.

"Shut up and fight. You can't die. If you go, I'll be all alone. You know how I hate being alone." Adam felt his Kevlar vest being ripped off and pressure being applied to the wound in his chest.

Shit, that hurts. Paine looks scared. Adam winced as Paine applied a bandage to his wounds. *Just like we've been trained. He's a good learner.*

"Hang on, brother. You've been through worse than this. We're going to get you to the medics now." Searing agony went through his body as Paine lifted him to his shoulder in a fireman's carry.

His vision blurry, Adam could just make out the door to the aid station. *God help me, I'm going to die.* He felt himself being thrown into the meditube. As the door close, he heard Paine say, "Please live. I can't go on without you."

*****

Ignoring his own wounds, Paine he waited for the machine to finish its work. He watched the telltale lights change from yellow to green. Feeling relieved, he went to the next meditube and got inside.

Paine's wounds were superficial. The machine quickly healed them. Once the doors opened, Paine went to see Adam.

"How's it going, big brother?" Paine laughed at their escape from death. "You look like hell."

"I feel like hell, too." Adam looked around to make sure no one could hear their conversation. "I'll make this quick. I think we were set up."

"What?"

"The guys who attacked you were just trying to disable you. The ones coming at me were going for the kill." Adam looked from side-to-side as if he expected to be attacked again at any moment.

Paine saw fear in his eyes. "You scared?" he whispered.

"I'm scared for you and mother. I got caught sneaking to her room. I made up a story about stealing from the kitchen, but I don't think Father bought it." Paine felt Adam's strong grip on his arm.

"He wouldn't kill his own son," Paine pulled his arm out of Adam's grasp. "No one would do that."

"He killed our sister. Mother told me that, and I believe her. He's going to kill me, I feel it." The look on Adam's face burned into Paine's mind. "Mother and I have a plan to escape. We're going to go during a major attack. She's ready to take us out of here. Get us away from him."

"Why haven't you told me this before?" Paine stared at his brother, wondering if he should be angry.

"If father knew both of us were in on this, we'd be dead now. Those guys could have killed you, but they didn't. Now you're the heir apparent." Adam dropped his chin to his chest. "You have to act like nothing is wrong. You were just doing what you were taught when you saved me." Paine felt the pressure on his arm again. "When I'm gone, you have to act like you don't care. Pretend you're happy. You're going to be his heir."

"He'll never hurt you. You'll be fine." Paine gripped his brother's arms with both hands. "So long as I'm with you, I'll keep you safe. That's what father ordered me to do, back when he first paired us up."

"Promise you'll keep mother safe when I'm gone." The hug from Adam almost crushed his chest. Paine heard him whisper, "Thanks for saving my life, this time. I love you, brother."

Chapter 6 – Fratricide

"Incompetent fools." Josh slammed his fist down on the desktop. The pain brought his anger under control. The men he'd contracted to eliminate Adam had failed miserably. Something had to be done quickly, and with discretion. He needed someone Adam wouldn't suspect to do the job. He brought up a list of Martin family members who had signed on with the Regulars when Josh established the mercenary group. They feared Josh, but all of them liked Adam.

He'd have to convince one of them to do his dirty work. Josh looked over the manning roster to see who would have the most to lose for not following orders. The knock at his office door irritated him.

"Sir, Albert Martin is here to see you." His adjutant, Rachel Miller, reacted to his glare by withdrawing from the doorway.

"Send him in," Josh commanded.

Albert had been a holdout. As a family member, he could live in the compound, but he never joined the force.

Josh watched as his disheveled nephew slunk into the office. He noticed blood under Albert's fingernails. Sitting back in his chair, he sneered, "What do you want?"

"I need to be gone, far from here." Albert glanced around the room, obviously agitated.

"You need to tell me why, or I will call my guards and have them extract the truth."

"I have a problem."

Josh made a come-on gesture with his hands.

"My cousin, our cousin, Mirabelle, she comes over to help Ma with Big Al, ever since he had that stroke. She been flitting around the house for a long time, always wearing those tight shirts and short skirts, running around barefoot. Well, yesterday, she came over to me and bent over right in front of my face while I'm sitting there on the couch not doing nothing. She just teased with me, but I wanted to teach her a lesson."

"What did you do?"

"When she went to go home, I followed her and caught up with her near the creek behind the house. I tried to hug her, but she slapped me."

"You've been slapped before."

"Not by her!" Albert looked down at his feet. "I can't stand being slapped. I might have punched her a little too hard, and she fell in the creek. I guess I just went mad. I could see nothing but red. When I finally come to my senses, she stood there, naked and bleeding. I had blood all over me, too. I don't know what happened."

"Then what?"

"She finally stopped crying and tried to gather her clothes, so she could get dressed. She said 'Wait 'till I tell my Daddy and brothers. They will be coming after you. They're going to kill you.' I couldn't let that happen." Albert looked at his bloody nails then stared into Josh's cold eyes.

Josh could see the emptiness, the lack of emotion in his nephew's eyes.

"When she climbed the bank of the creek, she slipped and fell into the water." Albert took a deep breath. "I hit her with a rock. I held her down until she quit moving."

Josh didn't care about the death of Mirabelle. Because of her, he had the perfect tool for his plan. "All right, I will have my personal guards take care of the body. You can join the Regulars, and I will make sure none of this gets out. There are a group of squatters over in Cave City we can blame. I want you to be in the unit that goes after them. Say you joined the Regulars to avenge Mirabelle's death. Everyone knows how fond you were of our dear, dead cousin."

Wincing at the last comment, Albert mumbled his thanks and stood up to leave.

"Sit back down, I am not through with you yet."

Frightened, Albert plopped back into his seat.

"You will do whatever I want you to, no matter the consequences, no matter the circumstances. Fail me and I tell our cousins what happened. Do you understand?" Josh's voice came out cold and hard.

"Of course, I will. I promise." Albert sat still, not sure if he could leave.

"Good, because I have a mission for you right now. It involves my son Adam." Josh paused for effect. "Adam is planning to escape with Ashley. They have been secretly stockpiling food for more than a month. I tried to have this cleaned up before now, but his brother is always there, watching his back. I had it set up so Adam would die in the last attack, but the boy shot the assassin before he could get the job done. In all the confusion, I convinced him that he had been the one who shot Adam. I think I can still control the boy. Ashley hasn't infected his thinking, yet. Adam is beyond hope. I separated them. I've assigned the boy to a different squad."

"What do you want me to do?"

"I want you to partner with Adam. When the time is right, do what you did to Mirabelle. Dealing with family members is the only thing you seem to be good at." Josh turned back to his paperwork.

"You want me to kill him?"

Glaring at Albert, Josh responded in a cold, flat tone. "Make sure it's lethal. Meditube technology is too good. It would be very bad for you if Adam survives."

"What about Ashley?"

"Not yet. If it comes to that, I'll let you have Ashley. She won't suspect anything. I plan on getting roaring drunk after the death to convince her that I grieve our loss, too."

Josh took out his personal communication device. "You can leave now, Private Martin." As the door closed, he called the commander of the Brandenburg Militia. "Mica, Josh Martin. I have a proposition for you. I'll make it worth your while."

Chapter 7 – Death Comes Knocking

Slipping a note to his brother proved harder to accomplish than Adam expected. Josh made sure they were separated by assigning them to different units. Paine's unit had responsibility for the north side of the perimeter, Adam's unit guarded the southeast side. They had different mess hall schedules, too.

He found it difficult to hide the disdain felt for his teammate. Adam knew Albert as a flake, someone who joined the Regulars last week. In a short time, he demonstrated that he did nothing but goof-off and shirk every duty possible.

Older that Adam, Albert thought he could tell him what to do.

"We need to make sure our chicken plates are in the combat vests. The last attack, some of the guys got wounded by shrapnel." Albert tapped at Adams's vest, hitting the center to make sure the insert had been properly installed. "Your plate sounds a little funny. Did you take a hit from something?"

"Keep your hands off my gear, or so help me, I'll beat you to a pulp." Adam jerked the vest out of Albert's hand. "There's nothing wrong with my equipment."

"Hey, I'm here to have your back," Albert protested. He held his hands up in surrender. "I don't want no trouble. Just tryin' to help."

"If you really want to help, stay out of my way." Adam left, slamming the door behind him.

Albert saw his chance and quickly removed the plate, replacing it with a different one.

The other soldiers left Adam alone as he stormed down the hall with a scowl on his face. He went outside, pacing the parking lot. He hoped Paine would see him and come outside. His prayers were answered a few minutes later.

Throwing his hands in the air, Adam began exercising. A passing sergeant looked at him quizzically. "I just need to release some steam." Sweating profusely in the August heat, he completed his side-straddle hops and dropped to the pushup position. He worked his arms until he collapsed, then wiped his face with a towel, throwing it into a nearby trash barrel.

He used sign language to spell out *note* as he walked past his little brother.

Hoping Paine would be smart enough not to pick it up anytime soon, he marched back to his room.

*****

The attack on Adam's side of the perimeter wound down to a few scattered shots. He ran forward, searching for any breach in the defenses. He felt like someone punched him in the back.

Albert fired six rounds through the plaster plate he'd put into Adam's vest. They punched through the flimsy combat vest and into his chest.

Rolling over, Adam looked up at his cousin and tried to talk. Then his nightmare reappeared. He saw his father appear above him.

"It's no use, Adam. You shouldn't have gone to see your mother. I can't trust you anymore." Josh stood over his son's bleeding body. He waited, making sure Adam drew his last breath. Then he cried out for a medic.

"There's nothing I can do. Sorry, but your son is dead." The soldier looked up at Josh. "I'll take the body to the casualty collection point."

Josh watched dispassionately as the medic carried Adam away.

"You second son is on the other side of the compound." Albert voice quivered in anticipation as he whispered. "Do you want me to take him out, too?"

The look Josh gave to his nephew made him draw back in fear. "Not yet. I think I can still convert him to my way of thinking. If I can't, I'll let you know."

*****

Paine noticed the blue bandanas the attackers were wearing. "These guys are allies. There from the Brandenburg Militia. Why would they be attacking us?"

"I don't know or care. There coming at us. We've got to stop them." Wesley Miner, his new partner, shot one of the attackers, then flinched as a grenade went off in front of the position. "Shit, Paine, I've been hit."

Paine gritted his teeth as he fought to keep his own fear and agony in check. "Yeah, shit. Me, too. You got to suck it up and keep fighting, no matter what. We can't let these guys break through the perimeter." Slapping a fresh magazine into his rifle, Paine took aim at a group of attackers. "Here they come again. Get ready."

The weapon bucked against his shoulder as Paine took down three attackers. The other two dove for cover. "I'll keep them pinned down, you go left. Flank them. When they break cover, I'll be ready." He fired three-round bursts at the ditch the men were lying in, keeping them from advancing.

Trying to watch the enemy and Wesley, Paine hoped his teammate would get there soon. He'd be out of ammunition soon.

The attackers jumped up when Wesley fired from their left. Paine mowed them down. He yelled, "Come on back, Wes. I'll keep you covered." Paine swept his weapon back and forth, searching for more targets. There were none.

He felt a body fall against him. Wesley had a serious wound, blood seeping from a hole in his tactical vest. Without taking his eyes from the avenue of approach the enemy had been using, Paine ripped open a Quickheal packet and handed it to his teammate. "Put this on, before you bleed to death."

"I...don't know...if" Wesley passed out from loss of blood.

The headset crackled. "Cease fire. All clear. Commanders, reestablish the perimeter. Consolidate ammo and personnel. Prepare SITREP. Send wounded to the aid station."

"I have two wounded at position three bravo," Paine called out to his squad leader.

"Hold in place until further orders," he heard his sergeant yell. "Go to the medics once your relief arrives."

Slapping Wesley with his hand, Paine yelled, "Stay with me, Wes. You'll be in the 'tube soon. Come on, look at me."

"We got this, Paine," he heard a voice from behind. "You guys get going."

Ignoring the wound in his left arm, Paine picked up Wesley and carried him to the aid station. He passed a litter team as they carried Adam's body out. Stopping in his tracks, he felt his heart would burst as he watched his brother being placed in the row of KIAs. Fighting back tears, he carried Wesley into the lighted room and put him on the floor next to an occupied meditube. He felt a slap as a tech put a Quickheal patch on his own wounded arm.

"Just a scratch," Paine waived off the medic looking for more injuries.

Turning his attention to Wesley, the medic took his pulse. Standing up, he brushed off his hands. "Sorry, Paine. Looks like you lost your partner."

"You lost your brother, too." Josh walked up right behind Paine.

Choking down his anger, he calmly replied, "Maybe if you'd kept us together, he'd still be alive."

"How can you say that, given your new bunk mate is dead?"

"I just know," Paine turned to stare at his father, willing himself to show no emotion. He almost broke, but maintained control. "But there's nothing I can do about that now. He's dead. I'm alive. I guess that makes me your heir, unless you want me dead, too." He handed his rifle to his father.

Paine could feel his father's eyes boring into his very soul. He did his best to look stoic.

He watched as his father pulled the bolt back part way, to see if the weapon had a round in the chamber. Paine didn't flinch as the bolt slammed forward.

"You are my only surviving son. You're going to take my place someday. I need you to be the toughest, best soldier in the unit." Josh paused. "I don't want you dead. I want you to be like me." He handed the assault weapon back to Paine.

"Yes, sir. I'll do my best." Paine thought about shooting his father but knew that would lead to his own death. It would not bring back his brother. He saluted his father, did an about face and walked out of the aid station.

Once he entered the shadows, Paine ran to the garbage can and kicked it over, He lay down behind it, away from the direction of the aid station. Using his flashlight, he searched the rubbish for Adam's towel. Tears streamed down his face as he read the message.

Escape planned for next attack closest to new moon. Darkness will help cover - We'll make it. Meet us at Mom's room. Good luck, P – ILY Bro

Chapter 8 - Charades

Followed by his bodyguards, Josh staggered into his apartment and sat down at the dinner table. "You make me sick."

Looking up from the stove, Ashley gripped the handle of the frying pan tightly. She imagined it flying into Josh's head.

The guards tried to blend into the background, not wanting to be noticed by their drunken commander.

"I can't even look at you, you miserable piece of filth." He started in on Ashley, "You're constantly trying to turn my sons against me. It won't work, you know." He sat down at the table with a thump. "I know how to get them to do my bidding."

Ashley knew that when Josh drank, he could be even more abusive. She kept her mouth shut and placed the food in front of him.

"This is cold." Josh yelled. He swept the plate off the table. "Clean up this mess." He sat there, glaring at Ashley as she went over to pick up the broken dish and clean the food off the floor.

Dumping the dish shards into the trash can, Ashley turned to Josh. "What is the matter with you?"

His next words came out slow and slightly slurred. "I'll kill you on the spot if you say another word."

Something bad had happened but Ashley didn't dare ask. Josh must have lost a big contract or a lot of soldiers. She prepared herself for the usual beating. Instead, Josh drank himself into a stupor and passed out in the kitchen chair. As she cleared the table, she looked longingly at the knife at Josh's plate, and then decided not to act. His guards were too good. They would stop her before she could finish Josh off. *It's not the right time, if they kill me, the boys won't be able to escape.* After finishing the dishes, her guard escorted Ashley back to her room.

As the door closed behind Ashley, Josh sat up. He stared at the guards for a full minute before yelling, "Get out of here." Once the door closed, he poured the bottle of colored water flavored with a little bourbon down the sink. The message he'd received from the Corvis Foundation yesterday preyed on his mind. *This could be the big break I've been waiting for.* He straightened his uniform and walked out into the night.

*****

Shortly after she went to bed, a soft tapping came from the door. Ashley recognized the code she'd taught Adam a few years before.

Her youngest son almost knocked her over. He buried his head in her nightgown, silent sobs wracking his body. Ashley looked down the empty hallway, and held him close.

"What's wrong, Michael?" She could feel his body shaking with silent sobs.

"Adam got shot during the last attack." He looked up at his mother, tears in his eyes. "He's dead. They didn't get him to the meditube in time."

After making sure the door would stay open, Ashley pulled her son into the room. They whispered until the first rays of light appeared on the horizon. Her heart ached as she watched him creep back to his room. The door locked as it swung shut.

The next day, at three o'clock in the morning, the key turned in the lock. She had been waiting for this, fearfully, ever since Adam had been killed. She kept her back to the door as footsteps approached her bed, then his weight made the bed sag. She knew what he wanted. Powerless to resist, she kept her eyes closed and thought about how much she hated sex.

He roughly pushed her onto her back and pulled up her nightgown. Pinning her arms to the bed, he forced himself on her. Josh mechanically finished with a barely audible grunt.

She heard him whisper in her ear, "I'll be back. You'd better get pregnant again soon. And it better be another boy, or it will end up in the compost heap, just like the first one." He pushed himself off her, went to the door. "I still have your computer files and copies of your DNA in a safe place. I'll turn them and you over to the NUS authorities if you don't do what I want." He locked the door behind him.

"Please God, get us out of here." Ashley turned her face to the wall. She cried herself to sleep.

Chapter 9 - Escape

The blaring siren caused Ashley to bolt up in bed. She looked at the clock. Had the attack come a half an hour earlier, Josh would still be in the room. Ashley ran to the door and found it locked as usual. Gathering her supplies from their hiding places around the room, she put them in a backpack and slid it under the bed.

"He will be here, I know it. Just like we planned." She waited impatiently for the knock. When it came, Ashley responded with the proper code. Paine opened the door.

"Come on Mom, we have to hurry." Paine grabbed his mother's hand. He dragged her down the darkened hall to his room.

Ashley whispered, "Has your father been here yet?"

Just then, footsteps pounded down the hallway. Paine pushed his mother onto the floor. He jerked the covers off his bed. Jumping on top of the pile, he whispered, "Stay down and lie still."

"Boy, what the hell is the matter with you?" His father entered already dressed in fatigues, carrying an infantry assault weapon.

Paine pulled himself up off the floor. "I got tangled up in my covers and fell down, sir. I'll be ready in twenty seconds."

Josh glared at him for a second then threw the rifle at his son, who barely caught it in time. "Stop being so damned clumsy. Get to your post now." He stood in the doorway, waiting impatiently.

Leaning the weapon on the bed frame, Paine pulled a set of camouflaged coveralls from his closet and slipped into them. He quickly zipped them. He slipped his combat vest over his head, struggling to get it in place.

Automatic rifle fire erupted outside. Josh ran out the door, yelling, "Hurry up. If you don't get moving, so help me…"

He waited until Josh left the room. "Mom, there's a pistol under the mattress, with a hundred rounds of ammunition. The key to your room is there, too. Get them and get out. I know you'll come back for me, some day. Don't worry, I'll be fine until then." Paine picked up the weapon, went down the hall and ran into the compound. If he didn't show up at his assigned post, his father would send someone to find him. He didn't want to see his mother beaten again, or worse.

The firefight raged on. Ashley ran back to her room. The attackers must have hit the generator because the lights went out. She found her way in the brief flashes provided by the constant gunfire and explosions.

Slipping into her room, Ashley grabbed the backpack she'd so carefully packed and slipped the pistol inside. Leaving the entryway during a lull in the fire, she sprinted to the mouth of the cave. The guards waved her in, they had enough to worry about. Another volley of mortar rounds landed in the compound. They had orders to keep Mrs. Martin in her building, but where could she go?

Ashley moved into the dark depths of the cave. She had been planning this for a long time. Ever since Adam began visiting her, she had rehearsed her actions in her mind's eye. She stopped at the rendezvous point hoping Michael would join her. She wanted both of her sons to escape with her but realized that could not happen. The death of her oldest son had spurred her to attempt the escape.

Checking her watch, she realized she had to move, or risk being captured. She ached inside thinking about leaving Michael with Josh. She experienced a bittersweet moment, remembering how Adam kept reminding her, "He goes by his middle name now."

Brushing the tears from her eyes, she pulled a headlamp out of her backpack and switched it on. She studied the map of the caves she'd copied while doing research in one of the Park Service buildings. Ashley ran headlong into the darkness.

The cave passageways became narrow as she headed down into the earth. She walked, crawled, and climbed for three days, worming her way deeper and farther away from her captivity. To conserve the batteries, Ashley turned off the lamp while she slept. When she opened her eyes, she couldn't see her fingers in front of her face. Ashley thought this must be what it's like to be blind. When the headlamp switched on, her eyes ached from the brilliant light. Her other senses became much more acute. She heard drops falling into water long before she came to the underground river.

She looked at the map and couldn't identify her position. *I'm lost and I'm going to die without being able to help my son.* Ashley sat down and tried to retrace her route on the map. She'd followed her planned route exactly. By her calculations, she had less than a few hundred feet before she reached an exit. The river presented a major obstacle. She couldn't get out of the cave. The water flowing water blocked her route.

I'm trapped.

There must have been a storm above ground because the water flowed into the cavern at a rapid pace. The passage she'd come through disappeared as the level rose.

I can't stay here. I'll drown.

Firmly securing the lamp to her helmet, she put her last three MRE pouches in the cargo pockets of her fatigues. Taking off the backpack and tethering it to her left leg, she stepped into the swiftly flowing water.

The current pulled her feet from under her. She barely caught her breath before her head went under. Swept along by the current, she bumped against the walls of the cave. She momentarily lost her breath as she slammed against a rock. Then the river dumped her into a large chamber.

Ashley gasped for air as her head broke the surface. The wildly swinging head lamp allowed her to see the river emptying out of the chamber a few feet ahead. She took another deep breath and prepared for the worst.

Lights flashed in front of her eyes, and she felt as if her lungs would burst. She suddenly realized the lights were real. She kicked and clawed her way to the surface and gulped in sweet, fresh air. She could see sunlight coming into the cave from her left, so she swam in that direction.

The current tugged at her, sweeping her along as the river continued its journey. With one final burst of energy, she pulled herself up onto a rock shelf. Huddling there, she prayed that the water wouldn't rise any more. The water-filled backpack threatened to drag her back into the river. She needed every bit of her remaining strength to pull it out of the current.

Gradually, the water level in the cave dropped.

Free for the first time in thirteen years, Ashley sat on the shelf, sobbing for her dead children and the child she left behind. She wiped her eyes on her soaked jacket sleeve. Taking a deep breath, she moved toward the light.

Chapter 10 – Chance Meeting

The sun beat down on the deserted stretch of highway. Ashley collapsed onto her backpack. She sat down in the middle of the old road that ran between Louisville and Nashville. Her MREs ran out two days before. She hadn't seen a soul in her three days on the road. She feared that Josh would find her and take her back to the camp. *Maybe he'll be more humane and just kill me and leave my body for the carrion-eaters.*

Knowing Josh as she did, she had little hope of a quick end. If he let her live, he would punish her for years over this escape. She shook the canteen. *Empty.* She needed to find water soon or Josh would be the least of her worries.

A soft humming came from the south, getting closer to her position. It didn't sound loud enough to be a vehicle. Too tired and hungry to care anymore, she pulled the pistol out of the backpack.

Paine had given her an old weapon, made by Colt. Heavy, solid, with a seven-round magazine of .45 caliber bullets, she liked the way it felt in her hands.

She thought about putting it to her head and ending it all. She didn't have the energy. Setting the gun into her lap, she buried her head in her hands and waited for the worst.

*****

William Whippette pulled his truck up to the Army hummer parked in the middle of the old highway. His wife Betty opened her mouth to ask a question and William waved her into silence. William rolled down his window and called out, "What seems to be the problem, Captain Cooley?"

The balding NUS Army captain looked up from his console with fear and confusion in his eyes. "There may be a trap ahead. There's a woman in the road, sitting on a backpack. She could have a bomb, or it might be a trap. I'm going to take a closer look, so just hold your horses."

Captain Cooley manipulated the controls of the small mini-drone and watched the monitor as the camera zoomed in on the figure in the road.

"She looks harmless enough," William mused, "More lost than a threat."

"She has a gun," Captain Cooley replied. "She may be waiting to ambush us."

"One pistol against a company of infantry?" William glared at the unit commander. "You've got to be kidding me."

As the drone made a wide sweep around the area, it picked up figures stealthily approaching the woman on the roadway. There were at least fifteen armed men moving toward the road bed, picking their way through the brush and fallen trees on the west side of the road.

Cooley put the remote platform on hover and turned to the Whippettes. "There's nothing we can do. My orders are to avoid contact with the indigenous people in this area. Intelligence reports indicate there are several contracted mercenary forces operating in this region, and headquarters does not want any fighting that might cause a future agreement to be placed in jeopardy."

"You mean you are going to let that woman die, or worse?" Visibly upset, William protested. "I thought we were here on a humanitarian mission."

"My orders, sir, are to protect you. I cannot do more than that."

"Then get ready to protect me." William gunned the engine and sped down the road. The captain shouted for him to stop, then got on the radio to alert the company to get ready to engage an enemy force about to attack the Whippettes' vehicle. The soldiers dismounted and spread out. They waited for orders as Captain Cooley looked at the monitor to determine his best possible plan of action.

Ashley looked up at the truck speeding up the road. Determined not to be taken alive, she picked up the pistol in her lap, gently stroking the barrel. The driver slammed on his brakes right in front of her as Ashley placed the weapon under her chin.

The door opened. A pleasant-looking man stepped out. He walked up to Ashley with arms widespread, revealing he had no weapon. The blond woman in the truck stepped out of the passenger's side, also empty-handed.

"Good morning. I believe we will be having visitors in a few moments, some of whom may try to kill us and hopefully some who will try to keep us from being buried beside this road. I suggest you get into the truck bed and hunker down." William turned to his wife. "Betty, please get into the truck bed with her while I try to fight off the approaching hordes." He dropped to his knee. Taking a pistol out of his jacket, he waved the muzzle toward where he thought the approaching men would appear.

Ashley, momentarily stunned, picked up her Colt .45. Shaking off her exhaustion, she sprang into action. She moved into the ditch ten feet away from William. "Thanks for the warning, but I can take care of myself. If I were you, I would get behind some cover, so you don't make such a large target."

William never looked in her direction. "William Whippette. The beautiful woman who also refuses to listen to me is my wife, Betty." Betty pulled a sawed-off shotgun out of the truck and moved to a covered spot, fifteen feet on the other side. "Don't let the scatter gun fool you. She can hit what she aims at most of the time." Betty stuck her tongue out and made a rude gesture with one hand. "I'm sure she's pleased to meet you, but I think we need to be quiet for a while. I hear footsteps."

They waited for what seemed like an eternity. Suddenly, a shot rang out, and a bullet passed between Ashley and William. William quickly dove into the ditch and looked over at Ashley. The "I told you so," look he thought he would get didn't appear. Ashley focused on looking for the shooter. No one moved, they just clutched their weapons a little tighter and searched for targets.

An amplified voice boomed out from the roadside. "You guys need to give up. We have you outnumbered six to one. Surrender and we'll let you live."

As one, Ashley, William and Betty fired toward the sound of the voice. They were rewarded with screams that gradually faded away.

"I guess we decided our own fate. These guys won't walk away from us, and my thought is that we will have about ten minutes while they figure out the best way to attack." Ashley looked at the pistol in her hand. She took out the three spare magazines and opened the full box of rounds so she could load quickly.

"Betty, I hope your husband would rather see you die quickly rather than be taken prisoner. I plan to keep one round for myself.

If the attackers are who I think they are, death is preferable to being captured." Ashley looked at the woman. "If I get wounded or knocked out, one of you please, please kill me."

William stared at Ashley for a moment and shook his head. "I think they may be in for a surprise. There are about a hundred soldiers from the New United States Army half a mile from here. If the captain in charge of them ever gets his head out of his rear end, he'll come charging to our rescue." Trying not to look worried, William grinned. "I just hope he decides that his orders not to interfere with the locals need to be disobeyed as soon as possible."

The sweat ran down her back in the hot sun. Ashley shivered as she thought about what she'd told them to do. She steeled herself to the fact that the last shot she fired would be into her own brain. She no longer feared death. To her disappointment, she would never see her son again.

"Well, while we're waiting, we might as well get acquainted. Like I told you, my name is William Whippette. I'm a doctor and my wife, Betty, is a research scientist. We're on our way to Lexington. I'm going to help stop the cholera epidemic there. Betty is going to study the resurgence of bluegrass in that area. We hope it'll provide us some clues on how to get hay to grow in other areas of Kentucky." He sounded as if he were lecturing to a group of college students. "This part of the state used to produce lot of beef. If the grasses start growing again, we can restore the cattle industry here."

"I used to work in research myself," Ashley heard herself say. Then she thought, *"What have I done?"* Trying to cover her admission, she said, "My parents were in retail sales. I just had to try something different."

In a soft voice that Ashley could barely hear, Betty said, "I followed in my father's footsteps."

Ashley looked at the woman hiding underneath the truck. Something gnawed at her memory that she couldn't put her finger on. She thought Betty looked vaguely familiar.

Something thumped near her leg. Ashley almost jumped up screaming a warning. Her training and determination not to be taken prisoner froze her in place. She calmly whispered, "I think someone threw a grenade near me. Cover your heads."

"Sorry, Ashley, it's a water bottle for you," Betty softly chuckled. "You look like you could use a drink."

When Ashley turned to pick up the water bottle, she looked at Betty to offer her thanks. She froze. "You said your father is a research scientist. What's his field?"

"Um, he just worked on some stuff he never talked about," Betty answered awkwardly. "He's dead now." She looked over at William for support.

"I knew him for a short while. He worked doing a computer analysis on emissions for an engine manufacturer. He didn't talk much about it."

Liar, Ashley thought. She stared at the blond woman's profile. "Oh, my God," she blurted out. "I've seen your picture before. You're Betty Amatto." Ashley could see the shock on Betty's face. "I recognized you from the picture of you and your Dad. He kept it on his desk."

"Yes, he's my father." Betty whispered once more. "Now two people in the world know where I come from, you and my husband. I've been hiding the truth from everyone else."

Ashley looked to her front, searching for a target. She took a deep breath. "Your father was a brave man and a great scientist. I worked with him on the project. I promise you he did everything he could to keep the plague from being used."

They both looked at her in wonder.

"I worked for your father on the Plague Project. He hired me right out of school. I watched the mobs attacking him. It was hard to see him die." Ashley sighed. "I'm Ashley Miller, and I am the one who developed the plague."

"My father didn't deserve to go that way." Betty kept scanning the road as she told the story.

"On night, he came home early. He never came home early before, so I wasn't expecting him. He stood in the hallway, just staring at me. He looked tired. When I asked him if everything was okay, he said, 'I've been trying to find a way to stop the blight that's infecting plants in South America. It's getting worse." She paused for a moment, took a deep breath, and continued.

"He tried to explain it all to me. 'Ever since your mother died, I haven't spent enough time with you. I immersed myself in my work and tried to block out the pain of losing her, forgetting I still had you. I am sorry for that.' He started to tremble, saying, 'Bad times are coming because I did a terrible thing. People will be coming after me. I want to protect you from my fate.' He stood up as the sound of an approaching car startled him. When a black sedan pulled into the driveway, a young man stepped out of the car."

"He handed me a bank book for a Swiss account. Then he pushed me toward the door, telling me, 'Leave before it's too late.' He grabbed me harder than he ever did before and yelled at me, 'The plague will kill everything. I created it and set it loose on the world.' Then he calmed down and pointed to the sedan. 'I have a trusted friend who will help you get out of the country to somewhere I hope is safe. His name is William. He's a very nice young man. He's waiting outside, and I want you to go with him now, before it's too late.'

"I wanted to stay, to help him. He just looked at me. 'I can't stop it. Nobody can. I tried, it's no use.' He made me swear on my mother's grave that I would never talk about this again." Betty had tears rolling down her cheeks as she finished her story.

William looked at her and dried the single tear that rolled down his left cheek. "I waited outside for Betty. We fled the country and ended up in Montreal. When the news came out that the government had caused the plague and the rioting started, we were sitting in a bar watching it on television. We watched as the mob pulled him from the airplane. I tried to shield her eyes, but Betty insisted on watching him being torn to bits by the crowd. We both cried that night. Then I asked her to be my wife, so I could keep her safe."

A bullet kicked up dirt five feet from where William lay. "Looks like I failed in my mission this time. I think they are coming from my side."

They were surprised by the final rush of the marauders coming into their tiny perimeter. A small, ferret-like man kicked William in the side of the head, knocking him unconscious.

Betty screamed. She ran to William. Two men converged on her, knocking her off her feet. They pinned her to the ground, ripping at her clothing while fighting with each other. Betty got her hand free and grabbed for her dropped shotgun. A third man clubbed her down. Then he beat both of Betty's attackers senseless.

"You can have your fun later, you idiots. Let's find out who they are and if they're worth anything first."

Ashley got off two shots. The first hitting an attacker in the chest. She turned the gun on herself. As she pulled the trigger, someone stuck her from behind, knocking her aim off. The bullet grazed her temple and took off the top of her left ear.

The attackers wrestled the stunned woman to the ground.

Chapter 11 - Decisions

"Blackhawk six, this is Blackhawk alpha six, please come in," Cooley's whiny vice crackled over the company net.

Ryan Flagehty, senior to the other lieutenants by a few weeks, motioned the other two platoon officers away from the hummer. "Look, guys, if we wait for Cooley to make a decision, both docs are going to die. I for one am not going to let that happen. Jack," he turned to the second platoon leader, "can you spread your guys out enough to cover my portion of the perimeter?"

Jack Pruit nodded.

"Great. Keep an eye on our fearless leader. Call me on my internal frequency if he does decide to do something." Flagehty took off at a dead run back to his platoon. The second platoon moved in to take over his unit's position. Waving his men and women forward, Flagehty took the point. All three squads followed him as he ran toward the Whippette's vehicle.

As they crested the hill, they heard shots and screaming. Everyone dropped to the ground. The lieutenant checked the video feed from the mini-drone and saw the Whippettes being beaten down by attackers. He spoke into his microphone.

"First platoon, move into position now and target the attackers." Flagehty clicked off his mike and whispered to his platoon sergeant, "Damn, I wish this wasn't happening. The captain is going to eat my ass for this one."

"Ask for forgiveness, not permission." Sergeant Tim Angle grinned at his platoon leader. "That's what my old first sergeant used to say."

"That's just great." Flagehty looked through his sights, putting the crosshairs on the leader's head. "First squad. Take out the four bandits on the left. Second, get the guys holding the Whippettes. Third squad take out the remaining five. I'm on the leader." He began a countdown in his head. "You have sixty seconds to get into position. Shoot on my command. Move out."

A shrill, familiar voice rang out in his ear bug. "Lieutenant, I told you we have to wait for orders."

"What's that, sir? I can't hear you. Say again." Flagehty replied.

Sergeant Angel, on the same frequency, looked at his boss and then shook his head, as if to say he didn't get the order either. His sister had been gang-raped and killed. He gripped the weapon tightly, his knuckles turning white. It took all his efforts not to shoot the two men ripping the clothes off Mrs. Whippette.

"Come on, sir," he growled. "We need to hurry if we want to save them."

Chapter 12 – Flagehty To The Rescue

The leader of the attackers stood in front of the three prisoners. "Well, lookee here. We have us some hostages. Don't hurt them." The leader of the attackers looked at the black-haired woman. "You're the wife of that son of a bitch that killed half my men."

"What difference does it make who they are, let's have some fun and then kill them," his second in command growled. "I like the looks of the blond woman, and I got first dibs." He never saw the rifle butt coming and sprawled in the dirt after the blow to the side of his head.

"Does anybody else want to question my orders?" the leader snarled. "I can do this without at least five of you guys, and I'd have fewer mouths to feed. We need to take the dark-haired one to the compound. I bet the commander there will want to get her back." He kicked the man he had butt stroked to a sitting position. "I don't care about the other two." He saw the look in his subordinate's eyes and continued, "Keep them alive if you want to have some fun later. I'll leave that up to you guys."

You," he pointed at Ashley, "are going to get us into the compound so we can settle the score with your old man."

Ashley sat silently, blood dripping down her neck from her tattered ear. Her head hurt like hell. The ringing in her ears prevented her from understanding what the bandit yelled. She watched as he moved form her to her new-found friends.

William and Betty sat beaten, Betty holding her torn shirt to her chest, while a large red blotch grew on the side of William's face. Both stared defiantly at the thugs surrounding them.

The leader picked up Ashley's pistol. He ejected the empty clip and replaced it with a full one. Releasing the slide, he stepped toward the couple. Grabbing William by the hair, he pulled him to his feet. Putting the pistol against William's forehead, he demanded, "Who are you? Why should I let you live?"

Still groggy from the kick, William mumbled, "We're doctors, trying to get to Lexington. We're working for the Red Cross and are going to provide medical aid to people sick from the cholera epidemic there."

William never saw the slap coming.

"Liar. We left Lexington a week ago, and I didn't hear nothing about no epidemic." The leader moved the pistol and pointed it at Betty's head. "Tell me why you're here, or I swear I'll shoot your bitch right now."

Ashley noticed the red light of the laser designators dancing on the remaining twelve attackers. "I suggest that you drop your weapons and put your hands up, right now, if you want to live."

The leader laughed and transferred his aim from Betty to Ashley. "Give me one good reason why…."

The hypervelocity round that cracked in the air erased his final words. It passed through his skull, hit the surface of the road, and whined off into the distance.

Ashley, William, and Betty were looking at each other through the fine red mist that surrounded them. The rifles of the platoon fired almost simultaneously, killing all thirteen bandits within a fraction of a second. Ashley, hardened by years of fighting to defend the compound, surveyed the scene dispassionately. She stood up and retrieved her pistol from the hand of the fallen leader.

William and Betty had seen their share of blood in operating rooms, but were shocked as they looked at the carnage. The combination of adrenaline, fear and the smell of death caused them both to throw up as the platoon raced down the hill to their position.

Sure that Josh had found her, Ashley couldn't bear going back into captivity. She turned the pistol on herself. The man leading the soldiers yelled, "Freeze! Put the weapon down. Now."

William put his hand on Ashley's and pulled the pistol down. He moved between Ashley and Lieutenant Flagehty.

He held out his arms to protect Ashley. "Easy, Ryan. This is Doctor," he coughed, "excuse me. Ashley Smith. She's a colleague of ours from Houston. She's also going to Lexington but decided against joining our convoy. Maybe she found out who's in command."

Flagehty shot a hard look at William. William could almost hear the unspoken *Bullshit.*

"She thought mercenaries would provide her better protection than the NUS forces operating in this area." William pointedly glanced at the dead marauder leader. "It's obvious she made a mistake. They were holding her for ransom, but she escaped. She's been running for the last three days. They finally caught up with her."

Flagehty looked at Ashley for a moment, as if trying to decide what to do.

Betty touched his arm. "Ryan, please help her. I appreciate your protection, and I'm sure that Ashley would appreciate your protection, too."

Flagehty waved his platoon medic forward. The medic placed a Quickheal patch on Ashley's ear and shined a light in her eyes. "She has a slight concussion, but I don't think it is too dangerous."

One of the soldiers, Private Neel, pulled a uniform jacket out of his rucksack. Blushing, he shyly handed it to Betty.

She put it on, smiling at the young trooper. "Thanks, Benjamin. I'll clean it and get it back to you tonight."

Hummers advanced down the hill. Their turret-mounted machineguns and automatic grenade launchers were searching for any possible attack. The lead hummer pulled up.

The first sergeant stepped into the roadway. "Sir, the commander is really pissed off. He's been trying to reach you on the platoon's net. Would you use my communications to call the captain and explain just what the hell is going on?"

"Where is old blood and guts?"

The first sergeant snorted at the reference to his commander. Careful not to let his disgust show in his voice, he replied. "Sitting on the high ground. Waiting in case regiment calls."

"That figures."

Stepping close to Ryan, he lowered his voice. "Sir, please get on the horn and tell him everything is okay. If he does get through, he'll call for the rest of the battalion to back us up. I don't want to have to face the command sergeant major on this one, and you damn sure don't want to face the old man."

"Fine. You tell him he just saved our doctors and rescued another one from certain death," Flagehty replied. "That will make for a good report to higher headquarters. Meanwhile, get the company medic down here, and get a fresh jumpsuit for Mrs. Whippette." He walked away to check on his soldiers.

Ashley caught William's eye. "Smith? You couldn't come up with a better name than that?

Chapter 13 – The Trip to Lexington

So, we're heading to Lexington?" Ashley sat between William and Betty in the front bench of the Hummer. Her head ached and her ear still oozed blood. She pulled off the Quickheal patch.

Betty put a fresh patch on her Ashley's head. "It'll stop bleeding, if you leave it alone. You're a worse patient than my husband."

"I may be a bad patient, but the leader of this convoy has to be a complete idiot. Doesn't he see the choke-point coming up? This is a perfect place for an ambush."

"He thinks drones are going to spot any problems," William gripped the steering wheel tightly. "You both need to be ready to unass this vehicle and jump in the ditch."

The lead vehicle flipped over as a rocket slammed into its side.

The entire company erupted with return fire as the commander's hummer slid to a halt, exposed in the middle of the road. The hyper-weapons carried by the NUS troopers slaughtered the attackers.

*****

"Ashley, come over here. I need your hands."

William tried to stop the blood gushing from a wound in a wounded soldier's neck.

"Put your finger here. Apply pressure while I try to clamp the artery."

"I don't know what I'm doing," Ashley whispered.

"You're doing fine. Just a little more pressure." William focused on the wound. "Got it stopped. Now I need to suture it."

He cut away the damaged part of the vessel, nicking his finger in the process. His blood mixed with the soldier's.

"Don't let go, Ashley. You're doing a great job."

Ashley felt the curved needle stab into her finger. She grunted in pain but did not pull away from the injured man.

"Sorry about that," William muttered as he finished sewing the artery back together. "Clumsy me." He smiled at Ashley. "Don't worry, I've had all my shots."

"How can you be so calm with all of this going on?"

"I could ask you the same thing. You've been a great help. Without you, this trooper would be dead. You can move your finger, now." William yelled over his shoulder. "Betty, could you get me some more plasma and a Quickheal patch?"

"I've been in worse situations over the past thirteen years. Blood doesn't bother me."

"Thank you for saving Private Mills."

Ashley looked up into the sun, shielding her eyes. She saw the lieutenant who saved them standing over her.

He held out his hand to help her to her feet.

"I'm all bloody," Ashley said. "I can get up by myself."

Ryan took a gauze patch out of his first aid kit. He handed it to Ashley.

"Thank you." She cleaned her hand, then held it out to him. "I'm Ashley Miller."

"I thought William called you Doctor Smith?" He looked at her with a question in his eyes.

"Smith is my married name." Ashley laughed, "At least, it used to be.

"You're not married anymore?"

"Not since last week. We just couldn't get along. We're both better off apart." She spoke the truth, so it sounded believable. "I took back my maiden name. This is the first time I've seen William and Betty since the divorce."

"Anyway, thanks again for saving my soldier." Ryan saluted her, then walked away.

"Pretty fast thinking, Ashley Miller." William smiled at her. "I thought we were going to have trouble. You used your real name. What if he decides to run a check on it?"

"Miller is almost as common as Smith. I doubt he'll find anything. Even if he does check, my name won't come up. Officially, I'm dead."

"I think the less he knows, the better." William handed Ashley another gauze pad.

She finished cleaning the blood off her hands in silence.

*****

"Lexington is smaller I remember." Many buildings were deserted and in disrepair. Ashley, glad to be there, worried at the same time. *What's going to happen now that the journey is over?*

48

"Well, we've finally arrived." William stared up at the front of the hospital. "Betty, Ashley, we'd better go inside." He shook hands with Lieutenant Flagehty. He apparently didn't see Cooley's outstretched hand. He nodded his head in Cooley's general direction. "Thank you, sir, for all your help." He climbed the steps after his retreating wife and friend.

"Thank God that's over. I could have been here three days ago without his help." Ashley muttered to Betty.

"Now, now, we'd all be dead on the side of the road if it weren't for Ryan Flagehty," Betty whispered, "The big question is what to do with you, now that we are here?"

As they entered the hospital building, William caught up with them and guided them toward the stairwell. He explained the plan to Ashley while they walked up the steps.

"Once we get to the third floor, go down the back stairs to the basement. Wait there until 2000 hours. Hide wherever you can. Betty and I'll meet you in this stairway at exactly 2005 hours. I'll be able to get you out of here and into our apartment without too much notice. Then, I think you're going to have to leave NUS territory. If anyone finds out who you are…." He left the rest of the sentence unspoken.

When the NUS unit left Lexington, William brought Ashley to the city limits. Betty insisted on coming along to say goodbye.

"I always liked your father. What a great man." Ashley smiled at the woman in front of her.

Tears welled up in her eyes as Betty hugged Ashley. "I want to help people, the way my father couldn't." Betty wiped her face with her sleeve and turned away.

"I'm sure you will."

William handed Ashley a bag of food and water. He gave her a hug before she got on the back of the truck heading north.

Waving goodbye, Ashley thought, *New York is outside the NUS. It should be a safe place to hide.*

Chapter 14 - The Real Pain Begins

Ten-year-old Paine stared at the ceiling of his stark barracks room. He tried to keep the tears from coming as he thought about the recent loss of his brother. He wished he could see his mother. She'd escaped this living hell, or so he hoped. The voice of his brother echoed in his head. *Be strong. You need to rest. You know Father will try to break you.* Closing his eyes, he tried to go back to sleep.

The blaring siren jolted him out of his reverie. Heart racing in fear, he rolled out of bed and quickly dressed in combat gear, donning the helmet with its communications equipment. Flashes from weapon's fire lit up the compound outside his window. Running to the arms room for a weapon, he hoped he wouldn't be late.

"Man all defensive positions," rang out over the address system.

The armorer threw a twelve-gauge automatic shotgun at him. Paine staggered under the weight.

"I need something different."

"It's all I got left, kid. Take it and get to your position. At least you don't have to be right on target to get a kill."

Running toward the perimeter, Paine could hear bullets passing over his head. Ducking down, he ran toward his position. He saw a marauder coming across the compound.

They both fired at the same time.

Double-ought buckshot tore into the man. Paine watched him go down, blood pouring from his chest. Something had hit him, but the shock kept him from feeling the pain. He tried to slow his breathing.

A voice rang out in his helmet's speakers.

"Boy, get to your position right now."

Paine fell as he tried to run. Two bullets had punched holes through the calf of his left leg. Seeing the blood, he almost passed out. It started to hurt like hell. *Fight through it. Don't show any weakness.* He applied a Quickheal patch and a tourniquet. Limping through the rest of the firefight, he lost all sensation in his left foot.

The battle raged around him. Vision blurred, shivering from the cold and blood loss, Paine still managed to kill three more attackers at close range. Breathing heavily, he collapsed against a wall. He felt light-headed and nauseous from the physical pain and from the death he had wrought. He'd seen plenty of death, but it never got easier to shoot someone. Shaking his head to clear it, he looked for more targets.

Something moved behind him. Without thinking, he brought up the weapon, squeezing the trigger. The hammer fell on an empty chamber. The weapon, ripped from his hand, slammed into his chest, knocking him to the ground. Paine closed his eyes, prepared for the end.

"Didn't you hear the all clear? The fight is over." A voice cracked in the humid air. "Get up."

Paine struggled to stand. Hard hands roughly pulled him to his feet.

"Stand up!"

Looking into his father's cold, hard eyes, Paine gasped out, "Yes, sir." He stood at a ragged attention.

Josh stalked away, then looked back. "Move, soldier."

Limping behind his father, Paine shuffled toward the medical building in the center of the compound, manned by personnel of the 338th Medical Brigade Headquarters from Nashville, Tennessee. Josh convinced the technicians to join the Kentucky Regulars after the government collapsed. They brought state-of-the-art medical technology with them.

As he entered the aid station, harsh white light momentarily blinded Paine.

"Change the sub-routine." Josh scowled at the medic when she hesitated. "Now."

Specialist Tillello looked at the unit's commander. "Sir..." she began.

Josh stopped her with a cold stare. "It will make him tougher. He needs to be a better soldier."

Tillello made the adjustments and opened the meditube door. The look she got from Josh made her stop short of helping Paine go inside.

Paine tried not to cry out from the agony and fear. He'd been in the meditube many times before.

Once he entered, the machine went to work.

Mechanical arms grabbed Paine, strapping him to the vertical table, immobilizing him. All his desperate prayers for unconsciousness were unanswered. The machine, impervious to his screaming, sealed the door as the table moved to the horizontal.

Ten arms snaked out, the surgical instruments attached to them flashing. One arm stripped away the uniform, exposing Paine's body to the coldness of the tube's air. High-pressure, caustic fluid washed away the filth and blood.

Two arms injected antibiotics and nanoprobes into Paine's right thigh. The nanoprobes were designed to remove blood clots and repair the damage to the blood vessels in his shattered leg.

Three more arms worked on his leg, their surgical blades a blur as they cut away skin, separated muscles and exposed the damaged tissue and tendons. They were sewn back together, and the muscles and skin sealed using heat and surgical glue.

Hoarse from screaming, Paine felt his throat burn. The machine didn't heed his cries and dispassionately continued its work. His shrieks faded to low moaning. He felt like he'd been flogged. The injuries the enemy inflicted upon his body were less painful than the cure.

The remaining four arms worked on the minor wounds scattered about his body. They cut away dead skin, replaced with plastic film. Capillaries cauterized, Quickheal applied, and stitches in place, the machine worked with all with the efficiency of modern medical science.

An eleventh arm emerged from the back of the table, its needle poised inches from Paine's neck. It quivered slightly as if in anticipation. The other arms finished their work. The compartment flooded with antiseptic gasses, the final step in the healing process. The surgical arms clicked back into ready position. The straps loosened.

The needle at the end of the last arm stuck forward like a snake. It delivered a general anesthesia to its limp, gibbering patient. Darkness overtook Paine as the tube door slid open.

An hour later, Paine regained consciousness. He ached in every part of his body. Standing up too quickly, he grabbed the technician's arm to keep from passing out.

Tillello steadied him. She looked at the identity disk hanging from his neck. "You'll be okay, Michael."

"I'm not Michael," he whispered to himself. "No," he shouted, jerking his arm away. Fighting back the tears that threatened to flow from his eyes, he choked out, "I go by my middle name."

He stalked out of the aid station, yelling, "Paine."

Chapter 15 – The Hunted

He'd been hit several times during the last firefight. Josh dragged his son to the meditube.

"No anesthesia at the end of the procedure, Specialist Tillello." He watched the medic make the adjustments. "I want to be here when he comes out, and he'd better still be awake."

The doors slowly opened. Unable to stop crying, Paine tried to stand up. He passed out.

"Wimp can't take his medicine." Josh glared down at his motionless son for a moment. "Be more like me." He yelled at the comatose boy. He gestured to the waiting medical technician. "I'm taking a team to Utah for a man-hunting mission tomorrow. Some worker killed one of the Mormon Elite, and they want us to bring him to justice." Glaring at Tillello, Josh growled, "Get him out of here. Wake him up in two hours and put him back into uniform. I'm taking him with me on the trip. He needs to be ready and on the shuttle by zero-five-hundred hours." Josh turned on his heel and marched away from the tube.

*****

The hunters moved silently through the scrub brush, tracking their quarry. The target, fleeing for his life, made good time over the rough ground. He ran with careless abandon over the boulders and through the vegetation. Colonel Martin clicked over to the command net and issued his orders.

"I want to see how he will react. I want the trees around him cut off at four feet. Don't hit him. Ready, fire."

Twelve rifles fired as one, neatly clipping off the aspens around the fugitive about waist high. He moved in a slow circle, his right arm raised, and middle finger extended, flipping off his pursuers before scurrying off through the brush. The lead scout keyed his mike. "He has a pair of balls bigger than the outdoors, Colonel."

"Guide him into the clearing about 100 meters ahead," Colonel Martin ordered. "I want this one watched after we get paid. No sense in letting him waste away here when we can find a spot for him in the unit. If they don't kill him, I want him."

Moving away from the cliff face, the fugitive skipped down the gravel slope, scattering stones and trying to stay upright as bullets rained down from above. He'd evaded at least four groups of bounty hunters, but this group wouldn't give up the hunt. He tried to hide in the new growth of aspen trees that covered the mountain. Flopping down on his belly, he wormed his way deeper into the foliage, to no avail. The bullets striking around him were guiding him, and he soon came to a clear area. The posse had cornered him at last. Resigned to his fate, he stood up, and with hands at his side waited for the bullets to come.

An amplified voice boomed, "Get down on your face."

The large, dark-skinned man refused to go down. He crouched and advanced into the center of the clearing, gripping his knife, waiting for them to come. Surrounded by 13 men and women, dressed in mottled-brown camouflage, he knew he couldn't escape. As he slowly turned and surveyed the soldiers, he noticed they were carrying thermal-sighted weapons. The leader walked up to him, stood with his hands on his hips and looked at the knife.

"You led us on quite a chase, boy." Josh sized up the young man in front of him. "If it weren't for the money and food bonuses, I would have killed you three days ago." His voice came out flat and emotionless, "The name is Colonel Martin, Independent Kentucky Regulars. What's your name?"

"Marcus."

"Marcus what?"

"It's just Marcus. My mother never told me about my father. I don't think she knew which one knocked her up. At least we know he's black." Marcus grinned for a moment. The smile left his face as quickly as it appeared. "Right after my fifth birthday, she died. It got me a one-way trip to an orphanage."

"All right, just Marcus." Colonel Martin pulled out a document, cleared his throat and read, "The duly appointed authority of the Young Nation deputized me. Therefore, by the power invested in me, I arrest you for the murder of John Collins." He carefully folded the paper and put it in his combat vest pocket. "The Mormon authorities paid me to bring you in, dead or alive. We can do that the easy way or the hard way. I get the bounty either way, but I get a bonus if we bring you back alive. It's your choice."

55

*****

Marcus looked at the faces around him and figured the hard way meant they would carry his body out of the wilderness. These hunters looked like they would shoot him without hesitation and cut him into quarters to make it easier to pack him out. Only the smallest member of the team looked at him with any kind of sympathetic eyes.

He weighed the options and decided he would take his chances with the Mormons. Marcus thought because they needed the manpower they would let him live. No one had liked that despicable bastard he'd killed. He flipped the knife in the air, caught it by the tip and handed it to Colonel Martin. Marcus stood quietly with his head up as they put plasticuffs on his wrists and prodded him onto the trail.

Two hunters were assigned to guard Marcus kept him from serious damage during the difficult trek to the main road. Colonel Martin intentionally took the hardest route, weaving in and out of boulder fields, staying off the trails. The hunters set a furious pace, even faster than the one Marcus had used in his effort to escape them.

Determined that no one would walk him into the ground, Marcus gutted out the last long climb to the top of a canyon. He finished ahead of most of the hunters and one of his guards, even though he didn't have the use of his hands. He grinned at Colonel Martin and worked up enough saliva to spit at the men and women behind him. "Screw you all. Even though I'm going back to hell, I showed them what I'm made of."

Colonel Martin looked at Marcus for a few seconds, as if gauging the man before him. He shook his head slightly, then pushed Marcus toward the waiting Mormons.

Marcus had a sinking feeling in the pit of his stomach. He recognized a face at the front of the milling crowd. Greg Collins, the brother of the man he'd killed.

Chapter 16– Vengeance is Mine

Collins pulled his fist back as two other sets of hands held Marcus still. Marcus watched the fist come in, ducking at the last instant. He momentarily lost consciousness when the punch stabbed into his face.

Spitting out a piece of broken tooth, Marcus tried to duck his head to avoid the next blow. His scarred skin split open as the blow stunned him. He laughed as he thought it would ruin a perfectly good brand, and then he passed out.

Rude hands slapped him awake. He managed a broken smile as he watched his tormentor shake his hand in pain.

"You killed my brother, you bastard." The fist smashed into Marcus once more. "You're going to suffer much more than my brother did, you pig. Just like his slut of a wife, the one you were fornicating with. She lasted a long time before I sent her to hell." Greg saw the look of hate on Marcus's face. "What do you have to say now, you murderer?"

Marcus moved his lips. The brother leaned closer. Marcus spit blood, mucous and bits of teeth in his face. He blacked out again as the man rained blows on his head in frenzy.

The informant helped load the unconscious prisoner onto the waiting vehicle. As it drove off, he took out the transmitter he'd gotten from the leader of the hunters. He turned it on. "They took him out of the building and loaded him on a truck. He don't look too good. I think he's still alive, but I can't be sure." He yelped as the single-use communications device heated in his hand. As he dropped it, it turned into a small puddle of melted plastic and metal.

*****

Josh watched the tracking tracer on the screen move. "Saddle up, troops." He waved his team to their feet.

*****

The intense pain woke Marcus. His shoulders, head and arms burned as if they were on fire. He struggled to blink the blood out of his eyes, but couldn't. His eyelids had been cut away. Raising his head off his chest, he looked around at his predicament through a red mist.

"Good. You're awake."

Spread eagle, stripped of his clothes, Marcus' arms were tied to the branches of a dead cottonwood tree. His feet were tied to stakes driven into the ground. Blood from several knife cuts on his lower abdomen seeped down into his pubic hair.

A voice came to him from a platform built into the branches above. "The fire is going to go out soon." Greg Collins whispered.

Fire burned in circle twenty feet from the trunk of the tree. It kept the pack of wolves attracted by the smell of blood at bay. As the fire burned lower, the wolves moved closer.

"I can't wait to see what happens to you when the first wolf gets here. They always go for the groin, so I made it especially easy for them to find their target."

Something stung Marcus' shoulder. A warm glow spread out from the injection site.

"I just gave you a stimulant," Collins voice dripped venom. "I want you to feel the pain. The doctors told me this will keep you alive even after serious damage. You'll be awake for the whole process. I want to hear you scream."

Marcus trembled as the stimulant took effect, not from fear but from the involuntary rush of adrenaline coursing through his body. Every cut, every bruise hurt like fire. The ropes burned where they dug into his flesh. He clamped his jaw shut, causing more agony as the raw nerves of his broken teeth sent waves of pain through his head and jaw. Determined not to cry out, he let a soft moan escape his tight lips.

"Glad to hear you suffer. Just wait, you fornicating murderer."

The fire burned lower. The coals turned to ash. One brave wolf jumped the embers and slunk toward Marcus. It bristled and gathered itself for a leap.

"Should be any time now, Marcus. Die like the scum you are." The voice cackled insanely as the wolf moved forward.

Two hypervelocity darts cracked through the air. The wolf died at Marcus's feet. Collins fell from the tree to land a few feet from the animal carcass. Marcus could see a neat hole in his forehead. The wolf pack scattered. Marcus tensed as he heard footsteps approaching from behind.

"Cut him down."

Due to the heightened sensitivity provided by the drugs, a searing fire tore into his body when he hit the ground. Marcus bit through his lip.

The medic plunged a needle into his neck. Marcus slipped into unconsciousness.

"Pick him up and get him into the lifter. He'll be a great addition to the team." Josh looked down at the broken body. "You owe me, now."

Chapter 17 – New Recruit

He felt almost human again. It only took ten days and three trips to the meditube. His missing teeth had been regenerated. His jaw hurt, and his speech slurred because of his reconstructed lips. Marcus had trouble seeing. His new eyelids stayed open while he slept, causing his eyes to dry out. He felt pretty good.

"I won't need to see you again. You'll be completely healed in a few days." The doctor looked at the old wounds that covered Marcus's body. "Unless you want me to remove those keloids."

"These tell my life's story. I'd rather not lose them." Marcus ran his hand over the multitude of scars on his arms. "I might forget who I am."

"Suit yourself. You can go back to your quarters." The doctor entered a notation on his tablet that Marcus refused treatment.

Marcus heard him mutter, "Those guys are all like," as the door shut.

Sitting on the bed in the two-person hospital room, Marcus looked up as a fellow patient walked in.

The tall, rangy soldier, as disfigured as Marcus, crossed his bandaged arms and leaned against the doorway. "So, what are you going to do now?"

Marcus scratched his face, finger running along a scar he'd gotten in some insignificant slave quarter fight three years ago.

"Where did you pick up all the marks, Jimmy?" Marcus pointedly looked at the soldier's face.

"Got them all serving right here in the regiment." His laugh sounded bitter to Marcus. "You ought a see some of the other old guys. Well, there aren't too many of us around. Mostly they're dead."

"Just what does the regiment do, besides hunt down runaway slaves for the Mormons?"

"Actually, kind of like what we did in Utah. We tracked you down, got paid very well for it, and then saved your sorry ass so we could invite you to be a part of all this." The soldier waved his arms in a wide circle.

"What do you mean?"

"The colonel wants you to join the regiment. He liked what he saw in the mountains, and you've got plenty of size and strength. How would you like to join us and kick some major butt? You look like the type who could do well in the regiment. Good pay, food, shelter and weapons, and all you have to do is be ready to die protecting this compound and to fight for the honor of the regiment."

"What if I say no?" Marcus tensed, ready to respond to anything that might be coming.

"Well, the colonel said if you didn't want to join us, he would arrange a trip for you. Said maybe you want to get back to Utah. I heard you cut quite a swath there with the ladies." Jimmy paused for a second. "And with their husbands."

Marcus laughed aloud. "Colonel figured that, did he? Well let me tell you what you can tell the colonel. I'll join, eat your meals and kill whoever needs killing, as long as I can walk away anytime I want to. I really want to be a free man for a change."

The lanky soldier shook his head. "It doesn't work that way. You take an oath, to the colonel, and swear it on the regimental flag. Dishonor your oath and it means death. Honor it and it means you fight whenever and wherever the colonel orders you to."

"Can I think about it?"

"Sure." He smiled at Marcus. "You have two hours to decide what you want to do. Join us. Or we'll take you back to the hell hole you came from. It is your choice."

Marcus promised himself he'd never be a slave again. Joining the regulars seemed no different than being sold to the Mormons. He didn't really have a choice. He knew there were only two choices, to join or die. "I don't need to think. I'm all in."

"Colonel figured you would be."

The following Monday morning, Marcus stood in front of the entire regiment with five other recruits. Colonel Martin held the end of the tattered regimental flag, blood stained in several places. At least forty battle streamers were attached to the staff which bent from the weight.

"Applicants, step forward and repeat after me."

"I swear by God this sacred oath, that I shall render unconditional obedience to Joshua Martin, the leader of the Kentucky Regulars, supreme commander of the armed forces, and that I shall at all times be prepared, as a brave soldier, to give my life for this oath."

The words broke over Marcus like a tidal wave. He thought Utah didn't seem so bad. Then the roar of hundreds of warriors echoed across the parade ground, yelling in one voice the age old "Hoo-Rah." Marcus found a home.

Chapter 18 - Marcus

"I have a mission for you. It will be long-term. All you have to do is report anything he does that might interest me."
"Yes, Sir."

*****

His footsteps echoed as he marched down the empty hallway. Walking up to the open door to his new room, Paine stopped and looked inside. The lower bunk almost contained the large, dark-sinned giant they'd brought back from Utah. He thought about turning around and crawling to his father, to beg him for another barracks assignment.

Instead, he stepped into the room. Paine tried not to disturb the sleeping man.

The giant moved with surprising speed. On his feet in an instant, he growled, "What do you want?"

Staring at the large knife in the dark man's hand, Paine could barely hear the raspy, threatening voice. He swallowed hard, squeaking out, "I'm assigned to this room, now." Deep scars covered the man's face and arms. Paine noticed a large, purple 'R' burned into his new roommate's forehead.

"What are you, ten years old?" Marcus laugh bounced around the walls. "You got to be the youngest soldier I've ever seen."

He hated it when that happened. Paine felt his face turning deep crimson. "I just turned thirteen. My father has had me fighting in the unit for the last four years, so don't think I'm inexperienced."

He felt a stirring of mixed emotions as Marcus stepped toward him. Paine looked at the muscles in his new roommate's arms and thought, *"He could rip my head off. Maybe he will, and I can be free of my father at last."*

"Welcome to our humble abode," Marcus extended a ham-sized hand to the much smaller Paine. It engulfed his in a bone-crushing handshake. Thankfully, it ended quickly. "The name's Marcus. Just Marcus. I never knew my father."

"I wish I didn't," Paine mumbled as he threw his bag on the top bunk. "Paine Martin." He hoped Marcus wouldn't recognize the name.

"You're the commander's son?"

Paine could feel the big man's eyes boring through him.

"Yeah. But don't think that will help either one of us."

"So, you don't want to talk about your old man?"

"Not really. He isn't much of a father to me. I'm just a soldier doing what he's been told to do." Paine leaned against the desk in the corner. "Can we just leave it at that?"

"Sure." Marcus lay back down on his bunk. "Do you mind if I tell you my story?"

"Go ahead," Paine checked his chronometer. "The next formation isn't for another two hours. I'm all ears."

"Let's see. Born in New Orleans. My mother did whatever she needed to keep me alive and well-fed. I remember guys hanging around the apartment. Sometimes they were there the next morning. I never knew my father." Marcus remembered what happened in the clearing where he met Colonel Martin and grinned. "You dad sure got mad when I told him, 'Just Marcus.' I thought he'd go ahead and kill me on the spot."

"You're lucky he didn't. He's not known for his compassion."

"I'm still alive." Marcus rubbed his chin, fingering a scar. "When I turned five, the Texas National Guard, part of the New United States military, moved into New Orleans to take it back over. They brought food shipments from the first orbital farms. All of us were ordered to turn over what food we had for redistribution. I guess my mom thought that was a bunch of bullshit, so she hid our supplies. They hanged her for hoarding. Sent me to an orphanage. They kept me there for four years, then got sent to Utah."

"Why Utah?" Paine, fascinated by the events of Marcus' life, leaned closer to hear the rest of the story.

"The Independent Young Nation, Old Utah State, offered part of their stockpiled grain seeds to the New United States for warm bodies to work the farms," Marcus replied. "All of us kids in the orphanages were sent there in the spring of 2050."

"That must have been hard for you."

Paine watched Marcus shrug. "I didn't make it easy on myself. I stole food, I ran off more than once. I spent one winter in the mountains and damn near died of exposure." He touched his forehead. "They gave me this after they caught me."

"What does the 'R' mean."

"Runaway. I'm surprised they didn't end my life, but my owner wanted to start a breeding program. I am a pretty fine specimen of a man." Marcus laughed as he flexed his muscles. "The others picked on me because of my skin. They don't have too many black people in Utah." Paine saw Marcus' eyes harden. "I learned how to fight, and how to win. They learned how to leave me alone."

His right hand still smarting from the handshake, Paine knew he didn't want to cross the giant man in front of him.

"Anyway, they started bringing women to our ranch. I guess you could say I had it pretty good."

"How many women did you have?"

"I lost count," Marcus laughed. "But my problems started with one woman."

Paine sat down on the desktop, intrigued by the story.

"Too busy to spend time with his five wives, the owner stayed gone on business a lot. One day, his youngest wife happened to walk by. I had my shirt off, and she started staring at me. Then she stuck her nose up in the air and passed by. I saw her drop something on the ground."

"What was it?"

"A piece of paper. When no one around, I went back and put it in my pocket. Later that evening, after everyone went to sleep, I went into the barracks latrine." Marcus grinned, his broken teeth shining.

"What did it say?"

"Thursday at midnight, master's chambers."

*****

Rachel snuggled up to Marcus and sighed. She never had this attention from her husband and felt guilty that she could make love to someone else. A sob escaped her lips.

Marcus woke with a start. "What is wrong?" He reached over to wipe the single tear from Rachel's eye. "Did I hurt you?"

Her tears flowed profusely. "I'm so unhappy with my marriage. I share my husband with so many others and he never has enough time for me. He says it is because I'm not worth his time." Marcus propped himself up on one elbow and looked at her with questioning eyes.

Rachel blushed and then continued. "Mister Collins never comes to me anymore. He says it is entirely my fault, and this is God's way of punishing me for allowing him to bed me. He calls me an abomination. I'm a slave in the house. He says that I'm not his wife, but a message sent from God."

Rachel took a deep breath, put her head down and continued, "He married me just after I turned thirteen. The law is we had to wait to consummate the marriage until I turned sixteen. He came to me in the night three days after we were wed. I never encouraged him. I feared God's wrath, and what might happen if we broke His laws. What could I do? He forced himself on me." She whispered, "He raped me. I got pregnant right away. We were excited and happy."

Rachel shivered and put her head into the pillow. Her muffled voice continued the tale. "After I started to show, I got really sick." She sobbed, "I lost the baby. Now I can't have children. When that happened, something broke down there," she rolled over and wistfully rubbed her mid-section, "and I can't get pregnant again."

Marcus leaned down and gently kissed Rachel just above the navel. The tears began again and Marcus took her in his arms and held her close.

"We'll run away," he whispered into her hair, "Somewhere we can be free." Something welled up inside of him that he'd never experienced before. "I think I'm falling in love with you."

Rachel and Marcus kept up the affair, meeting every time her husband went away from the farm. Rachel feared that something would go wrong but couldn't stop seeing Marcus. She made them both pray for forgiveness every night after they'd made love.

It ended as suddenly as it had begun.

One fall evening, Rachel's head rested on Marcus's shoulder. Stroking her hair, Marcus began kissing her ear.

"How touching." Rachel and Marcus bolted up in bed, staring in disbelief at John Collins. "I come home and find a filthy slave fornicating with my wife." He slapped his riding crop against his thigh. "I guess I'll have to do something about that now, won't I?"

He pointed the whip at Marcus. "Stand up, slave, and prepare to take the righteous punishment of a believer. I'll personally castrate you before I have you stoned to death."

He shifted his glare to Rachel as Marcus got out of the bed. "And you, harlot, will die before the dawn."

Collins hit Rachel across the face with the whip. As he drew back his arm to strike again, Marcus jumped on his back.

To strike an owner meant death for a slave. A dead man either way, Marcus attacked to kill. Wrenching the whip from Collins' hand, he put it under his chin, falling backward.

Collins' eyes bugged out as he gasped for oxygen, then drew his knife and tried to stab Marcus. Marcus punched him in the temple, dropping the whip as he ripped the knife from the stunned owner's hand. He plunged the blade deep into his attacker's heart, holding it there a moment, then twisting it until Collins stopped breathing.

Marcus pushed the body away and pulled on his clothes. "Rachel, we have to go, now."

Rachel sat up and stared at her dead husband. She explored the cut on her face gingerly. Staring at the blood on her fingers, she moaned, "This is God's way of punishing me for my infidelity. I'm cursed." She lay back down and pulled the covers over her head. "Leave me now. I never want to see you again."

Marcus reached out, touching Rachel through the blanket. She kicked his hand away. Looking at the lump on the bed for a few moments, he then turned and ran out of the room.

*****

"After I escaped, my owner's brother hired you guys to find me." Marcus looked at Paine. "I remember you now. You were on the mission to catch me. Maybe I misjudged you. You kept up better than some of your friends."

"My father doesn't like it unless I'm better than everyone else." Paine whispered. "I hate his guts."

"I like him all right. You know, your father saved my life."

Paine couldn't stop the explosive laugh from escaping his lips. "Saved you!" Paine snorted. "If he didn't want you for something, you'd be dead now. He almost killed you in the clearing. He would have, if you hadn't dropped the knife. He turned you over to your masters. They could have killed you on the spot."

"Yeah, but they didn't, and I'm here now." Paine could see Marcus mulling over his words. "He did kill the bastard, and the wolves. He brought me here." Marcus waved at the room.

67

"He saves me all the time, after putting me where the fighting is toughest." Paine's eyes grew dark once more. "Then he throws me in a meditube that has no anesthesia. The pain is unreal." Paine looked at the dark man in front of him. "Watch out. He wants to use you for something. He'll expect you to deliver once he calls in his favor."

"OK, I'll watch my back. I'll watch yours, too." Marcus clapped his hand on Paine's shoulder. "As long as we're teamed up, we'll take care of each other."

Chapter 19 - Gabby

"Today, you get to use your new weapons." Colonel Josh Martin stood in front of the unit, looking over his soldiers. "You are now armed with the latest technology. Hypervelocity carbines, rocket launchers, and plasma rifles, coupled with your fighting experience, makes you an almost invincible force. You are a force to be reckoned with."

The assembled soldiers cheered loudly. Josh waited for the noise to abate.

"We're deploying to Florida, to clear out squatters who are claiming the land around Cape John and Ted Kennedy." Taking out an archaic document, he held it up for all to see. "We have been contracted by the NUS State Department to make the area safe for the spaceport workers." He looked over his assembled soldiers. The ranks had swelled thanks to the hefty fee he got for this mission. "We are the best fighting force in the world."

Once again, yells and cheers filled the air.

Josh motioned for Captain Rachel Miller to come forward. She and the command sergeant major unpinned his colonel's eagles and replaced them with the stars of a major general.

"I proudly accept the promotion to flag rank." Shills Josh had planted in the ranks began a chant, "General, general. The others quickly picked up the mantra.

Because of his size and strength, Marcus carried a rocket launcher. Paired with the undersized Paine in the newly formed weapons platoon, he grinned as he yelled with everyone else.

Paine staggered under the weight of three rockets in addition to his brand-new hypervelocity carbine. His father assigned him to that difficult position to make him tougher.

In his last assignment, he carried the M206 infantry assault system, a 5-millimeter rifle over a 20-millimeter grenade launcher. He loved that old weapon, but Paine immediately fell in love with the accelerator carbine. He shot expert on his first try, and would have been prouder of his accomplishment if his father hadn't slapped him for missing one of the 40 targets.

"I'm in rare company," Marcus whispered to Paine. "Nice to have a friend who knows the commander."

"I warned you. Don't be so sure that's a good thing," Paine replied.

Sergeant Gabby Lee, a pretty, jovial, 35-year-old plasma rifleman in charge of the weapons' squad, yelled, "Knock it off, you two." An old-timer, one of the original Kentucky National Guardsmen, the first to join the volunteers, she ardently supported Josh Martin. "Let's get ready to move out."

****

Rain fell in sheets as the squad moved out to pull perimeter security. Gabby passed the time telling Paine stories about her little boy, Bobby.

"That rascal just up and ate all the biscuits. He didn't even leave one for his ole mother." She laughed and looked over at her young soldier. "He's only seven, but pretty soon, he'll be old enough to join the Regulars. You know, he looks like you. You guys could pass for brothers. Maybe you could keep an eye on him, if'n anything happens to me."

Paine looked at the older woman. "I won't have to. You'll be here long after I'm gone. You don't have 'General' Josh Martin as a father." Paine dug into his soggy rations. Closing his eyes, he relived the torture of the meditube.

"Did I ever tell you how I came to meet your daddy?" Gabby moved closer to Paine and pointed out his area of responsibility. "You keep your eyes peeled that-a-way while I tell you what happened."

"I joined up before the plague hit, so I could have some money to go to school. I always wanted to be a nurse." She had a faraway look in her eyes. "Course, that never happened after the shit hit the fan. Anyways, we were waitin' for orders when bad things started to happen. People were killin' and fightin' and we were havin to defend ourselves against folk searchin' for food."

"Then he and your mama come a roarin' up to the Kentucky National Guard Armory back home in Bowling Green. Your daddy stood on the hood of his H3A, that old hydrogen-powered hummer hovercraft under armor, waving an infantry assault weapon and demanding to talk to the commander." Paine noticed she closed her eyes and shivered slightly. "In that big voice of his, he yells out, I'm representative from the US Army."

"Well, Captain Bill Baldwin had been in charge, but he took off for the hills when the mobs came. He never had no guts when it came to confrontations, especially when it came to killing folks. Staff Sergeant Jones, acting first sergeant, he stands at the doorway and yells out 'I'm in charge, the captain took off.' Your Daddy looked hard at Jones for a full minute. 'Is that any way to report to an officer?' he says in that cold voice of his. Jones, sort of stunned by the question, he straightened up. Looking real sharp, he goes an brings his weapon to present arms. 'Staff Sergeant Percy Q. Jones, 233d Maintenance Company, Kentucky National Guard, sir.' he shouts out."

"Your daddy slung his weapon over his shoulder, come off the top of that vehicle smooth as silk, walked up and returned the salute. 'You people get all the food you have here and load it into your vehicles. I want every weapon in the armory, all your spare parts and all the ammunition you have.' He had a way of cutting through the crap and getting right down to business. Well, one of the new boys, who never had no real training, he'd always been kinda cocky, pushing civilians around and always shooting at folks for coming too close to the compound, he got his dander up. I think he had just joined up for the food and the fancy guns. Anyway, he walks up with his rifle held on your daddy. He poked the muzzle of the rifle in your Daddy's chest. 'Just who the hell do you think you are?' he said, kinda nasty like."

"Never seen a man move so fast. Next thing you know, the muzzle of the boy's weapon pointed at the sky. Your daddy swept the legs out from under that boy with a swift kick. The boy fell on his back, trying to catch his breath, when this knife come out of nowhere and your daddy buries it in his heart, just like that. We all just stood there, some of the guys fingering their weapons, wondering what to do, watching that boy bleed out onto the ground and die."

"Then he looked up from the corpse and yelled out, 'By the authority vested in me by the Congress of the United States, I am assuming command of this unit,' real slow-like. He just stood there, with only a bloody knife in his hand, facing down forty rifles. Then he bent, wiped the blade clean on the boy's shirt and puts it away. He looked around the compound with those cold eyes

71

of his. 'I expect my orders to be obeyed, and I'll kill anyone who doesn't follow them. Is that clear?' Everybody just backed down."

"Sergeant Jones, he spits on the ground and says, 'You heard the lieutenant, troops. Let's get the show on the road.' And that's how your daddy come to take charge of us." Gabby looked over at Paine. "That's enough storytellin' for one night. Wake me in two hours."

The squad had been moving through the swamps for days, looking for the enemy camp, but seeing nothing more than a few alligators, one swiftly departing swamp deer, and a lot muddy water. The flat land came as a relief for Marcus, since he had spent so many years in the mountains of Utah.

Paine hated the water. Gabby took Paine under her wing, showing him how to move through the swamp silently, stay dry in rainy weather and cook field rations under the worst conditions.

The weapon's squad headed for another possible enemy encampment. Water sloshed around them as they headed deeper into the swamp.

Feeling the hair stand up on the back of his neck, Paine froze. The rest of the soldiers stopped in response to his actions. Marcus looked over, hands flashing in the combat sign language all the Kentucky Regulars used while on patrol. "What is it?"

"I don't know," Paine signed back. "I just have a bad feeling about this."

Gabby looked at Paine and grinned. She signed, "If I stopped every time I had a bad premonition, I'd still be in Lexington." She jutted her chin in their direction of movement.

An involuntary scream escaped her when she stepped into a spring-trap with her left foot. The squatters waiting in ambush opened fire when they heard her cry out in pain. All six weapons' squad members were hit, none badly. They responded immediately and cleared the ambush with the fire of the three plasma rifles and two carbines. A lone sniper kept shooting at them, trying to keep them in place. Thankfully, he couldn't hit anything.

Paine worked frantically to free Gabby's foot as the sniper's bullets splattered around them. The radio implants in the ears of the team came alive. "KR Six to all hands. Move in now."

Paine practically screamed into the radio, "Gabby is trapped, and we are under fire. Orders."

"Pick up her plasma rifle and get it into action, now." His father's voice rang in his ears.

"If I leave her, she won't make it. If I can get her loose, we'll have two guns." Paine's voice had a pleading tone as he pulled on Gabby's leg. "I just need another second." A bullet skipped off the water inches from Paine. As he ducked, the hot back blast of the rocket launcher blew past him.

Ignoring the pain from bullet that had ripped through his left forearm, Marcus raised his launcher one-handed and fired a 40-millimeter rocket at the heat signature signifying the location of the shooter. The rocket went through it, sucking the sniper through the back of the sandbagged bunker. It continued for another two miles before splashing down in the swamp.

They weren't taking any more fire.

The General's voice crackled over the command net. "Move out or I'll come get the weapon and shoot you myself. We need you to support the attack now."

Paine looked in Gabby's eyes. She smiled. "Go on Paine. I know you tried." She reached under the water, pulled out an antique 9-millimeter pistol and worked the action. "Besides, I can take care of myself."

Paine clumsily pulled the hand grip out of his carbine and took the plasma rifle from Gabby. He ejected her grip, replaced it with his own and slung his carbine over his pack. He pulled the strap of the plasma rifle over his head. Weighed down even more than before, Paine struggled as he waded through the waist-deep water. He finally caught up with the rest of the squad as they moved toward the enemy forces. The additional firepower of the weapons' squad helped the Regiment defeat the squatters and destroy their camp.

The scouts were mercilessly shooting down the survivors trying to escape. Sporadic shots echoed through the swamp as Paine waded back to the place where Gabby had been trapped. There were four bodies floating in the water, dressed in the ragged clothes of the squatters. When Paine didn't see Gabby, he plunged his hands under the water and contacted a body. He cried as he pulled Gabby to the surface. Her throat had been cut, and she had at least 10 stab wounds in her chest. The attackers took her combat vest, with her personal weapons.

Marcus found Paine with Gabby in his arms, tears streaming down his face. "OK, let me help." Marcus slid his hand down Gabby's leg to the spring-trap. It took him less than 10 seconds to free her foot from the trap.

Touching Paine gently on the shoulder, Marcus whispered, "Let her go, man. Just let her go." He tried to pry Paine's hands from Gabby's body.

"Leave me alone." Paine roughly pushed Marcus away. Taking Gabby's dog tags, he held the body for a moment, then released her. The body slipped beneath the surface.

Paine stared at Marcus for a few minutes after the corpse disappeared. "I swear on Gabby's body that I'll never leave another soldier behind again." He brushed the tears from his face and defiantly stared at Marcus, daring him to challenge his oath. Marcus simply nodded, not trusting himself to speak.

They added Gabby's name to the wall of the dead back at headquarters.

Josh charged Paine for losing Gabby's gear and personal weapon.

Chapter 20 – Fulfilling Promises

"I just can't figure the old man out," Marcus shook his head as he and Paine sewed new rank onto their combat vests. "First, he busts you to private, puts you on water only rationing for three days and fines you for losing Gabby's weapon. And now you're a sergeant. Ouch...son of a bitch, that hurts."

He could see mirth on the young squad leader's face. Paine focused on his own needle as he stuck a verbal one into Marcus. "Like that hurts. You've been through so much hell and are worried about a little pinprick?" Paine held up his vest. "Perfect." Putting in on, he told Marcus, "Don't even try to figure my father out. He has ways of making things difficult beyond normal human comprehension. Just go with the flow, and hope there's medical help nearby."

"I'm older and wiser," Marcus laughed aloud at the look on Paine's face, "OK. I'm just older. I just don't see why he promoted you over so many other qualified individuals."

"Like you, for example?"

"Well, you have been in the unit since you were in the womb," Marcus stopped when he saw a hurt look appear on Paine's face. "You know what I mean. I know you miss your mother."

"She's dead and gone, as far as I am concerned. We agreed not to talk about my family. Just let it go." Paine put the vest on, striking a pose. "How's this look?"

"Great. Maybe you can use those boyish good looks to attract some women?" Marcus tried to sound sad, frowning and looking down at his feet. "I could use a little female companionship."

Paine doubled over in laughter. "You have them coming out of the woodwork. Maybe if I had a few more scars, I could do as well as you do in the romance department."

Ignoring the last comment, Marcus continued. "Back to my original point, I can't figure it out. From PFC to buck private to sergeant in five months. What's the colonel doing?"

"He wants me to be just like him. That means I must learn every job in the unit, and maybe someday, I'll replace him as the leader of the Regulars." Paine got a faraway look in his eyes as he whispered. "Just like him."

"I won't ask again, but I have to say these sergeant stripes aren't going to get wet on their own."

"I'm only fifteen, Marcus."

"You're almost sixteen, as you keep reminding me. Only seven years younger than me." Marcus slapped Paine on the shoulder. "Old enough to put money on the bar, old enough to drink. Let's go have a beer to celebrate, while we still can. Rumor has it we're going on a mission tomorrow." Seeing the quizzical look on Paine's face, Marcus grinned. "My luck with the ladies also helps with information gathering. Some of them like to talk, you know, after."

They walked out of the barracks room and headed for the mess hall.

*****

The unit deployed to North Georgia to chase down the rebellious squatters who escaped the Cape Kennedy and Canaveral raids. NUS wanted them either captured or killed, and hired the Regulars to finish the job they'd started.

Paine's squad led the platoon's advance. He received orders to cross a rock slide, move to high ground, and set up an ambush overlooking a trail coming through the pass.

"Lieutenant Shafik, I don't think we should go that way," Marcus heard Paine's complaint on the company frequency.

"Came from the top. The battalion commander has eyes in the sky and says it's okay to move there. Enemy forces are three kilometers away. You need to be in position and ready to conduct the ambush in twenty minutes. Get moving, sergeant."

Marcus ducked as fire erupted in the boulder field. Pinned down by heavy rifle and machinegun fire, the second squad, the one Paine commanded, couldn't move. Marcus gave orders to his own seven troopers.

"Move up on the left, prepare to lay down covering fire so Paine's squad can pull back," Marcus yelled as he waved his unit forward. "By the tree line over there."

Jogging over to the woods as enemy bullets cracked around him, Marcus yelled to his wingman. "Forget your plasma rifle, the range is too great. Use your carbine." He fired at an enemy position, muttering, "A rocket launcher would be a big help right now."

76

The attackers increased their fire.

"Paine, you need to mark your position. I don't want my guys to hit you."

A puff of blue smoke appeared on the edge of the field. "Identify blue."

"Negative blue, that's enemy smoke," Paine replied. "Shoot at the smoke, keep them down."

"SITREP," Shafik called out over the net.

"Three WIA, five effectives." Marcus tried to hear anything in Paine's voice to indicate he might be wounded, then focused on shooting anyone near the blue smoke. "Popping smoke now."

"Identify white," Marcus yelled.

"Just don't hit any of my guys," Marcus could hear Paine's labored breathing. "Moving to checkpoint five now."

Marcus could see a figure dragging a body through the field, stopping every few meters to drop it and fire at the unseen enemy. The other five members of the squad were running toward Marcus' position.

"Come on, Paine, move!" Marcus waved the first trooper into his line. "What the hell happened?"

"We got hit as soon as we got to the edge of the boulders. They were waiting for us. Sergeant Martin took one right through the arm, and Mills and Bushey were hit in the legs. He told us to get back here and cover his retreat."

"Then cover his damned retreat." Marcus yelled. "Fire at anything that isn't our guys."

The combined squads poured hypervelocity rounds into the suspected enemy locations.

Dust and rock shrapnel filled the air, giving Paine some concealment from the attackers. Slinging his rifle, he grabbed the wounded soldier by the combat vest, dragging her up the hill toward the tree line.

"Keep it up, guys." Marcus saw the attackers break cover. He screamed, "Paine, get down!"

He saw Paine drop to the ground and roll over, bringing his weapon up and spraying the attacking soldiers. Marcus added his own fire. The enemy disintegrated in the hail of fire.

Running toward his friend, Marcus yelled, "I got her, Paine." When he reached the wounded soldier, he slung her over his shoulder and sprinted back to the cover of the tree line. He turned to see Paine running in the opposite direction.

"What in the hell is he doing?" Marcus screamed.

Private Mills, dangling from his broad shoulders, croaked out, "He told Private Bushey to stay put. That he'd be back for him." She winced in pain as Marcus laid her down on the ground and looked at her wounds. "Sarge always said he'll never leave anyone behind. I thought it was all bullshit until he stuffed Bushey in a big crack in a rock. He covered the opening, then dragged out of there." She grimaced as Marcus put a Quickheal patch on the open wound on her thigh. "He's hit worse than me, but he's going back for Bushey."

"Jones, take care of her. I'm going out there." Marcus grabbed Mills' ammunition and headed down the hill, in the direction Paine took.

Marcus slowed his approach as enemy fire intensified to his front. He could hear conventional and hypervelocity shooting being exchanged. It stopped suddenly. Careful not to be caught in an ambush, Marcus crept forward. He came upon a bloody scene.

Six enemy soldiers lay dead on the ground. Paine sat in the open with Bushey's head cradled in his lap. He used his own first aid kit to try to stop the bleeding.

Marcus could hear the death rattle as Bushey breathed his last.

"Paine," Marcus whispered, putting his hand on his friend's shoulder. "Come on, buddy. We've got to move before they come at us with more." He tried to pull Paine to his feet.

"We need to take him back. His family should be able to bury the body." Paine struggled to get up. "He has a girlfriend and a baby son."

Marcus noticed not all the blood came from Bushey. There were two holes in Paine's left sleeve. Paine's blood seeped through his combat vest from a shoulder wound.

"I'll get him. You okay to walk?"

"I've been better. Just get me to a meditube and I'll be fine." Paine passed out from loss of blood.

"We got this, sergeant."

Marcus spun around to see the five unhurt soldiers from Paine's squad standing there, watching for enemy action. "He would die for us, so we figured we could die for him. Can you give us some help?"

"You two get Bushey. I'll take care of him." Marcus slung Paine over his shoulder and headed for the safety of the perimeter. He called Lieutenant Shafik. "We need medevac for two wounded and one KIA."

*****

The light hurt his eyes. He opened them slowly, seeing the tech standing at the door to the meditube. He flashed back to the torture he went through every time before. That scared him more than his wounds. He started to get up.

"Hold still, Paine." Marcus pushed his friend down. "Don't worry. Kaitlyn and I are going to become good friends when we get back to base." Paine saw him look at the blushing pretty, young woman. "She told me she had orders. But she might be willing to overlook them if we could share a drink, or something."

Watching Marcus wink at the girl made Paine want to laugh, but his shoulder hurt too much.

"I also have a friend who is looking for a little male companionship." Kaitlyn gave Paine the once-over. "I bet she'd think you're cute, without all the blood."

Looking at Marcus's mischievous grin, Paine did laugh. It hurt.

"Okay, one drink, I promise." He turned to the tech, "What are you going to do?" The fear began to subside.

"Well, I'm going to modify the procedure, just like you-know-who told me to do." Kaitlyn inserted a syringe into a small bottle.

"Before you go inside, she's going to knock you out." Marcus smiled at the young woman. "That way, no orders will be broken and you won't have to go through hell in there." He patted Paine on the uninjured shoulder. "I told you I'd have your back."

Paine felt a pin prick on his arm. He heard Kaitlyn say, "Count down from ten."

"Thanks Marcus, I really…." His world went dark.

Chapter 21 - Trisha's Torment

Staff Sergeant Paine Martin looked over his assembled squads. "We're going to California. Our orders are to eliminate the bordellos in the city and rescue the children being exploited there."

He looked over his soldiers. They kept their feelings hidden, but he knew from their profiles that some of them had been abused as children. "The Corvis Foundation is moving their space-control operations to San Francisco. Steven Corvis hired our unit to clean out the red-light district centered around the old Fisherman's Warf area. We've been assigned to the most notorious establishment. The place is a child-sex factory, with children as young as six years old being sold to clients."

Corporal Mills muttered, "I hope we don't have our hands tied on this one."

"The rules of engagement are pretty loose. Corvis got a special decree from the NUS president. We can use whatever force we deem necessary to accomplish the mission." Paine could see the gleam in Mills' eye. "That doesn't mean you can kill everyone. I know what some of you went through, but let's not turn this into a blood bath."

*****

Trisha's parents survived by scrounging food from the deserted buildings in and around Los Angeles. They often had to fight off other scavengers to keep what little they found.

"Trisha, come here." The small, blond girl walked out of the culvert her parents commandeered for their home. "These nice men are going to be taking care of you from now on."

Trisha looked at the shopping cart full of canned goods parked in front of their shelter. Jason, her nine-year-old brother, stood outside. One man had his hand on Jay's shoulder.

Her mother knelt in front of the children.

"You two be good and do what they say. They're going to take you to a camp where there are other children, and schools, and lots of food." She cried as she hugged them close. "Everything will be just fine, you'll see."

The cart disappeared into the culvert. Trisha could see her father hungrily opening a can and wolfing down its contents.

The man who had her by the hand laughed until they were out of sight. Then he grabbed her arm and pulled her close.

"You're better off with us than with your parents," he whispered, pawing at her skinny body. "Those cans are as rotten as they are. What were they thinking, giving their kids to a bunch of strangers?" The other two men were disrobing her brother as she closed her eyes and screamed.

The men, with the children in tow, returned to the drain pipe two days later. There were four open cans on the ground outside the opening, and the smell of death filled the air.

One man put a cloth over his mouth and nose and went into the pipe. "Yup, they're dead." He pushed out the partially empty cart. The men had a good laugh. Trisha felt nothing as they set fire to the bodies and moved along in search of more victims.

The men found additional starving families and traded for seven more children, five girls and two more boys. They were almost out of the canned food they were trading for the children, so they tried one more time before they left the area. They hit the mother lode.

Five children, all beautiful, big-eyed girls who ranged in age from eight to twelve, were standing outside on the broken sidewalk. The negotiations were going on.

"I need to talk to your mother," Trisha whispered to the oldest of the girls.

She gasped as a hard hand gripped her shoulder. "Now we don't want to start any trouble, do we?" The hand turned her around. She could see another man holding her brother by the back of the neck.

"No, please don't hurt him anymore." Tears welled up in her eyes as she remembered what they'd already done to her little brother. She closed her eyes, trying to block out the memories.

Two days later, the girls wailed and tore at their hair when they saw their parents, stomachs bloated from gorging on the poisonous food, dead in the street.

The men took the children into San Francisco. Trisha and the rest of the newly orphaned children were sold to a sex factory. The leader of the gang assured the owner that the children were already well broken in. They were stripped of their clothing, put into cages on display and sold to any who could pay with either food or snarf, a new synthetic drug.

One of the lucky few, if you could consider it lucky to live for six years in the hell hole of the back-alley bordello, Trisha managed to survive. Most of the boys and girls who came with her were already dead.

Returning to her cage after a disgusting encounter with a client, she saw her brother. Stopping by the cage door, she called out, "Jason, are you all right?"

He turned toward the sound of her voice. Frightened when she saw his eyes, she knew he'd given up. He'd lost all hope. Now one of the living dead, he simply waited for the breathing to stop. The guard leading her jerked her back to reality, pulling her away from her brother's cell.

Later that night, her neighbor whispered through the mesh cage. "Jason's dead. He made a rope out of his blanket and hanged himself. At least he's free from all this."

"I will survive. I'm not giving up hope," Trisha kept telling herself. "One day, I'll get my revenge on those bastards."

More children committed suicide over the next few days. The pimps removed all clothing and blankets from the cells. When they came for Trisha's things, the pimp leered at her. "It will add to the presentation, seeing you naked like this."

Trisha became the favorite of one pimp. He liked to torment her. Trisha finally snapped. She attacked the pimp when he came into her cell. Retaliation swiftly followed.

Bruised and aching from the beating she received. Trisha curled up in the fetal position in the filth on the floor of her cage. They'd hurt her but caused no permanent damage. Surprised they let her live, her hopes were shattered when the man she'd beaten walked up to her cage.

"This is your last day on earth." The pimp carefully stayed out of reach. "But don't think your gonna just die. You're part of a show." He mounted several cameras around the cage. "Gang-raped until dead. We're getting lots of money for this show, and lots of people signed up to be a part of it." He grinned evilly. "Lots of your old customers want to see you die."

She needed to find a way to kill herself. She tried to use her fingernails to open the veins in her arms.

"Go ahead, you know we'll stop the bleeding. You're worth too much to die now." Her pimp laughed aloud.

Scratching wildly at her arms, Trisha watched blood began to flow. The pimp pushed a shock-stick into the cage, sending electricity through her battered body. "Just let me die!" Trisha screamed, grabbing the prod, feeling the voltage course through her body. Then a miracle happened.

The crack of hypervelocity bullets filled the air. When she saw the head of her tormentor explode, she cheered the sound. She reached through the bars of her cage and splashed her hands in his blood, laughing hysterically. Another pimp came running toward her cell. Seeing the crazed look in her eyes and her bloody, clawed hands reaching out for him, he backed away from the cage door. As he ran away, the crack came again. He stumbled and fell. Trisha watched in glee as more blood pooled under his mangled body.

A large soldier shot the pimp again, finishing him off. He approached the cage containing the cringing girl.

"I'm Sergeant Marcus. I'm here to help you," she heard him say. Trisha backed away as he reached for the door handle. Anger flashed in her eyes, along with a thirst for revenge, a longing for justice. She hoped Marcus would recognize it.

He silently released Trisha from her cell.

Trisha straightened up and ran bloody fingers through her matted hair. Then she pulled the knife out of the dead pimp's belt. Spitting on the body, she carved on him, not leaving any way of determining if the gender of the corpse.

Holding the bloody knife, Trisha walked toward the soldiers who were herding the surviving pimps toward the front of the building. The hardened mercenaries stepped back from the bloody, wild-eyed girl. The prisoners held their tied hands up in front of their faces, trying to protect themselves from Trisha.

"Die, you fucking assholes." She swung wildly, killing three and stabbing a fourth before Marcus wrestled the knife from her.

"It's over, you're safe now."

Trisha laughed hysterically. She flinched when Marcus took her hand but let him lead her away.

A soldier shot the last pimp behind the left ear.

Chapter 22 – Security Council Meeting

The Security Council meeting room felt stuffy. The air conditioner, on the fritz again, struggled to cool the room. Allan Baum looked at the list of member countries. The change in global politics showed in the composition of the United Nations. Many of the former members no longer existed as countries. Of the 211 countries that made up the UN General Assembly in 2038, only 42 remained. Five new countries had been admitted, two of which were space colonies. The UN represented the "civilized" nations of the world.

He called the meeting to order.

"We have an opportunity to establish a workable world government." He sat back as the council members stared at him in disbelief. "It will involve gaining control of the rest of New York. My military advisor will be coming in to discuss plans for eliminating any resistance from the factions in New York, so we can make this a reality."

Lin Chow Tsing, the ambassador from China, represented the most populous country in the world. He spoke quietly. "Mister Secretary, why would China want to be under someone else's rule? We are still the most populous nation on earth, and our government has been stable, through the worst of days."

China's population at the start of the plague stood at 3.5 billion. The ravages of starvation reduced the population to a mere 115 million. Tales of cannibalism had come from a trickle of refugees to the island nations, but China had closed her borders to all outsiders. No one discovered what happened to the dead. The government maintained a strict hold on all incoming and outgoing information.

"We have no idea what's going on in your country," Oshara Tdaki responded. "Japan also suffered terribly, but the government stayed intact." He turned to Andre Chevalier of France. "Our beloved Emperor made an impassioned appeal to the people of Japan to do what they could to save the children. He spoke to us about duty, honor, and national pride. His speech ended with the following, 'I ask the people of Japan to do what they can for the future of our great country. I beg you to do what you can for our children, the future of our land. You must do what you think is best to protect their future. As for me, I hereby abdicate my throne to my great-grandson, Hidecki. May he have a long and prosperous reign.' Then he knelt on a reed mat."

"We all know the story, you've told it so often." Andre spoke in a fake Japanese accent. "His personal guard, in ancient samurai dress, walked up behind him with a drawn sword and took up a fighting stance. The Emperor picked up a short sword lying on the mat and bared his upper body. He bowed low to the camera, grasped the sword in one hand and as he drove it into his belly cried out, 'Banzi!' The guard's sword flashed, and the Emperor died."

"You mock me, my country and my emperor." Tdacki's glare caused Andre's heart to skip a beat. "If we were in my home country, I would have you killed."

"Sorry, I meant no disrespect."

"Japan lost sixty percent of its population over the next three days, but we had enough food to survive the ravages of the plague. Our civilization remains intact." Tdacki looked straight ahead as he delivered his own dig at his counterpart. "We did much better than France."

"I've heard the story, too." Ian Burns, the Irish delegate sat back in his seat. "You might have saved some of your people if you did it the way we did."

"You blockaded your ports and kept refugees from coming into the country. The plague didn't affect you but let the people of Great Britain starve to death. It no longer exists." Tdaki shook his head. "That's genocide, not sacrifice."

"They deserved it after what they did during An Drochshaol, the Great Famine."

"Oh, my God, Ian. That happened more than two hundred years ago." Allan's exasperated voice rose in pitch. "It's that kind of thinking that keeps us from having a world government."

"Doesn't matter, now. We have repopulated the islands with decent folks."

"You've also laid claim the Maritime Provinces, Massachusetts, and Maine." John Gutenberg, representing the New United States, chimed in. Tall and rangy, he sported a handlebar mustache that made him look more like a villain than a diplomat.

"We don't dispute your claim, but don't want you to take any more of the old United States territory."

"You Irish kept everything for yourself instead of helping others." Gerhard Mueller, the German ambassador, pointed his finger at Burns. "We lost many of our people while you grew fat. The asteroid mining colony of New Germany only had ten percent survive, before we could ship food to them."

"We had to feed our own first," Ian Burns retorted. "No one got fat, I can promise you that."

"Perhaps, but you also vetoed New Germany becoming a state, part of our country. They had to become their own country."

"Those mining spheres provide us all with precious metals. Without them, we wouldn't have materials for the farming platforms." Ian leaned back in his seat, glaring at the German ambassador. "We couldn't let you control all of that. And don't blame it all on Ireland. France and Poland also vetoed the admission request."

"Yet neither France nor Poland insisted their mining colonies be independent since the combined population is only five thousand." Gerhard leaned forward, glaring at the Polish and French ambassadors. "Your excuse that many of the workers were from other countries doesn't make allowing them to join the UN legal. Thank God we can grow plague-resistant wheat."

"That you Germans stole from us," Szymon Tajek started on a tirade. "Who is first to grow disease-free grain? Poland. We Poles brought peace and food to the ancient lands of the Kingdom of Poland and to Slovakia, Bulgaria, Romania, and Hungary. We gave our wheat to Ukraine, so they could be strong allies with us against the gangs that raided our borders from the Russian wasteland."

"So Ukraine would side with you in case Germany decided to expand its territory once more." Andre Chevalier, the French delegate, sipped his latte before continuing. "France also developed its own strain of wheat and one of barley. We have plenty to eat today because of our great scientists." He looked across the table at Mueller. "We are a strong country, one that will not tolerate any expansion of the Germans on either side of their borders."

"Why must you assume Germany would do any such thing?" Allan thought Mueller might explode.

Andre looked disdainful. "History, Herr Mueller. The two phases of the European Wars. The Second and Third Reich, and now you're calling yourselves the Fourth Reich."

"That's a lie, perpetrated by some here who would besmirch the German race." Mueller came out of his seat, pounding the table in front of him. "You wouldn't let New Germany be a part of our country, yet you keep your space colonies under your own control. That's outrageous."

"I, for one, would like to see a return to the status quo." John Gutenberg spoke again, breaking the tension. He represented the New United States, one of three nations created from the original USA. "I know we'll never get everything back. Utah seceded from the Union in 2041 proclaiming itself the Mormon State. Louisiana, Mississippi and Alabama formed a confederation, the New South. Parts of Massachusetts and Maine are now in the overseas holdings of Ireland."

"We won't be giving them back, you know." Ian looked at Gutenberg.

"I'm not asking for them," Guttenberg replied. "The government in Austin has no claim on those areas you control. We only want to get New Jersey, Connecticut, and New York back. They're a no-man's-land."

"Aye, we've not been able to go in there, either. Every time we try, we lose people." Ian sat back in his chair. "It's a lost cause, for now."

"As much as my president wants to return New York to the NUS, if we can get it under control, he's all for it."

"Under UN control, you mean," John Wilson Smythe, the Australian ambassador, waved his hand contemptuously. "We did what needed to be done, just like our Irish friends. I admit that stopping immigration caused a few deaths, but the benefits outweighed the cost. If we need to do something similar in New York, then we'll do it for the common good."

Gutenberg laughed aloud. "You sank ships full of people, then machinegunned survivors so they couldn't get to shore. Now you want us to believe it is justified?"

"We all did things we considered necessary. Your government began the problems in New York by killing every man, woman, and child in the international terminal at JFK Airport when the plague began. No wonder the New Yorkers hate you so much. If we must kill some so others survive, so be it."

"The old USA did that, not us."

"You hypocrite. Your government keeps the people of South and Central America from coming into NUS. They're living in poverty, stuck in massive border towns near the border. The Mexican government rules through martial law, stealing what the workers make as they work in Corvis-built factories and facilities in the desert." Smythe pointed in Gutenberg's direction. "Corvis is the real power in NUS, you're just puppets."

"That's not true." Gutenberg yelled.

"Gentlemen, you can see why we need to form a government that controls everything, so we can stop this petty bickering," Allen Baum smoothed the hurt feelings around the table. "We must work together, or our world will be plunged into another disaster. Old hatreds will lead to what happened on Luna Colony."

Refugees from India and Pakistan settled there with help from the USA, China, and Japan. Luna's eighty thousand inhabitants helped maintain software for the many computer systems built by the Corvis Corporation.

"We debated for weeks whether to admit Luna as one or two countries because its population had separated themselves into Muslim East Luna and Hindu West Luna." Baum seemed to lecture the assembly. "Even though people from both groups sought their own nation, we agreed to admit Luna as one nation, with one condition. They had to establish a dual presidency. The civil war caused by this decision held up their admittance. After a short, violent battle by rival factions, who were all killed when the dome they were fighting in lost pressure, the remaining population passed a referendum to accept the terms."

"Now the colony is at peace. See, some had to die to make it a reality." Smythe smiled, sure he made his point.

"True enough. Let's hope the plan to establish a world government won't result in more death." Baum stood up and walked to the door. "All of you will receive a briefing from our military specialist. He'll help us solve this dilemma."

Chapter 23 - Cleaning up Atlanta

"How do I look?" Paine stood in the outer office of the regimental headquarters.

Captain Rachel Miller, the regimental adjutant, looked at the young man standing in front of her desk. Brand new gold bars glittered on his shoulders. He wore clean boots and a fresh uniform and obviously had recently shaved.

"Pull the tissue off the razor cut." She smiled at Paine. "Other than that, you look fine." The comm on her desk beeped. "The General will see you now."

Paine marched through the open door and stopped three feet in front of his father's desk. "Serg... Lieutenant Martin, reporting as ordered, Sir." He stood there as Josh continued to read his computer screen. Paine squirmed uncomfortably as he waited in the warm room.

"I have a mission for you. I don't want to send you, but I have no one else available." Josh's voice came out in a monotone, emotionless. "Keep in mind if you screw this up, you'll be a sergeant again." He looked at his son. "If you're lucky."

Paine stood silently, flushing from resentment and embarrassment.

"After the Old US killed immigrants trying to get into the country, NUS put several restrictions in their constitution. Those restrictions keep them from doing what needs to be done to eliminate problems. We don't operate under those rules, and the NUS State Department looks the other way as long as we get the job done." Josh pushed an icon on his desk-top screen. "They recently resettled Atlanta, opening factories to build space platforms."

The screen behind Josh lit up. A chart appeared.

"This shows the crime rate in the occupied part of the city. Most of the problems center around the drug trade." Josh looked as if he would spit on the floor. "I hate drugs, and I hate dealers more. They're pushing snarf on the workers, hooking people and causing them to steal to get enough money to buy more drugs."

"Why doesn't the NUS send in police?"

"Did I give you permission to speak?" Josh's voice came out low, full of malice. "Don't interrupt me again."

Paine's face got even redder as he closed his mouth.

"The drug of choice is snarf. They get it from New York. It's ten times more addictive than cocaine, and generates a high that lasts for days at a time. However, the physical dependency it creates causes them to take any risk to get a fix. NUS wants it stopped."

"You'll be facing modern weapons. The drug cartels have guns at least as good as what we have in the regiment. The police don't have the will or the manpower to take on the street gangs, much less the drug lords." Josh swore as he continued. "Damn it all. If President Brown had any balls, he'd send in the army and wipe out the city's entire criminal population. But he doesn't. The state department received bids from several mercenary groups. I want that contract. You and Marcus will go to Atlanta on the noon shuttle. Engage and eliminate the undesirable elements terrorizing the workers. I want it filmed, and I want it done within three days."

Paine stood there, waiting for his father to continue.

"What are you waiting for? Get out." Josh went back to his reading.

Heading for the landing pad, Paine motioned for Marcus to join him.

"I have the briefing packet on Atlanta right here," Marcus held out a chip reader to Paine. "Looks like the city is in sorry shape. Most of the infrastructure isn't working. The workers are in tenements. They've blocked off the first floors of most buildings to keep the criminal element out."

Paine looked at recent pictures of the housing areas. "What's all this?" He pointed at the litter in the streets.

"People are too lazy to put their trash in the dumpsters. They just throw it in the street." Marcus shook his head as he read the intel report. "The sewer system is completely clogged. Looks like they're using chamber pots for human waste." He pointed out wads of toilet paper in a puddle. "This job is going to stink."

****

Paine gagged as he neared the tenements housing the spaceport workers. The stench permeated everything.

A misty, cold rain muffled the sounds of the night. The city streets were deserted, except for the vermin that listened to approaching footsteps. A single unbroken lamplight flickered off and on as a man passed in the shadows, trying to blend into the background. A huge black rat, larger than the rest, stood unafraid on its hind legs and watched as he passed by, then dropped to all fours, and scurried off.

Tired of wandering around, Paine welcomed the whispered curses coming from behind him. Paine thought the gang members would find him much earlier than this.

It could have been his expensive clothing or the meandering path through the streets that had lulled them into a sense of complacency. They'd discover their mistake shortly.

Trying to look lost and searching for some place of refuge, Paine punched a random number into a staircase platform control panel. The access-denied light flashed. He swore bitterly, and moved toward a nearby alley.

His potential attackers were sloppy. He could hear them sloshing through puddles of waste. One of them turned on a flashlight, the beam slicing through the misty darkness, revealing their position to Paine.

There were five assailants, one laboring under a heavy load, probably a plasma rifle. Although that made his mission a little more dangerous, he figured it would add to the sales presentation. As Paine neared the corner, he prepared for the coming confrontation. The rush of adrenaline surged through his body, so he took a few deep breaths to slow his rapidly beating heart.

Turning into the alley, Paine flipped a grenade up onto a retracted stairway. The rattle caused his attackers to freeze. He opened his coat, pulling out the fully-automatic assault carbine. Thumbing a flash-bang grenade to explode on impact, Paine threw it around the side of the building.

Diving out of the alley, he flopped down in four inches of stinking muck. His eyes were closed as the blast went off. Paine could see the assailants blinking in stunned confusion as he attacked.

He tapped the trigger.

Steel darts cut through the first attacker. They continued into the second man, standing close behind. Both had looks of surprise on their faces as their shredded torsos flopped down into the bloody street.

Paine spotted the largest of his assailants, a bearded, tough-looking man, taking aim with the plasma rifle. The other grenade exploded, sending a shower of shrapnel into the street.

Bleeding profusely, the man collapsed. The weapon slipped from his hands. As it clattered to the ground, the plasma weapon discharged and burned a two-meter-wide hole in the alley wall. The remaining assailants tried to shield themselves from the flying metal and debris.

Paine changed from automatic to burst fire, activated the laser designator, and got into a kneeling position. He targeted the heads of the last three. They died quickly.

Wiping his hands on his coat, he looked at the carnage. Most of the weapons were antiques. He picked it up the plasma rifle. Paine moved into the light to get a better look at the weapon. An older design, he decided not to save it. He ejected the hand grip and then reinserted it into the magazine well. Putting on a fire-resistant glove, he activated the trigger mechanism. The weapon self-destructed when it didn't recognize the palm print of the user. It glowed a dull red as the grip fused to the receiver, making it useless. Dropping the melted rifle into the muck, he proceeded to disassemble the remaining firearms and scatter their parts.

"Marcus, did you record it all?"

A deep rumble came from behind a dumpster. Marcus emerged from his hiding place. Paine noticed that in the dim light, his friend's scarred face looked as though it had been pieced together from spare body parts - more like a monster than a human.

"Got it," Marcus replied glancing dispassionately at the carnage in the alleyway. He picked up a small, empty tube. "These boys were really stoned. They must have been after some of that snarf you were supposed to be carrying."

"When you sent me to contact the gangs, I ran into a wall of silence. People were afraid to talk." Marcus chuckled. "I guess they thought I was a narc. I let it slip I knew about a snarf mule carrying a big shipment in from New York. They all know New York snarf is the best. This one approached me." He kicked the body of one of the dead men.

He riffled through the pockets of the men as he spoke. All the thugs had several empty vials on their bodies. "It looks like they were using up what snarf they had once they took the job." Marcus shook his head as he looked at Paine. He added pointedly, "These boys were really high. Probably the only way they could get up the nerve to attack someone crazy enough to walk these streets alone at night."

"Shut the hell up, Marcus." Paine visibly shook as he came down off the rush of combat. He felt slightly ill even though he'd seen much worse death than this during his twenty-four years. He checked himself for wounds. "Did you get it all on disk? This is an important contract. I hope you didn't screw it up."

His side throbbed. Reaching down, he felt a hole in his shirt. His hand came away bloody. Paine suddenly froze. He didn't think he suffered major damage, but he felt lightheaded.

The vest must have dislodged when he hit the ground. A piece of shrapnel sliced a five-inch cut on his side. "Come here and check my wound out." His voice sounded strained as he pulled up his jacket, exposing the vest where it overlapped the groin protection. Blood oozed out of a tear in the seam between the two appliqués.

"For God's sake, Marcus, look at this, will you." Paine had a flashback – a vision of a trip to the meditube. He saw his father's face sneering at his weakness.

Walking over to his friend, Marcus examined the wound. He laughed, "Jesus, Paine. It's just a scratch." Paine shot him a hurt look. "What's with you, anyway? You've been hit a lot worse than this before."

Paine slapped a Quickheal patch on his side, settled the armor in place and pulled down his jacket. He stared at Marcus. His voice came out flat and without emotion.

"This video recording is for my father's sales pitch. You know how he is about casualties." Another wave of nausea hit Paine. "I just don't want us to lose this contract." A new thought made him pause. "Is that damned recorder off? That son of a bitch is not going to get to see his son's blood again. I'll destroy the disk and start all over again if I have to."

"Relax, I stopped it right after the closeups of our fallen friends here." Marcus sounded irritated. "I know how to run a vidcorder."

"Forget it," Paine snapped. "And don't forget to call me 'Sir' when we get back. Last time you called me 'Paine' in front of my father I thought he'd kill you on the spot."

Marcus drew himself up to an exaggerated position of attention and snapped a salute. "Yes, *Sir*, you still wet-behind-the-ears-puppy-lieutenant, sir. Just remember when I saved your ass in that Florida swamp. You were fifteen and a buck private."

Paine's face clouded up as he thought back to that day in the swamp. "I remember. That's when Gabby got killed."

"Sorry to bring that up." Marcus gently punched Paine's shoulder. "OK, boss. I'll be good."

Paine's face hardened again, so Marcus made light of the situation. "I mean, *sir*, yes *sir*." He saluted sloppily. "I hope the lifter is flying with the doors open, boss." He sniffed in Paine's direction, "You really stink. Let's get the hell out of here."

Activating his communicator, Marcus gave the code word. Both men raised their weapons as an air car approached. They didn't lower them until the lights flashed the correct recognition signal. The lifter's weapons shifted to the surrounding area as Paine replied with the countersign. No one let their guard down anywhere in this part of the NUS, especially at night.

The air car hovered two feet over the alley, fans at maximum, causing the fluids in the street to spatter both men. Marcus yelled, "Son of a bitch."

They were both covered with blood and human waste.

Paine solemnly looked at his drenched friend. "Who stinks now?"

Gritting his teeth, Marcus grumbled, "Wait until I catch that pilot in a dark alley."

Paine grinned and held his nose. Laughing, they leapt into the air car. The pilot went to full power, and they were pressed into their seats as the lifter shot into the dark evening sky.

They left the corpses for the rats.

Chapter 24 - Whippettes in New York

The NUS surveillance technician followed his target down the broad avenue. The sensors of the tiny flying surveillance platform picked up the signal emitting from the device embedded in the lining of the black Stetson that Doctor William Whippette wore. The computer linked to the sensor platform recorded the greetings William called out to passers-by. The faces of the people and their conversations were recorded and stored for analysis by a special code-breaking program. The trip home seemed uneventful, the technician thought, but one could never be too careful these days.

****

William rode the elevator to the fortieth floor. He walked down the hall to his apartment. He threw the Stetson across the room toward the hat rack, intentionally missing it. "Damn!" He hoped he knocked the tracking device out of synch. Closing the door, he looked at his wife.

Betty, forty-six years young, maintained a rigorous exercise regimen. He admired her from behind as she ran on the treadmill.

"You still have a great ass."

She wiped the sweat from her face with a towel. William motioned for her to play along, subtly pointing to the camera hidden in the light fixture in the living room.

"Looks like you need a shower." William moved across the room and took his wife in his arms. He rubbed her sweaty body against his. "And now I need one, too." He whispered into her hair, "We need to talk."

Betty playfully pushed him away. She strutted toward the bathroom, swinging her hips from side to side. "Since we're both dirty, we might as well enjoy it."

William shed his shirt and pants as he walked across the room, causing the microphones built into his clothing to boom in the ears of the technician as they hit the floor.

The tech grinned at his partner. "Larry, come on over here and get a look at this. We're going to get another show. Man, do these people ever get tired of each other?" He activated the camera in the bathroom and expanded it to full screen.

One watched with great interest as Betty Whippette removed her sweaty clothing and stepped into the shower. The other only had eyes for William. The two techs enjoyed the show until the shower door fogged up from the steam.

William held his wife close as they made love and whispered in her ear, "I'm right. We're being monitored. I think the FBI is surveilling us, on orders from the White House."

Betty leaned in and as she bit his ear she whispered, "Son of a bitch. You suspected something, but I never thought the government would let this kind of thing happen."

"We have to find out if the rumors of a new plague are true. My source says the Corvis Foundation has been working on a pathogen that attacks the nervous system. We need to find out if that is what caused the recent peak of unexplained deaths New York." William ran his hands over Betty's back, washing off the soap. "There is a group in the city that has agreed to let us help, if we can get there."

"Didn't we learn anything? We damn near killed everything on the planet twenty years ago. Now NUS is planning to start killing people again?" She pulled away and looked at her husband. "What can we do?"

"We go ahead with our plans to go to New York as a part of the United Nations relief effort." William gasped as Betty squeezed him tightly and shook with suppressed sobs. "Take it easy, baby. The worst thing the NUS can do is kill us. We might as well enjoy until then." They concentrated on each other, trying to forget about their impending problems for a little while.

*****

The pilot of the lifter spoke into the intercom. "Relief operations are difficult, but none is more dangerous than our missions to New York." Heavily armored aircraft circled just out of small-arms range as the larger and slower relief carriers moved in to drop off supplies. The heavy aircraft hovered above street level. Gunners manned plasma rifles mounted in the door hatches. They constantly scanned the area, watching for any sign of attack.

"Doctors, you have to get ready to go. Once we unload this pile of relief supplies, we'll go vertical, break away from the main group and fly directly to the Chrysler Building. You only have a few seconds to get out, so please have your bags and equipment ready."

He looked back over his shoulder at them and spoke again. "Technically, I'm not responsible for you once you leave my aircraft, but there are a few things you need to be aware of. When you get out, drop everything, take two paces forward and stand with your hands up. The UN guards are still a little jumpy after last week's attacks against the compound. If you make any kind of sudden movement, or lower your hands, they will shoot at you." The pilot glanced at the two passengers sitting behind him. "Odds are they'll miss, but I wouldn't take the chance. Even a blind rat finds a corpse once in a while."

They nodded thanks to the pilot and got ready to disembark. The lifter dropped the last of the supplies on the ground and the formation leapt into the sky. The Whippettes watched hundreds of New Yorkers swarm the piles, fighting over the food and medicine piled on the ground. In the time it took to the lifter to reach a thousand feet, the load and most people were gone. They could see a few bodies lying where the pile of supplies had been. They were too weak or slow to survive the crush of people.

William tightened the straps on his wife's backpack, touched her gently on the shoulder. "Get ready. Hold on." Their lifter dropped out of formation and descended quickly to the empty street in front of the Chrysler Building. The door gunner pushed the Whippettes' luggage out with his foot as the crew chief shoved Betty and William out the door. The lifter leapt back into the air as the Whippettes fell face down on the cracked pavement.

The lack of activity unsettled them.

Betty turned her head toward her husband. "We'd better do what we were told." They stood up, dusted off their clothes, then took two steps away from their baggage and put their hands into the air. "I just hope your information about the resistance is correct. If not, we're in deep trouble."

After what seemed like ten minutes, a lone soldier wearing the blue-black uniform of a UN Guard came forward. Obviously buzzed, he'd either been drinking or high on snarf. The guard looked scared, probably because of the numerous muzzles that appeared in the blown-out windows of the first three floors of the building. They all pointed into the street. The guard's words were slurred as he spoke. "Drop them backpacks and move toward me." The Whippettes complied. The guard moved to them and scanned them with an explosive detector. He stepped back with a look of relief on his face. Turning toward the windows, he yelled, "All clear."

The soldiers in the windows pulled back their weapons and went back to their card games, videos, or other diversions inside the building. The guard motioned the Whippettes to follow him. As they recovered their bags, a manhole cover opened in front of them. A neatly thrown club caught the guard in the center of the forehead.

The hand that emerged from the manhole motioned the Whippettes forward. They quickly dropped their rucksacks into the sewer. Betty went into the hole first, followed by William. The lone soldier at the front door turned around and saw the guard on the ground and William disappearing into the hole. He sounded the alarm as the manhole cover clanged back into place.

Forty weapons fired wildly into the street. The sound, muffled by the manhole cover, was barely audible. One hypervelocity round ripped through the side of the hole, showering the Whippettes with debris, inflicting razor cuts on their faces and hands.

The smoky, flickering torch held by a hooded figure lit their way in the darkness of the sewers. They couldn't see the guide. The shielded torch only reflected in their direction. As they stumbled through the dank smelling water, hidden obstacles tripped them. They were drenched in foul water and sweat. The guide kept up a frantic pace. Even though they prided themselves on keeping fit, both were panting when the guide finally stopped.

"Stay where you are." The guide moved away, farther down the sewer. The light faded into the distance.

Suddenly, the entire sewer pipe lit up with a soft red light.

"Strip." an amplified voice rang out. "Take everything off, including jewelry. Put your wedding rings in the bag to your left. Leave everything else in the water."

After the Whippettes complied, two sets of coveralls and two pairs of boots were thrown at them from the darkness, splashing them with filthy water. "Put them on." They pulled on the soaked clothing and stood waiting for instructions. The red light went out and a string of tiny lights flickered on and off leading into the distance. "Follow the lights."

They walked through the sewers for at least an hour. The route twisted and turned. They were lost. Suddenly, the lights went out. William and Betty stood still and waited.

"Shield your eyes, please." The voice sounded pleasant and vaguely familiar. The lights came up, and the Whippettes were facing a bank of flood lights. "I have a few questions for you. Why did you come to New York?"

"We need to know who's asking before we answer any questions," William shielded his eyes, trying to peer at the person behind the lights. He could only make out a shadow.

"Suffice it to know that if you don't answer my questions now, you won't leave these tunnels. Not alive, anyway." William heard a something splash at his feet. He jumped back.

"Don't worry. It's not a grenade." Laughter echoed in the chamber. "It's just a canteen. You look like you could use a drink."

Something about that statement sounded familiar. William also thought the undercurrent of jocularity seemed out of place, given the situation. He remembered that he'd spoken those words years before, on a stretch of road in Kentucky. "Ashley?"

The glare softened. Ashley stepped forward into the light, laughing. "You guys look pretty good for a couple of old farts. It's a wonder you could keep up with me." Betty and William quickly moved to Ashley and gave her a hug. Ashley pulled away. "We can catch up later. Right now, I need to get you into some dry clothes."

Betty looked around the tunnel. "Where are your people?"

"I won't let them do anything I wouldn't mind doing myself, and to be honest with you, I really didn't trust that it would be the two of you down here. None of my people are familiar with you two. I had to be sure this wasn't a trap." She stopped for a second to pick up the automatic rifle she had leaned against the wall. "If it were anyone else, I'd have shot first and found out who they were later."

Shocked, Betty breathed in sharply. "You're kidding, right?

Ashley answered the question by changing the subject, "Let's go get you cleaned up and into some dry clothes." She led them through a branch of the tunnel to a stack of equipment.

Betty looked through the items in the pile. Their clothes were not in the bags and none of their personal items were anywhere near. "What happened to our gear? We had some medical devices that could be critical to our work. And when do we get back our phones? We need to contact our daughter Elle and tell we're all right."

Putting her arms around her friend, Ashley held her tight for a few seconds. Her eyes misted over.

"I'm well-acquainted with the feeling of what it's like not being able to talk to your children. Understand that you must trust they'll be all right. If they aren't, pray that the end is quick, and they don't suffer. Just try not to let it eat away at you." Ashley wiped her tears as she turned away. "Believe me. I know how hard it is."

As they moved into the light, William looked at Ashley. It seemed like she'd gotten younger in the years since he had last seen her. "What's happened to you? You look even better than you did on that road in Kentucky thirteen years ago. What's going on?"

Ashley blushed and then laughed aloud.

"When I got to New York, I had a run in with a gang of muggers. They robbed me, beat me half to death and left me in the middle of the street to die. A group of Technos - scientists who survived the plague and formed a gang here - were moving from one safe house to another. They found me."

"They fixed you up?"

"Not right away. After arguing whether to let me die or help, they took me to their headquarters and got me into a meditube. Turns they scrounged from the fashion district."

"I'm getting the picture," William grinned.

"The 'tube had been modified for runway models. It treated my wounds, then took out the wrinkles, tightened up the flabby parts, fixed the varicose veins and even gave me a nice manicure and pedicure. I felt great when I got out. You still look pretty good." She raised her eyebrows and stared hard at Betty's face. "If you want to change those crow's feet in for smooth skin, let me know."

Ashley ducked the half-hearted punch Betty threw. They walked arm-in-arm, laughing softly as they headed down the tunnel.

Chapter 25 - White House Visit

Dust rose as the UN lifter settled down on the parched earth. Texas, in the midst of a heat wave, felt like a furnace. UN Secretary General Allan Baum and his assistant walked up to the front gate of presidential residence.

"It's just like the old White House in Washington, isn't it, Monica?"

Dabbing the sweat from her forehead, Monica looked at the white mansion. "Just like the pictures in my history books."

Baum stood with arms extended as the security scanners did their work. The personal defense weapon he carried in a shoulder holster had already been surrendered at the front desk. They even took the small pen knife he used to open correspondence. Monica gave up her weapon and handed over her purse for inspection.

"Ma'am, what is this?" the secret service agent held up a small aerosol can.

"It is hair spray. I can show you if you wish."

"Please step into the chamber and actuate the spray," the officer ordered.

She complied, taking out a handheld mirror and carefully running a brush through her blond hair before spraying it in place.

Baum leaned over and whispered in the agent's ear, "Vanity seems to have returned to the world, even after all the mess we've been in."

The scanner turned green, indicating that no toxic or dangerous biological compounds were found in the spray. The agent glanced at the printout. Satisfied nothing could hurt anyone in the White House, he passed Baum and Monica through security.

Baum, visibly agitated as he waited outside the Oval Office, nervously paced back and forth with the cup of water an aide had given him. He had intentionally arrived early, planning for this opportunity. He gave a veiled nod to his assistant. She stood and walked up behind him.

"Mister Secretary, could you please...."

Baum spun around as she touched his shoulder, spilling the water down the front of her jacket.

"I'm so sorry," Baum turned to the agent. "Could you please have someone take Monica to a place where she can clean off the front of her dress?"

The secret service agent led her through a small corridor to a rest room.

Once the door closed, Monica pulled out the hairspray can and directed it into the return vent for the air conditioning unit. Depressing the plunger, she held it until the can emptied. Then she cleaned the water from the front of her dress and returned to the waiting area.

"Sorry, Mister Baum. It was very clumsy of me."

Brown's secretary, Kelsie, looked up from her console. She interrupted his reply. "The President will see you now."

When Baum entered, President Bob Brown told his advisors to leave the room. He called out to his secretary, "Kelsie, I don't want to be disturbed for the next twenty minutes. Hold my calls, and don't let anyone come into the room, no matter what. Understood?" Kelsie nodded, then left the room and went back to her station.

As the door closed, the smile left Brown's face. He held up his finger and then reached under the desk to shut off the recording device.

Baum glared across the table at the NUS president. "You are a completely incompetent fool. How could you let them get away?"

President Brown looked up from the paperwork littering his desk. He hadn't slept in nearly a week, agonizing over the decision he had to make. "When you told me about the plan, I increased the level of surveillance on the Whippettes. We had them both covered, we even bugged their wedding rings. I don't know what happened. Besides, your people let them get away, not mine. Go bother your security chief and leave me alone." The president glared back at Baum.

Baum walked over to the desk and stood behind the president.

"Bob, don't get me wrong. If word of what we're planning gets around, it will be the end of all of us, so we need to figure out something. You're old enough to remember what happened to the government when the Coca Plague information leaked out. The Whippettes have a daughter. Maybe we can get one of your mercenary groups to take her hostage," Baum suggested. "I've been dealing with Colonel Martin of the Kentucky Regulars. He seems competent enough to make something like that happen. That may give us the leverage we need to keep them quiet long enough to eliminate the problem."

"Martin promoted himself to general." Brown corrected him. "He's doing a lot of other things for NUS right now. I'd rather he not be pulled away."

"Martin is also doing work for the United Nations," Baum interjected. "Maybe we can cut our costs and have him kill two birds with one stone, if you'll pardon the pun."

"I can't do it. I have to stop this madness." Staring at Baum for a full minute, President Brown rubbed his eyes and slumped forward in his chair. "I cannot do what you want me to do. I won't be party to kidnapping or murder. Leave this office right now and never speak to me again."

Secretary Baum moved to the other side of the desk and put his left hand on the President's shoulder. "You don't really mean that, do you, Bob?"

Brown jerked up out of the chair as the needle in Baum's ring stabbed into his neck. "What have you done?" His legs crumpled beneath him and he fell back into the chair. He tried to reach for the panic button under the desk.

Pushing Brown to the floor, Baum stood over the paralyzed man. "Just a little test, Bob. I gave you a small sample of the nanoprobes carrying the virus to see how well it might work." He saw terror in Brown's eyes.

"I know you're thinking about your family and staff. Don't worry about the other people in the building. They're breathing in an antitoxin that my assistant released into the building's air conditioning unit. That will keep the nanoprobes from jumping to another host once you're gone. I know how paranoid you are, and I know this room has its own filtration unit, so don't worry, you won't have to breathe any of it." Baum looked at his watch. "Five minutes. It'll begin working any time now."

The president's head ached as the virus attacked his nervous system. He could hear Baum's voice somewhere in the enveloping darkness. The UN secretary watched as the president's body convulsed as he fell out of the chair onto the floor.

"Sorry, Bob." Baum watched the twitching decrease as the nanoprobes did their work. "Thanks for being a good test subject. This virus makes you sick, and the nanoprobes attack the nervous system and the blood system. It causes your blood to weaken the cellular structure of your major arteries, deteriorating them. It also speeds up your heart rate, causing a corresponding rise in blood pressure. You'll be stroking out in a few minutes. By the way, the nanoprobes and the virus self-destruct if there is no host nearby, leaving no evidence of an infection. It will look as if you died of natural causes." Baum stepped up to look at the struggling man on the floor. "You've been under a lot of stress lately, Bob."

His heart pounded in his chest as Brown gasped for breath.

"It seems like the virus works very well," Baum checked his watch once more. "However, as my scientists predicted, I think this strain works a little too quickly. After all, we can't have the virus spread if the infected people die right away, now can we? Maybe by the time we get ready to execute the plan..." he laughed aloud, "I crack myself up sometimes. Sorry. Anyway, by the time we get ready to clear out New York, the nanoprobes will stay in the body for a while before attacking. That way it'll kill slowly enough to keep people running and spreading the disease."

Baum could see the president's lips moving. "I reminded you to get the vaccination, but you just didn't want to talk about it," Baum leaned down to whisper. "Oh, and Bob, I won't ever talk to you again. I promise."

The president's eyes rolled back in his head. Baum hit the panic button and screamed for help.

Chapter 26 - Elle

"New York is outside of our authority." The rep looked down at her desk. "We haven't been there since 2069."

Elenore Whippette sat in front of a NUS War Department representative. She tried to keep the frustration out of her voice. "You mean you won't help me?"

"The last time we sent anyone there, five thousand paramilitary police went into the heart of New York City. The force, equipped with the latest technology and the most advanced weapons, should have taken control of the city." The rep looked at the young woman in front of her desk. "We lost."

"I think we studied that in school. Was it really that bad?"

"Worse. The commander of the force believed the technological advantage made his force invincible. As one pundit succinctly put it after the massacre, he turned out to be 'dead wrong.' The official story is that a well-organized mob surrounded the force in Times Square. They were massacred. About thirty thousand attackers also died."

Elle looked at the War Department representative in disbelief. "That's pretty much what I learned. Is that why won't you help me?"

"Yes. We wrote off New York after the Times Square Fiasco." The War Department representative, polite but firm in her response to the distraught Elle, looked down at her desktop monitor. "Standing orders."

"My parents went in on NUS aircraft as part of a UN humanitarian mission. They are citizens of NUS and deserve your protection."

"Young lady, don't try to lecture me. Your parents went into the city without gaining the proper exit visa from the NUS. We arrested the commander who flew them into the city. He will be punished. We have no responsibility for their safety. They were under the protection of the United Nations."

The lost look on Elle's face made the official hesitate. She motioned her closer. "I really shouldn't be telling you this, but...." She leaned in, her voice low. "You might consider one of the mercenary units. There are at least twenty different groups out there. The best one is the Kentucky Regulars. They've been particularly effective when we've hired them. They cleaned up the tenements at the Atlanta Space Port three weeks ago."

Television coverage showed NUS forces conducting the raids, ending gang control in the city. Elle remembered the stories. The surprise must have shown on her face.

"But I thought…"

The rep cut her off. "NUS cleaned up Atlanta like the news reported. We just paid someone else to do it for us. Mercenaries can do things we can't do. To be bluntly honest with you, they aren't constrained by our laws of land warfare. Whatever else they are, they're very effective, even though their methods are unorthodox and sometimes more than a little bloody."

Elle, concerned about using hired thugs, considered walking away. The thought of her parents being held captive somewhere in the city flashed into her mind. She realized she had no other choice. "All right, can you tell me how I can get in touch with them?"

After Elle left the building, the War Department rep called the number she'd been provided. "She's on her way to you." Five minutes after sending the message, her computer announced that she had a message. Her bank informed her that a large deposit from the Corvis Foundation had been made to her account.

*****

Waiting in the foyer of the Kentucky Regulars leader's office, Elle realized the mercenaries were her last hope. She looked around the hallway. The walls were covered with at least a hundred small plaques, each inscribed with a name and date.

Intrigued, she turned to the guard at the desk. "What do all these plaques mean?"

He looked at her for a full thirty seconds and then dropped his gaze back to the monitor on his console. Elle felt very uncomfortable. She wondered why he wouldn't answer her question. Her thoughts were interrupted by another guard stepping into the foyer. "The general will see you now, Ma'am."

The room, bare except for a bulky metal desk in the center, seemed colder than the foyer. There were no decorations or pictures anywhere, nothing hung on the walls.

Elle shivered as the guide led her to a plastic chair, set precisely three feet in front of the desk. Four heavily armed men stood silently in each corner of the room, their backs against the wall. Eyes and weapons were trained on Elle. She looked at the large, well-built man of about fifty-five wearing stiffly starched fatigues, sitting behind the desk.

He stared at the petite blond woman standing in front of him until she squirmed uncomfortably. The man's voice, devoid of emotion, echoed slightly in the nearly empty room.

"My name is Martin, General Martin. Sit down." He waited until Elle settled into the uncomfortable seat. "I understand you are looking for military support to get some people out of the New York area."

Elle took a few seconds to fight down the lump in her throat. Taking a deep breath. she tried to speak in a forceful tone. Her words came out weakly.

"My parents were – are - doctors, working for the United Nations relief effort in New York. I spoke to them via sat-phone two weeks ago. They told me they were on their way to the Chrysler Building and not to worry about anything." Elle stopped to take another shuddering breath. "I haven't heard from them since. I know New York is a bad place, but they were under the protection of the UN."

Josh's voice cracked like a whip as he spit out "UN!" He shook his head, leaned back in his chair, and composed himself. "They can't even protect their own building. NUS forces have to do that, and even they can't do that well. The UN Guard Force is lucky if they keep their soldiers for more than five minutes after payday. They're a bunch of snarf addicts and drunks. Why we even allow them to exist is beyond my comprehension. They are completely useless."

He looked at the young woman as if seeing her for the first time. "Let me be blunt. The city is a cesspool. Order has not been restored in the thirty years since the plague hit. Few who go out of the UN compound and into the city come back. NUS police forces found that out in '69. The chances are that your folks are dead."

Elle felt as though she had been kicked in the stomach. She fought to regain her composure. She resolutely sat up straighter, forcing her voice to come out evenly. "I refuse to believe they're dead. I'm asking for help in trying to find them. I've done my homework. Your people are the best at this sort of thing. I understand that one of your units managed to clean up part of Atlanta."

The elder Martin's voice came out cold and flat. "That mission is supposed to be secret."

"The War Department person told me you did it."

"She did?" He looked at Elle for a full minute before speaking again. "We did a good job. Two days to set up and less than a week to execute. The gangs terrorizing the Atlanta Space Port Housing Project were neutralized with very little cost in terms of casualties. We only had two soldiers wounded, both minor. We took no prisoners. Space Port problem solved."

Elle winced at the iciness of his voice.

Josh touched the surface of his desk. A screen descended from the ceiling behind him and the lights went down. An empty alley appeared on the screen.

Elle watched as a young man entered the alley. The high-quality, high-definition recording enabled Elle to see faint stubble on his face and sweat beading on his forehead. She watched as he took a few deep breaths, then she saw him reach inside his pocket and throw something over his head.

"We contracted with the NUS War Department to conduct operations on the eleventh day of September." Josh continued, "As you can see from the date on the screen, we set up the first of our many ambushes in record time. It only took one of my officers to eliminate the first five gang members."

Elle watched as the screen played out the ambush in excruciating detail.

Using a red laser pointer to accompany his narration, Josh continued. "This action shows how quickly their most dangerous weapons were neutralized, the resulting confusion and the killing of the remaining criminals. My man did expend more rounds than necessary on the first two kills, but I took that out of his pay. Subsequent operations went as planned. The gangs were eliminated. We did it efficiently and effectively, exterminating the vermin terrorizing the Atlanta workers."

Bile rose in the back of Elle's throat as she watched the heads of three men explode. She had to swallow several times to keep from spitting it on the floor.

The soldier in the video looked very young, but his actions were fluid and sure. She noticed his face as he turned toward the recorder. *He's handsome.* His eyes looked just like those of the man trying to sell her the contract. Then she realized they were very different. She thought the young soldier's eyes had a haunted, hunted look. They showed feelings. The general's eyes showed no expression or emotion.

"All I really need is for you to find my father and mother." She fought to keep her emotions in check. "I've had no notes, no phone calls, no e-mails - nothing at all about why they were taken. There's no ransom request, no reason explaining what happened. I have to find out if they are still alive." As Elle uttered the last word, her voice trembled. On the verge of tears, Elle fought for control. She blurted out, "I have money of my own, but I'm not sure if it's enough."

"Here is my proposal." Leaning forward, Josh continued. "I'll send a platoon. The total cost is $10,000 a day, with guaranteed results in ten days or double your money back. That's $100,000 NUS, half up front." Josh sat back in his chair. "That's my only offer."

Elle quickly rose to her feet. She didn't notice the weapons of the guards snap to the ready. Shocked at the cost, and oblivious of the weapons trained upon her, she spun around and walked quickly toward the door. She stopped as she remembered the smiles on her parents faces the last time she saw them. She slowly turned and walked back to the desk. A guard stepped forward and blocked her way with a massive arm. Elle looked sternly at the general.

"I have $10,000 with me that I can put down as a deposit."

Elle reached into her purse.

"Don't move," the guard growled, grabbing her wrist.

"Stand down, she isn't here to hurt me."

The guard released her, but didn't back away.

She pulled out a bundle of cash, setting it on the desk. "I can get the rest of the money to you in three days." She hesitated. "For that kind of money, I want the best." She pointed at the video screen. "I want that man to lead the mission."

Elle didn't think it possible, but General Martin's face became even more expressionless. After a barely perceptible pause, he nodded. "Done." He dropped his head and returned to work. He didn't notice the woman's extended hand.

Elle stood there for a moment until she realized she'd been dismissed. Red-faced, she dropped her hand and walked away.

*****

Josh didn't watch Elle leave. He typed a note on his desktop reminding him to talk to his son about not screwing up this mission. He'd been paid by Steven Corvis to set this up. The UN also sent him a lot of money to increase Regular troop presence in New York. He could lose the platoon and the money Elle paid him, but needed to have the mission itself succeed. He buzzed his aide. "Get Lieutenant Martin in here." He turned abruptly to his personal guards. "Dismissed." As they marched out of the room, he set his personal protection system to the armed mode. Josh trusted no one, especially his own son.

Chapter 27 - Do What I Say

Careful not to do anything that might trigger an automatic response, Paine entered the office and stood at rigid attention in front of the massive gun metal desk. He could sense the weapons behind the wall panels following his every move.

Josh didn't respond to Paine's presence for several seconds, adding to the palpable tension in the room. When he looked up, no sign of emotion appeared in the gaze directed at his sole surviving son.

"The woman wants you to lead the mission. I'm giving it to you against my better judgment."

Paine's voice came out level and strong, "I heard that she did, sir."

Josh made a note to find out who on his staff had a big mouth. He thought *it's probably Rachel Miller, my adjutant.* She liked the boy too much. They all liked him. Whoever leaked the details of the mission would enjoy his or her reassignment to a line unit.

"The regiment cannot afford a failure." Josh allowed some emotion to enter his voice as he sneered, "I don't think you are ready."

"*You never think I'm good enough,*" Paine thought, "*but I always manage to prove you wrong, you bastard.*" Then he responded, "I understand the importance of the mission. I'll not let you down."

"I'm letting you go because she insisted. You will find her parents. Once that is done, stand by for a change of mission."

"What might that be, sir?"

"You'll know when you get new orders. It can be accomplished with the assets I'm sending with you." He tapped the desktop. A personnel roster and equipment list showed on the screen.

"I'm putting you in charge of the scout platoon. Sergeant Marcus will be your platoon sergeant. Don't get any crazy ideas that I won't be following your progress," Josh turned his attention back to the papers on his desk, effectively dismissing Paine.

"Sir, I have no doubt you'll follow my progress every step of the way."

Josh lost control. He came halfway out of his chair, caught himself and slowly sat back down. He stared at his son for a good thirty seconds, watching the red glow appear on Paine's neck and cheeks. He spoke softly in a flat, emotionless voice. "Shut your mouth. Do not speak unless spoken to. If I want you to talk, I'll tell you."

"Ever since your mother left us, you've hated me. You must understand that I don't care what you think as long as you do what you are told," Josh informed his son. "I get results because I demand results."

Paine quickly suppressed the rush of anguish caused by the memory of his mother. He remembered how his father had verbally and physically abused her until she could no longer stand it. They were supposed to run away together. When the situation presented itself, she had no choice but to escape alone from the fortified compound where they'd been imprisoned. Ashley told him she would come back. She never returned. Although he could not prove it, Paine thought his father somehow made sure she couldn't. A bounty had been placed on his mother's head, and Paine feared it had been paid.

"I do what I have to do. I've tried to teach you to do the same. Soldiers die in battle, civilians die in cross fires, and families fall apart." Josh's voice took on a hard edge as it got steadily louder. "You'll never be a good leader until you understand that things happen that are beyond your control. The end justifies the means. Don't ever forget that." He stared down his son for a few more seconds and spoke slowly and forcefully, "Now get out of here and don't screw up this mission. Dismissed."

The general watched his son perform a crisp salute, do an about face and march from the room. As the door opened to let Paine out, Josh saw the wall of memorial plaques in the outer office. He muttered, "That boy better not add any more names to the wall, unless it's his own."

He drafted two notes, one to the United Nations Secretary General and one to Steven Corvis. Then he dismissed his son from his thoughts. He dropped his eyes to the paperwork on his desk.

Chapter 28 - Scout Platoon

The small office had no windows. The desk practically filled the room. Paine called it his locker. Hot and musty, it smelled like old socks.

"You'd think the commander's son would have better digs." Marcus ignored the glare from his platoon leader as he scrunched in behind Paine, looking over his shoulder at the screen. "So, what's the plan?"

"We have no status with the UN." Paine studied the map of New York. "Not even my father could get us permission to land within weapons range of the UN buildings. The UN fires on unauthorized aircraft flying toward their compound."

"Most of the guards are so scared of an attack by one of the splinter groups operating in New York that they shoot first and ask questions later." Marcus scratched the scar on his forehead. "And I have it on good authority they hate mercenaries even more than the NUS military. We have to come up with another way into the city."

"We go in under the cover of darkness." Paine showed Marcus the map on the computer screen. "This is Neo Luddite territory. They won't be able to detect us. After we land, you and I will infiltrate UN territory. We contact the guards on the edge of the green zone. A few bribes will get us in. Then we find a delegate to sponsor our motion for freedom of action on the floor of the General Assembly."

"It'll take more bribes to get the motion passed. Just how much do we have to spend?"

"Enough, I hope. I'll use what little money I have to accomplish the mission." Paine replied. "Once the vote goes in our favor, we'll use the UN compound as a haven from which to operate."

"Cooperating with the UN is getting increasingly difficult."

"Insertion will be here." Paine highlighted Times Square. "No one with any sense of self-preservation walks the streets after dark. The Neo Luddites are our biggest threat. The good news is, they despised all technology. We go in with thermal sights. They won't have any way of seeing us in the dark."

Nighttime provided concealment as the three troop lifters carrying thirty-one passengers flew toward New York. There were a few camp fires burning in Central Park, but the target area appeared completely blacked out. Eight occupants of the lead lifter were dressed in phototrophic camouflage, which made it hard to tell how many people were in the cramped compartment. They had their hands exposed so they could talk in patrol sign while on the way to the target. Elle could only see hands flashing, seemingly detached from their arms.

Paine fingered the new first lieutenant bars on his collar. His father reluctantly promoted him after the Atlanta mission. He looked around the dimly lit compartment of the troop lifter. Whatever else Paine thought, his father wanted this mission to go right. The platoon under Paine's command comprised the best fighters in the division. *I pray I get them all back in one piece.*

Seated across from Paine, Marcus slept fitfully. Paine envied the way his platoon sergeant and friend could doze off as soon as he fastened his harness, well before the carrier lifted off. Paine studied his face.

Marcus woke up with a start, his huge hand moving with blurring speed to the pistol in the combat harness. He cracked a broken-toothed grin at his commander and slowly moved his reconstructed eyelid down in a grotesque mockery of a wink.

*****

Trisha Jones, the third member of the command team, busily fiddled with her communications equipment. No longer resembling the bruised, half-starved creature Marcus had pulled out of the cell in San Francisco, Trisha belonged to the Regulars. After months of psychiatric care, she'd been declared fit for military service. The doctor told her she needed to find a home. He said she would make a fine addition to the force. She had a knack for communications and became a sergeant at the ripe old age of twenty.

She'd been assigned to Marcus's squad after joining the force. On her first mission, the unit went on a particularly bad deployment where they lost several soldiers. General Martin had thrown them a drunken party. Almost everyone reported to sick call the next day. Marcus saw his young charge in the day room, waiting to see a medic. She looked green. He handed her a glass of his personal hangover cure.

"What is this stuff?" Trisha looked at it with trepidation.

"A mixture of beer, tomato juice and hot sauce." Marcus took a big swig, grinned and sighed, "This is a bloody eye."

Trisha dropped the tumbler, turned away, becoming violently ill. "Get that filth away from me." She fell against the wall, hyperventilating, and covering her face with her hands.

Marcus backed away and waited for Trisha to calm down. After a few minutes, her breathing became more normal.

"What's wrong, Trisha?"

"Sorry, Marcus, it's just that in the brothel you rescued me from, I had this pimp who fancied himself a vampire. He used to come by my cage every so often and drink some of my blood. He didn't want to mark me up so badly that I'd be worthless as a whore, so he cut me above the eyebrow and sucked on the wound. One day when he came by, I had a little surprise for him. I opened the cut over my eye myself and stood up. When he saw the blood, he forgot himself and came up to me without tying me up first. I kicked him in the crotch until the others came and beat me senseless." Trisha closed her eyes, remembering the beating and the threats. She regained her composure and continued her narrative. "That's the day before you guys arrived. My punishment? To be gang raped until I died. The pimps put out notice that it would be quite a show and anyone who wanted to could get in on it. The bloody eye is what they called me, and they told me they were going to start the show by gouging out my eyes. I thought I'd buried those thoughts thanks to the shrinks until now." She shivered. "Just having a little flashback. I'll be all right."

Marcus reached out and gently touched Trisha on her shoulder. She flinched, but didn't pull away.

"Well, you got even with the bastards," Marcus remembered the girl with the bloody knife in her hands. "Now that I know the whole story, I'm sorry I stopped you from carving them all up."

Chapter 29 - The Flight In

Lightning flashed outside the lifter as the pilot flew through a thunderstorm. The craft rocked violently, causing the passenger next to Paine to grab his arm. He resisted the urge to pull away.

Distinctly uncomfortable in her camouflaged clothing and combat vest, Eleanor Whippette constantly shifted in her seat, trying to adjust the unfamiliar uniform and equipment. She had insisted on coming.

Paine knew from experience that the rucksack digging into her back and crash-straps holding her in position in the seat were chafing her skin. The constant turbulence caused her to turn green.

Some of the soldiers were using patrol sign to bet on when she would throw up. A one-finger cutting motion and a look from Paine stopped their silent wagering.

Paine protested when his father told him about Elle coming along.

"Miss Whippette paid all the money up front, so in effect, she bought you. She wants to go, so she goes." Once his father spoke, there could be no argument. Paine never learned.

He dared to raise his voice as he talked to his father. "Damn it all, she'll be a drain on resources. She has no training, she doesn't know where her parents are. I'll have to put at least four troopers with her at all times to keep her from getting killed."

Josh didn't even look at his son. "If she gets killed, there's no one to refund the money to. The regiment wins no matter what the outcome of your operation." He handed Paine his orders and continued to work on the papers in front of him. Paine had been dismissed.

The soft hum of plasma jets filled the lifter. Elle leaned over to talk to Paine. "I think my parents were going to go work at the relief station in the Chrysler Building, if that will help."

A strong gust of wind struck the transport. It dropped like a freight elevator.

Elle threw up her dinner on the front of Paine's camouflage jacket.

Paine choked off the expletive forming in his throat and glared at the trooper across from him to stop him from sending the message to the rest of the platoon. The trooper's hands stopped moving. His shoulders shook as he made a valiant effort not to laugh while pretending to look out the window. Paine turned to Elle.

"Thank you for that information, Miss Whippette. I'll keep that in mind as we make our plans."

"Call me Elle, will you?" She wiped the vomit from her mouth and then laughed. She couldn't help herself. "After all, I just threw up all over you. That's about as close as we can get up here, isn't it?"

Paine looked at her for a moment, smiled briefly. "OK, Elle. Is there anything else you want to bring up?" Elle smiled back at his weak pun.

Marcus looked around the compartment, reading the patrol signs flashing from soldier to soldier. The troops were already gossiping. One signed, "Looks like the old man has a girlfriend."

Sergeant Chris Curtis, a tall, rangy red-headed boy from the small town of Smith's Grove, Kentucky, wagged his fingers in reply, "First time I've ever seen him smile."

"Remember when Sergeant Curtis threw up on his first mission, the old man just took over as squad leader. Paine damned near took his head off and the barf was at the other end of the compartment in a helmet. All the cutie gets is a goofy smile."

"I had a good excuse. I was still hung over from the night before when you guys helped me celebrate joining the Regulars. Don't think I've forgotten that or will ever forgive all y'all." Chris looked down the center of the aircraft. "Anyway, we'd better take good care of this one. I mean, he lost his mom and his squad leader. If he loses another female…"

Marcus signed "Shut up" as he saw Elle try to clean the front of Paine's battle dress. He grinned as he watched Paine and Elle and thought maybe having this woman along wouldn't be so bad.

Chapter 30 – Insertion

The weather over the target area cleared. The storm they'd flown through hadn't reached New York yet.

"We've got good weather for the next three hours." The pilot looked back at Paine. "Should we go ahead?"

Paine gave her a thumbs up.

The lead lifter moved under the craft carrying the heavy weapons' squad, both hovering high above Times Square. A hook extended from the top of the flight crew compartment and latched onto the undercarriage of the aircraft flying above it. The crew chief signaled the scouts to get ready. As the upper lifter increased the thrust of its engines, the pilot of Paine's lifter cut her plasma engines. It dropped like a rock.

Both side ramps opened on the way down. Air rushed through the compartment. The cable stretched as the lifter fell, slowing it to a stop a few feet above the cracked pavement of Times Square. As the red light went to green, the eight-man security force jumped from both sides and fanned out, each pair forming the corners of a square for maximum protection. The carrier leapt into the air as the cable snapped back. Elle grabbed the seat, afraid she would fall out of the open doors and even more afraid her stomach would erupt again.

"I think they used to call this bungee jumping," Paine explained. "I don't know why. Don't worry, you won't fall out."

Paine never looked in her direction as he scanned the position of his security force with thermals. He looked deadly serious as he explained, "I haven't lost anyone on a bounce in at least four months."

"Marcus, did you see anything we need to be concerned about?"

Scanning from the other side of the carrier, he responded once the pilot restarted her engines. "Not yet, Paine. I have the two teams on my side, but nothing on thermals and no movement anywhere." He paused, looking at the display. "Wait a minute, hot spot on the north side." He touched the communications switch. "Team one, you have a hot spot at the corner of Seventh and 43rd. Check it out. Report."

The voice on the other end whispered, "One-one. On it."

The carrier slowed to a stop and hovered once again as the plasma engines came back to full power. Paine and Marcus waited for two full minutes while the northern security element moved to investigate the thermal sighting. It seemed like a much longer time when the communicator finally came back on line. A text-only message appeared in the upper right corner of their thermal displays, tapped out by the lead scout of north team. The message read "One target. Adult male. Seems to be sleeping, no visible weapons. Orders."

Marcus looked at Paine, who made a cutting motion with his left hand. "Take him out. We can't afford to be blown." Marcus sent the message.

Paine's lead scout, Imani Jamal, approached her target carefully. She'd survived enough missions to know that one could never be too careful. Her left hand held an antique firearm, a center-fire pistol with a long silencer attached to the barrel. Her partner often made fun of the weapon.

"It may be a piece of shit that can't even fire supersonic to you, but that's what I like about it." She lovingly hand-loaded each round, each with enough powder to do the job. "The projectile stays in the target, the sound is negligible, and there's usually no collateral damage. It's effective for close combat, and it saved my ass more than once."

Quietly slinging her carbine, she crept forward. All but invisible in her phototrophic camouflage, she stood five feet away from her target. Taking up a two-handed grip, she centered the pistol on the target and took up the slack on the trigger.

*****

Walter sniffed. Something different floated in the night air. He couldn't figure out the smell, and that troubled him. Living on the streets, as he had for the past twenty years, gave him an acute awareness of his surroundings. That's why he liked being on guard post. He stayed still, trying to choose what to do, then decided the worst they could do for a false alarm would be bust his chops for a few days for getting everyone out of bed in the middle of the night. At least if that happened, he wouldn't be the only one losing sleep. He tripped the alarm just as he felt a hammer blow in the center of his chest.

"Five, One. Target down." She moved to the fallen guard and searched for a pulse. "Target is neutralized. I'm searching the area." Imani found a cable connected to thin air. She pulled out her scanner, running it over the cable. No sign of any power registered. "Wire tied to his wrist. Not connected to anything, no voltage running through it. No power source anywhere nearby. Orders."

Paine had to decide. He could go ahead with the mission or leave the security team on the ground and try to recover them later. Dressed as they were, they would have no problem conducting an escape and evasion mission. If they aborted, the security team had orders to move north to the emergency pick-up point.

Paine could recover them anywhere along the Hudson River and try to insert the platoon the next night. That would be a problem. His father wanted results in 10 days, and Paine couldn't afford the delay. He decided not to have the scout risk turning on a light and searching the ground around the corpse.

"We go as planned."

Imani moved back to her position on the perimeter of the landing zone. Because of the thermal sights, she failed to see the pigeon droppings near the end of the cable. No one saw the pigeon flying high above the street. Imani, oblivious to the impending danger, gave the all clear.

Acting on the available intelligence, Paine ordered the landing the rest of the platoon.

The three aircraft land in a perfect "V" formation and the rest of the platoon dismounted in fewer than two seconds. The aircraft went to full power and began their return to base.

Even though she'd been told what to expect and when to go, her designated guards practically dragged out Elle out of the lifter. The side of the lifter scraped her left arm as it took off. She hurt but bit her lip and clumsily pulled on her goggles, so she could see in the dark.

The platoon spread out in classic over-watch formation, scouts out front and on the flanks, weapons and command team in the center, everyone ready to support the others, if needed.

The two-person teams never moved simultaneously. One person stayed in a covered position, ready to support the other with fire in the event of hostile action. It took a long time for the last element to move out of the Square and head east on 42d Street.

As the platoon cleared the Square, silent figures moved in. They discovered the body of the dead sentry.

****

The leader of the Neo Luddites woke from a deep sleep, roused by her personal guard.

"Miss Pickers, a small force landed in Times Square about twenty minutes ago. It's moving toward the UN complex."

Annie Pickers looked at the runner in the flickering candlelight. "What else do we know?"

"The force is moving out of Neo Luddite territory, but we can still catch them if you want."

"Did we suffer any casualties?"

"Walter Chavez is dead. They found his body with a bullet in his chest." The runner knew that Annie and Walter had been lovers at one time. "I'm sorry, he never had a chance to defend himself."

Annie Picker's face hardened as she learned about Walter's death. She made her plans and sounded the alarm.

Miley Pickers, Annie's daughter, couldn't lead the mission. She'd reinjured her bad knee and still experienced intense pain. "Some defense force leader I am." Grabbing her crutches, she hobbled over to her second-in-command.

"Brad, push out the interlopers. You don't have to kill them, just get them out of our territory." She limped toward her mother's house as Brad ran off toward Times Square. "Let me know when you accomplish the mission," she called out as he moved into the darkness.

Chapter 31 - Counterattack

Moving at street level, the platoon remained vulnerable to attack by anyone hiding in the deserted high-rise buildings. The ruined shop fronts also offered hiding places for possible attackers. Reports from the scouts indicated heat signatures at all levels of the buildings. Paine had a sinking feeling in his gut as the unit moved slowly toward Bryant Park. Just another damned good place for an ambush, he thought. He glanced at Marcus.

Paine could just make him out in the darkness. Remembering a saying his mother used, he thought Marcus looked wound up tighter than a banjo string, whatever that was. Just before the lead elements reached the Avenue of the Americas, he keyed his mike twice, paused and keyed it once again. The unit immediately formed a 360-degree perimeter, blending into the background.

Paine crouched by a burned-out ground effects vehicle. Making a pointing sign at his feet, he held up two fingers, then five, and made a circle over his head, Paine knelt and waited for Marcus and Trisha to come to his location.

"Marcus, I think I made a mistake. This whole thing stinks of an ambush." Paine looked around at the towering buildings and signed, "I just have a gut feeling about this. It isn't a good one."

Marcus glanced at Paine, then turned to Trisha. "Alert all the troopers to be especially vigilant. I learned a long time ago to listen when the boss has a funny feeling." He fingered a long scar running down his left arm, a reminder he kept so he would never forget a time when he ignored a warning from then fifteen-year-old Paine.

Elle watched the three soldiers from five yards away and wondered what they were doing. She saw their hands flashing, not making a sound, yet they seemed to talk to each other. She saw Trisha type on a wrist-mounted key board, then watched Marcus move toward the point with surprising grace for a man so large. Paine moved in her direction. Just as the three split up, a desk crashed down in the space they had occupied.

"Jesus H. Christ!" Paine yelled as he threw himself to the right and ran into the middle of the street. "Ambush, twelve o'clock."

Soldiers ducked for cover as office furniture equipment rained down on the street. Paine roughly pushed Elle out of the way. A computer console crashed into the space where she'd been standing.

"All elements, get against the walls, but watch out for assaults from the windows and doorways. Move now." He reached down and grabbed Elle's arm, pulling her to her feet and propelling her toward the nearest wall.

The rain of objects from above ended as quickly as it had begun. Corporal Patterson, on the east side of the perimeter, had a broken ankle, smashed by an office chair thrown from the rooftop. He would be fine once they got him in the meditube, but right now he was a drain on the force. Paine ordered his spare power cells to be distributed to the other members of his squad, and then mentally debated what to do next.

Seconds later, Paine shook his head and yelled across the street to the troopers he had detailed to guard Elle, "Two of you take care of Patterson. We leave no one behind. Is that clear?" One team moved to Patterson, splinting his leg, and helping him to his feet. The other shifted to flank Elle. "No point in being quiet now, Marcus. They know we're here."

Marcus snorted, "No shit! So now what, boss?"

Paine thought for a moment. "Plan B, and I repeat, don't leave anyone behind."

Plan B had the force moving to Grand Central Station, then navigating through the abandoned subway tunnels toward the UN Complex. Paine glanced northward toward Times Square, noticing approximately a hundred New Yorkers carrying torches already filling the streets, moving in their direction. He ordered the unit to move straight to Grand Central.

Imani spoke into her mike, "I have at least two hundred more hot spots moving through Bryant Park. No power sources. They must be Luddites."

Paine and the unit were in trouble unless they moved now. Thankful they weren't being attacked by one of the more dangerous armed groups. Paine figured he would have enough trouble with the Neo Luddites. He made his plans quickly, calmly issuing his orders to the platoon in the clear.

The unit sprinted toward the Avenue of the Americas and turned left, heading toward 44th Street. The crowd, armed with sticks and clubs, emerged from Bryant Park and saw the last of the troopers run down the street. The cry went up, "Kill them all."

The crowd ran after the retreating soldiers, torches waving in the darkness. The scouts were crouching on either side of the avenue, invisible in their phototrophic uniforms, waiting for the leaders of the pack to get close. They opened fire when the crowd closed to fifty yards. Eight carbines on full automatic cut large swaths in the crowd, and the torches went out as the survivors turned and ran back for the safety of the park. At least forty laid dead or dying on the broken pavement. More than 100 were wounded. Paine had given orders to shoot low and cause casualties, so maybe some attackers would help their wounded comrades. Hope died as the crowd left the wounded and regrouped for another charge.

The main body had already turned on East 44th Street and the troopers were picking their way through the abandoned vehicles that littered the street. Paine keyed his communicator.

"Scouts, rear guard. Give us five minutes." A single click on the radio meant they understood and would comply.

They ran down 44th. Elle had a hard time keeping up. The two soldiers Paine had detailed to keep an eye on her practically dragged her down the street. Two others were carrying Patterson, the trooper with the crushed ankle, between them.

Elle gasped for breath even though she carried only 20 pounds of food and clothing. Her guard's packs weighed at least twice that, plus they were dragging her along. They barked directions to her as they ran, pointing out possible ambush sites and discussing what to do if they came under fire. Her ears were ringing, and she tasted copper in the back of her mouth. She thought she would be sick again when they finally stopped. Elle collapsed on the pavement.

Paine couldn't worry about Elle. He didn't have the time, and, besides, the soldiers knew what they had to do. He motioned the lead troopers onto Vanderbilt Avenue and called the scouts for a situation report. He didn't like what he heard.

"Six, this is one-one. Two-two and three-one are wounded, ambulatory, coming to you now. Teams one and four will act as rear guard. Estimate more than five hundred hostiles will be at your location in two mikes."

Team Two appeared first. The lead scout for Team Two, Sergeant Chris Curtis, had one arm around the waist of his partner, Paul O'Malley. The flesh wound in Paul's leg slowed him down but made good time despite it. The phototrophic camouflage had picked up the blood, and he looked like a red-painted specter moving through the night. Paine yelled at Chris to deactivate Paul's phototrophic system.

Team Three appeared, with a scout being dragged around the corner, unconscious. Paine detailed one of Elle's two remaining guards to help get the other casualty into the perimeter and then told Chris to get the power cells from the injured troopers.

Paine gathered the power cells Chris had collected and taped them together. As he worked on the connection, he looked over the vehicles littering the street. One newer-model cargo vehicle caught his eye. Pointing at it, he screamed at Marcus, "Get that hauler on its side and against the wall."

Marcus and three other soldiers strained to lift the vehicle. Two more ran to help. With one mighty heave, they pushed it over.

Jumping on the vehicle, Paine crawled inside the cab. He cut open the engine compartment with a hand-held plasma torch, careful not to cut into the engine itself. A careful pass with the torch disabled the governor by melting the components inside, allowing the engine to run at maximum power. A quick and careful pass with the torch melted the components inside, allowing the engine to run at maximum power. Putting the power cells in the receptacle, Paine made the final hot-wiring connections and the ready light came on. As the vehicle went to standby mode, he thought, "So far, so good."

After jamming a metal rod against the accelerator, Paine grabbed the remote starter and scrambled out of the compartment. He ran to the hastily erected barricade his men were crouched behind, his mental clock telling him he had less than a minute left. The four-man rear guard appeared from around the corner, firing furiously at the attacking New Yorkers. Many attackers went down, but the others still came on, hoping to get to the troopers.

Paine yelled out the age-old adage "Mad minute" and every one of the twenty-three remaining weapons in the unit went to rapid fire, filling the street with bodies. The rear guard sprinted into the barrier, quickly turning and adding their firepower to the defense. The crowd still surged forward, clawing their way over the bodies of their companions. As the mob came abreast of the upturned vehicle, Paine triggered the remote start and all hell broke loose.

With the governor off and the accelerator depressed to the floor, the vehicle's engines went to full power. Paine got the results he hoped for as the jets spewed white hot plasma across the street.

Those unlucky enough to be on the periphery died an agonizing death. They had body parts burned off. Some tried ducking into doorways or broken shop windows. The blast wave went by them, the burning plasma sucking the oxygen away. Some attackers suffocated in the vacuum. The lucky ones were those who were directly in the path of the plasma. They died instantly, becoming unrecognizable lumps of charred meat in a split second.

Paine figured the vehicle would run for six seconds before the power cells burned out but didn't hang around to see his handiwork. He and his soldiers ran into Grand Central Station.

The cavernous building echoed with their footsteps as they sprinted toward the entrance to the platforms. "Use your flashlights. The thermals are no good in this cold."

"We need to head down the red line track towards Queens," Trisha yelled. "The tunnels flood at high tide."

According to the data in Paine's computer, low tide would occur in about 10 minutes. They would have to move quickly to get to their destination before the water came back in.

Once again, Marcus and Trisha joined Paine for a conference.

"I believe they figured out we want to get to the UN Compound, so maybe we go in the opposite direction. What do you think?"

"If I were the New Yorkers, I would watch the Green Zone." Marcus pointed at several spots on the screen. "They have enough people to cover all the possible crossing sites. If we take our time getting there, maybe they'll give up and go home."

"I doubt it." Trisha looked at her commander. "When the UN created the buffer zone, destroying the buildings within two old city blocks of the compound, mobs engaged in three days of nonstop assaults. They didn't quit until total casualties exceeded 20,000. I don't think they'll just let us go on our merry way."

"Maybe we can go back the way we came, but underground." Marcus looked at the computer screen. "This tunnel looks like it takes us right back to Times Square. We move that way, we can either call for extraction or work our way back toward the UN."

Paine grinned at Marcus. "That's my plan, too. It's amazing how smart I think you are when you agree with me."

Trisha shook her head. "Cut out the mutual admiration society meeting, will you? Trouble is, guys, if we go underground, we can't communicate with base. Internal platoon commo will be fine. The walls reflect the signal. It may sound a little fuzzy, but we'll be able to understand voices. Text messaging is no problem at all."

Paine thought about his options. "Can you get me any outside communications? If we do have to request a pickup, the lifters have to be there on time, or we won't get out in one piece. There are just too many eyes out there. It only took them a few minutes to pick us up after our insertion."

"Sorry, Boss," Trisha looked at the signal indicator on her comm device. "There's no way to talk unless there's a break in a tunnel that goes all the way to the surface."

Paine looked at his two assistants. "Our chances are nil if we go above ground, so the tunnels it is." He keyed the all-hands button. "Scouts - out front and in the rear - baggage in the center. All hands watch for any movement. Thermals only, no lights."

Elle realized the wounded needed to be carried above the water. Four stretchers were assembled. The wounded were loaded, and the platoon leapt into the knee-deep water and moved into the tunnel.

Paine motioned for Elle to get on one of the stretchers.

"I'm not getting on that thing. I can walk."

"You just make too much noise on the water. Don't argue."

Feeling foolish, she climbed on. Elle gasped and held her nose as the mud disturbed by passing feet floated to the top of the dark water. She bounced slightly as her two guards moved to catch up with the others.

Five minutes later, a shot rang out in the darkness.

Chapter 32 – Urchin

The formation stopped. The troopers settled down into the water, only their eyes and the tops of their heads breaking the surface. Scout One called Paine forward. Paine submerged and swam the 20 meters to Imani's location. When he resurfaced, he saw Imani, helmet light on at low power, with her arm under water, shaking as if holding on to something. The scout grinned and then pulled up a struggling girl who looked like she could be about fourteen years old.

"Sumbitch, why you do dat, you bitch." The urchin had both of her hands on Imani's arm. She struggled to get out of the grip. The scout quickly dunked her again. As bubbles appeared, Imani lifted the girl's head back out of the water.

"Quiet, please, or I won't let you up next time."

The girl opened her mouth and then shut it as Imani ducked her back into the water. The scout grinned. "You learn fast."

"I found her perched on a ledge, with the pistol in her hand," Imani explained, handing Paine an old auto-loading pistol. "I must be slipping. She heard me moving through the water and shot at the sound. Damn near hit me, too."

Paine put the pistol in his combat vest, looked at the girl for a few seconds, then held out his hand to her. She shied away, but Paine persisted. When the girl resisted, the scout threatened to put her back under water again. She took Paine's hand.

"You want wa all da boys want? Costya big time for short time. Be easy, never didt afor now." She wrapped her legs around Paine's waist and moved up and down.

Paine grabbed her hair, pulling her head back. She released the grip on his waist. "That's not what I want. What's your name?"

The girl looked sad. "Usta be call Carole, then Joy fo a wall, now jus Carole agin. Got too ole for the ole man."

"I need information. What are you doing down here?"

She paused as she worked out what to say. "I wook here. Lotsa folk come down to do bidness. Come down true the sewers. Make lotsa food money, doin things mos doan do topside. So far dis year, mo money den I kin eat. Kep it fo m'self, a course, no pimp fo me."

"Where did you come by a pistol?"

"Found it, it's mine, din steal it." The girl looked guilty and didn't meet Paine's eyes.

Paine had been steadily moving toward the main body and signed the nearest soldier to get Trisha to his location as soon as possible. He needed someone who understood what the girl had been through, and who could wheedle information out of her quickly.

"I want you to talk to a friend of mine. She used to be just like you." The girl looked at Paine, her face screwed up as she tried to understand the unusual accent and new words. Paine shifted into the slang he had learned as a young man on his first mission. "She got lotsa food. Need news bout topside. Jeet? Yauntoo?"

"Be hungree, wontoo, needta eat." She smiled her best come-on smile at Paine. "You goan wanna get sum fo trade?" Paine turned away as the girl provocatively moved her slender hips. Trisha came up, and he gladly turned the urchin over to her.

A wave splashed over Paine as Marcus swam up. "Your father would have just kept her head under water."

Paine snorted in disgust. "Marcus, how many times do I have to tell you? I'm not my father. Besides, she may know something that could be useful. Trisha will get information out of her, or she'll drown the little whore herself."

Chapter 33 - Carole

Trisha listened to Carole's story in fascination.

"My da was kilt on a raid, the UN compound, I been tole. Mama says he was a nice guy, I neva knowed him. I hadta beg and steal food. Wudden gonna go work for no pimps. They was afta me to be a ho. I was inna alley, lookin through some rags for warm clothing when dis ole man walks up. 'Joy," he yells out an asks me where I been. He says he been looking for me. Says his name is Bannick. He takes me to a big billin on Central Park." Carole had a strained look on her face as if struggling to remember. "It had letters 'E sex Ho e' over da fron door."

"First night, I wait a long time for the man to come visit my bed. I figgur I'd do whatever, cause my belly wa full and I was warm and dry. He din't show up." She looked disappointed. "I din't know if'n I was mad or happy. So I goes to sleep, and next morning, asks him what his problem was. He says, 'I jus want to spend all my time with you, an never want to lose you agin.' I figure he's just old crazy guy, but like da food, so I play along."

"Second night, I wait til he's sleepin and go explore. Founda room wid a lock, but knows how to break in. I find a dead guy, wid my gun. I figure the ole man kilt him, so I watch out. Keep the gun unner my pillow." Carole grinned at Trisha, "No one surprises me an gets away wid it."

"Anyhow, he gives me food I can give to momma an my sisters. The one day he goes crazy, screamin "what did you to do Joy? Where is she?' He runs aroun and falls flat, dead on the flo. I stay long as I kin, then some bad guys break in the partment an say they lookin for scarf. Says Bannik makes the best scarf onna market, so where is it all? I din know I was in a drug king's house. I figgur I bedda get out, so I takes the gun and sum food and runs outta dere."

The girl turned out to be a treasure trove of information. She knew the sewer system well. Trisha gave her a quick lesson in map reading. After one or two quick dips underwater, she identified several unblocked routes under the streets. Trisha brought her to Paine and Marcus, who had set up their command post on a shelf, just inches above slowly rising gray water.

"Carole speaks a lot better English than she let on, don't you, Carole?"

Carole furrowed her brow as she slowly spoke, concentrating on forming her words, "Bannick wanted me to speak properly. He was always on me to talk – speak – more better. Taught me to read some, too, because his eyes were really getting bad. I always tried round him, but it was hard. When I escaped down here, I just kinda lost it and fell back into my old speech patterns."

Carole hung her head. "I'd been on da streets for three weeks, hidin from the pimps who had been waitin for me to get throwd out and avoidin the snarf addicts who thought I had the secret to Bannick's snarf fixins. I decide the only safe way to go was underground where I could live or die on my own terms. I been down here fo mebbe ten months, least I think it's been mo' dan six. Is kinda hard to figure when you got no light, no way to tell day or night."

Marcus looked down the sewer pipe. "How often do topsiders come down here?"

"Most time durin high tide, when there aren't that many places to hide. They come down lookin for anything they can take from us…" Carole stopped. "I mean me, of course. Bannick is dead now," she ended lamely.

Marcus shot Paine a look that said "liar" and opened his mouth, but Paine signed to let Carole continue.

"It is usually a group of at least 10, all armed with knives, clubs and spears. They are the Luds, the ones that don't want no electricity or lights or nothing. They know no one down here has anything much, but they want to make sure it stays that way. When they catch you, they cut you up bad. I seen it happen once. That was enough for me. Dis old man was lookin for some spare parts for a thing he calls a radio. He yell at me from across the water, askin me if I had seen 'bat rays', whatever they are. I told him I didn't know what he was talking about, I seen 'bats' but never seen no 'rays'. I did tell him I had me a can of spam I could trade if he could get me some bread from topside. He just laughed and turned to walk away, and den deese nets drop over him like it fell from the top of the tunnel. Three men with spears pulled it tight and dragged him away. I followed them aways, until they went topside and got to this big openin where dere were more people than I had ever seen."

Trisha touched the map on her screen, and Paine looked at his own display. The path the girl had followed led her to what had been called Radio Music Hall, a cavernous building still mostly intact. The briefing Paine had gotten on New York identified the music hall as the headquarters of the Neo Luddites.

"There was dis big ole woman up on a big ole stage, with all dese people standin around and all up in the buildin. I kinda slip into the crowd and move so I could hear what was going on. The woman was talkin, sayin the man they brought in was in violation of the rules of New York and he would have to pay." She stopped and shook her head as she looked at the glowing wrist displays, goggles and weapons of her captors. "They gonna kill all you dead."

"Let me worry about that." Paine kept his voice calm, to soothe Carole's fears. "Please go in with your story."

"He wasn't the only one. Most of the folks caught had radios. One had something called 'pewter', and one was making lectricity for bad purposes. I heared lots of what I didn't understand, but I sure understood what happened to those poor people. The lady, she pronounced them guilty of crimes against humanity, and that they had to die for their sins. They were thrown off the stage into the waiting crowd." Her eyes got a faraway look. "I seen a lot of people die, but all them waiting knives and spears were too much for me to bear. I got out of there fast and came back down here."

"Have you seen more of these Luds?"

"I see them from time to time." Carole sniffed. "I usually smell them coming. They don't take baths much and stink bad."

"You reek." Trisha stifled a laugh. "How much worse could the Luddites be."

Paine looked at Carole, sopping wet from the dunking, clothing clinging to her young body. He knew Trisha only had the clothes on her back because ammo is more important than a change of clothes to a combat veteran.

Paine motioned Elle over. "Do you have any spare clothes in that backpack of yours?"

"I have a couple of things she might fit into, but I may need...."

Paine cut her off as he pulled the backpack out of her hand and handed it to Trisha.

"Find Carole something suitable and try to dry her out a little bit. I need to think about what we are going to do with this information." He turned to the surprised woman. "Thank, you, Elle."

"You're welcome, Michael," Elle tartly responded.

A flash of surprise appeared on Carole's face, then it vanished. Carole went back to looking at the new clothes.

Dressing in the clothes taken from Elle's pack, Paine thought Carole looked pretty good for someone living beneath the streets the last six months. She seemed well-fed and had good muscle tone. He noticed her teeth were straight and clean, unusual for a street urchin. Although he tried not to look as Carole pulled the rag she called a shirt over her head, he saw a thin white line running down her shoulder toward her left breast. That had to be a tan line. He decided he would have Trisha keep a close eye on this one.

"The best way to the UN Compound is through the sewers." Carole splashed her hand in the water. "The tide is comin up pretty fas, and dem topsiders be coming down soon. If we wanna be clear of dem, we bes be goin."

Looking at the schematic of the sewer system downloaded from the Old US Homeland Security archives, Paine realized Carole made a good point. "We can move directly to the UN Compound by following the main line of the sewer system. We'll have to cut their way through the manhole covers but can do that easily with the plasma torches."

"I'd rather be above ground. More room to maneuver."

"Marcus, I like the idea of staying down here. With our rifles and carbines, any two of us could protect the entire formation from the Luddites."

Marcus studied the display. "Yeah, but if one of the other groups, like the Technos or the Cartel, comes after us with the captured weapons they have, we are all dead meat. The tunnel walls will help them as much as they help us, and if we get surprised, we'll be killed before we can react."

Trisha chimed in. "Carole has been a big help, maybe too big a help. I think she already lied to us once. She told you, '... they take from us...' so who is they and who is us? And her story about the Luddites doesn't match what intelligence I've seen. They don't arbitrarily kill people for using technology. They just don't use it themselves. I also noticed she had a little more color than someone who lived underground for as long as she did. She also reacted when she heard your name, Boss."

"I thought I saw a tan line." Paine shook his head. "What choice do we have? We can't go topside. They'd be on us in a heartbeat." Paine worried about his soldiers making it out of this quandary alive. "We have to go with the best possible option. Trisha, I want you to sit on Carole. First sign of trouble, take her out. We go in five minutes."

Trisha looked over at the girl. She understood what kinds of things Carole had been through and had a lot of sympathy for her. She even starting to like her. But evidence mounted that Carole wasn't all that she professed to be. Like her or not, Trisha would kill her in a second if the soldiers in the platoon were threatened.

The unit moved out right on time. They quietly slid through the rising water ever closer to the UN Compound. Twice they had to backtrack and go down a different branch of the sewer because the tunnel had collapsed. Paine led, with Trisha and Carole right behind. Elle and her two-man security force were in the center, along with the wounded. Marcus brought up the rear, ready to respond to anyone following the platoon. They had seen only sewer rats as they made their way through the deepening water.

Carole asked if she could talk to Paine. She seemed to change her demeanor as she sloshed through the slowly rising water, Trisha following closely behind her. Carole took a deep breath and slowly let it out, trying to calm her nerves. When her voice came out, no trace of street-talk appeared her words.

"We are under First Avenue right now. The tides are coming in and water will fill this part of the sewer in 10 minutes. We can't go back the way we came." Carole had tears in her eyes as she fingered the clothes she had been given. "You have nowhere to go but up into the street."

"I say we cut her throat and swim our way out," Marcus growled.

The water already passed his waist, and the four tunnels leading out of the large cistern they were in were under water.

Paine knew how long he could hold his breath. He would drown before he got halfway to the next cistern.

"Marcus, we don't have a choice. The only way out is up. Once the water gets over our heads, the best we can do is tread water. I really don't think we can make it." Paine turned to Carole. "What now?"

"You need to break the welds on the manhole cover." Carole glanced at Marcus. "Then we get out and make our way to the UN compound."

Paine used the butt of his rifle to bang on the cover, loosening it enough for him to push it open. Light flooded in. Paine, momentarily blinded, blinked rapidly. His vision cleared enough to see the muzzle of a plasma rifle pointing directly at his head. Careful not to make any threatening moves, he climbed up to the edge of the manhole, set his carbine on the cracked pavement, and held up his arms.

Rough hands slammed Paine to the ground. A hood covered his head. He tried to speak, to tell his captors to take care of his people.

"I had to lead you into a trap. I had no choice. The girls are just babies." Carole's voice failed as she tried to talk, the words barely getting past the lump in her throat. She croaked out, "I couldn't watch them be tortured anymore."

His world went black as a well-placed blow hit him in the back of the neck.

Chapter 34 – Captives

He could feel the restraining arms of the meditube. Waiting for the torture to begin, a bucket of ice water shocked Paine from his dream. He opened his eyes and looked around. He woke to a sterile room, sitting at a steel table. His hands and legs were strapped to a chair. There were guards behind him, but Paine could not see their faces. An audio speaker and a camera were on the table in front of him. The speaker came to life.

"What is your purpose for coming to New York?"

"Martin, Michael Paine." Paine almost bit through his tongue as an electrical shock went through him. He shook his head to clear it as the voice came back over the speaker.

"Your purpose?"

"Martin, Michael Paine." Ready for the shock this time, he decided these guys couldn't hurt him any more than that damned meditube had in the past. As the shock ended, he grinned at the camera, and then spit on the lens.

Josh didn't expect the glob of spit to hit the lens and involuntarily jerked back as the camera smeared. He could make out a figure moving forward and saw a cloth rubbing the lens clean. He got angrier than he thought possible. His anger abated when the UN General Secretary tapped him on the shoulder.

"You have a well-trained man there. I think he will die rather than answer any questions. Besides, we already know the answers. We want him to do our bidding, not break his body. Perhaps we shouldn't waste any more time." Baum paused and thought for a moment. "You should increase the voltage."

Reigning in his anger at Baum's interference, Josh thought about what the UN leader proposed. "Torture is no good against this one. I know, I trained him myself." He had to find another way. He made up his mind and gave the orders.

*****

Paine had been sitting for four hours. His arms and legs were cramping. He had already urinated on himself during the shocking and felt like it might happen again. His guard grabbed a handful of hair, jerking his head up. He found himself looking at a monitor. The voice came back over the speaker.

"Recognize your friends?"

Paine looked at the screen and saw Marcus, Elle, and Carole, all wearing orange jump suits. They were tied to posts in front of a pock-marked wall.

"You have a choice. You can talk to us, or you can watch your platoon die one at a time. We'll start the executions with these three. The choice is yours. You have 10 seconds before the big man dies. Nine, eight, seven, six, five, four, three…"

Paine had a flashback to the swamp in Florida. "Stop. I'll answer your questions if you let them live. And let the girl go. Didn't you use her enough?" The voice didn't respond. "I promise you this. I'll kill you if you hurt them."

Josh couldn't' contain a chuckle. "That is mighty big talk from a tied-up man. I think you better look out for your own hide and not worry about taking mine." He paused for a moment. "The price for your soldiers isn't high. Infiltrate Neo Luddite territory and get me information about their movements, their intentions. You'll receive a full list of the critical information requirements I need. Carole knows how to contact us - use her. You can take the large one and the other woman with you. They may be of some help." The screen changed, and Paine saw his soldiers in a large cell, sitting in small groups. "Fail me and every one of them dies."

Paine looked at the monitor. Marcus was the only brother he had now. Even though he wasn't a blood relative, he was the only family Paine claimed. He remembered the look in Carole's eyes as she talked about her two sisters. The picture of his platoon stayed on the screen. A vision of Gabby's dead face floated in front of his tear-clouded eyes. He violently shook his head and gave in to the inevitable.

His voice came out in a whisper. "I'll do whatever you want. Just let my people live."

Paine made a promise to himself. If he got out of this alive, he would find the person responsible and make him pay.

Chapter 35 - Return to Duty

The cell walls were closing in on the members of the platoon. They'd been given food and water, but had no idea where Paine, Marcus and the two civilian women were.

"We should be doing something." Trisha pounded on the door. "Get us out of here, you assholes."

"Relax, Trish. If they wanted us dead, we'd be floating in the sewer right now." Chris leaned back against the cement wall. "Try to get some rest."

Trisha kicked the door. It surprised her when it opened.

The soldiers jumped to their feet.

"General Martin, what's going on?" Trish looked behind him for Paine and Marcus.

"You don't have a need to know." Josh stood with his arms crossed, glaring at the platoon. "Your mission is officially aborted on my orders. I've arranged for your release and transportation back to base."

Without further explanation, the platoon loaded onto lifters and went back to Regimental headquarters. No one saw Paine or Marcus, but they knew better than to ask questions. After five hours of questioning and a complete debriefing, Josh granted the platoon ten days of rest and relaxation.

*****

"We're still on for the same bet?" Trisha pushed her way through the crowd to an empty table. Most of the troopers were well into the night's drinking. The last one standing took money from the front breast pocket of the one who passed out and paid for the drinks. The survivor then loaded the loser into a cab and get them both back to the hotel.

Chris had paid the last four nights. Three hours later, it looked like he'd be paying again.

The military police entered the building, looking around the crowded bar.

"What are those assholes doing here?" Chris snarled, drunkenly. "Trying to screw up our fun?"

"Shhhh!' Trisha snickered, "Jus don' get into any trouble. It's 'hic' prolyl nuthin."

The MPs walked directly to Chris and Trisha's table. "Sergeant Trisha Jones?"

"Just who the hell wants to know?" Trisha slurred her words so badly that Chris started believing he might have a chance of winning this round.

"You have been called as a witness in a court martial. Please stand up." The larger of the military policemen held out his hand to help Trisha to her feet.

Looking at the MP with a surprised expression, she stood up. The second MP jabbed her arm with a syringe. He held out a bucket. She swayed for a moment as the sober-up shot coursed through her body, then regurgitated most of the beer she'd been drinking all night long. Her vision cleared quickly, and her mind began working overtime.

"What are my orders?"

Chris had a hard time following everything.

"Come with us now. You'll be back before noon tomorrow, so you can finish your R&R."

Trisha threw a roll of money at Chris. "You were winning this one, so I'll pay. Don't worry. We'll finish our game when I get back."

*****

Things were different when Trisha returned early the next night.

"I need a lot of drinks." Grabbing the mug of beer out of Chris' hand, she drained it.

"What the hell happened?"

"You know better than to ask that." She ordered herself a pitcher of beer. Foregoing the mug, she drank herself to oblivion and stayed that way for the rest of the time they were on leave. She never talked about why she'd been called to testify.

When they got back to Regimental Headquarters, a lot more things changed.

The scout platoon shivered in the cold morning air. Chris stood in front of the formation, his new rank shining on his epaulette. He wondered how Patterson, the trooper with the crushed foot, was holding up. When the platoon got back, he'd had been first one sent to the meditube. He still had a few days of rehab left to complete. The two newest members of the platoon were ordered to hold him up if he fell.

Paul, Chris' former teammate, stood at the rear of the formation. His leg wound had responded well to Quickheal, and he had been given a clean bill of health after two days of treatment. Paul now wore the stripes of a Sergeant First Class.

Trisha went on sick call right before, leaving a hole in the front rank of the platoon.

The rest of the regiment, except those units on deployment or perimeter guard, lined the parade ground. Chris brought his eyes back to the front, listening to the general's voice crackle over the speaker system.

"Several days ago, one of our units failed to accomplish its mission. The Regiment does not tolerate failure. It has been determined that the entire unit will not be punished."

Chris mentally thanked God to hear that. The last unit to fail had been sent to a mining sphere to reestablish European Union control after a rebellion. Chris always had a weak stomach. Zero gravity made him want to puke.

The general cleared his throat and continued. "Its leader compromised the mission when he violated the rules of the regiment by surrendering to a hostile force. He conspired to do this with another member of the regiment and two civilians. It cost a lot of money to get the unit released. I convened a special court martial to hear the case. The results will now be published." The general stepped back and motioned to the adjutant.

Major Miller stepped to the microphone and unrolled an archaic parchment. She read in a slow, measured voice, "First Lieutenant Michael Paine Martin and Sergeant First Class Marcus No Last Name are charged with violating orders while on a mission to New York, consorting with the enemy and treason. A duly appointed court martial found them guilty of violating orders, mutiny, treason, and consorting with the enemy. The punishment for these is reduction to recruit private, forfeiture of all pay and allowances, and execution by plasma firing squad. Carole Bean, a civilian working for an outlaw group called the Neo Luddites, has been found guilty, by duly appointed court martial, of espionage. The punishment is execution by plasma firing squad. Elenore Whippette, the civilian who involved the Regiment in its efforts in

New York, has been found guilty by duly appointed court martial of working with the Neo Luddites to bring dishonor on the Regiment and of using counterfeit Euros to pay for the services of the Regiment. The punishment is execution by plasma firing squad."

Four hooded and shackled figures in orange jumpsuits were marched out to the far end of the parade field. The figures shuffled along, feet chained together, and hands cuffed to a belt around each waist. They were taken to four metal posts rammed into the ground. A heavy weapons squad from the newly formed Yankee Company had been ordered to perform the execution. Chris thanked the heavens his platoon had been exempt from the selection process. The prisoners were shackled to the posts, followed by a sustained drum roll. Chris involuntarily flinched as the plasma rifles fired.

Smoke and the smell of burnt flesh wafted across the regiment as the general stepped back to the podium. "No one, no matter who he or she is, violates the rules of the Regiment." Josh paused for about 10 seconds, then shouted, "Commanders, take charge of your units and return to duty." He returned the salutes of his subordinates, turned, and marched off the stage to a waiting lifter.

Lieutenant Curtis dropped his salute and turned to march the platoon off the field. As the platoon moved off the field, Chris had thoughts running through his mind. *The general is a hard man, but this is unbelievable. Cripes, Paine's his only son. If the platoon gets trapped with no way out, we're sure as hell going down fighting.*

The communicator buzzed in his pocket. He halted the platoon, pulling it out to read his unit's new orders. "Get ready to deploy, boys and girls. We leave today."

Chapter 36 – UN Meeting

The lifter spiraled down from 10,000 feet to avoid possible weapons fire from the ruins surrounding the UN. It touched down on 1st Avenue. Josh straightened his uniform jacket, motioned to his aid to stay with the aircraft, and marched purposefully to the UN Headquarters building. He scornfully ignored the salutes of the guards at the front entryway, stopping momentarily to look them up and down, noting the sloppy uniforms and rust on one weapon. He audibly snorted in disgust. He hated coming here, but he had to come today.

The Secretary General waited at the door to his office.

"Come in, my friend. We need to talk." Alan Baum motioned Josh inside.

His hatred for the UN threatened to burst out of him in that instant. Josh's expression never changed as a thought flashed through his mind. He wondered how long it would take him to crush the slender throat of the Secretary General with his hands, then got his feelings back under control. *This is business. The UN is paying me a lot of money for what we're about to do. Steven Corvis is in this up to his neck, providing technical support to the UN and my soldiers.* Josh thought to himself, *Once I get what I want...* then put it out of his mind.

"What else is there to say? The plans have been put into motion. Now all we can do is sit back and wait for the results. My son is on his way to find the leader of the Luddites. He will do his duty, and if necessary, he will kill her." Josh wasn't concerned. He knew that either his son and or his personal watchdog, Marcus, would succeed.

The Sec Gen smiled, then led Josh toward the Security Council conference room.

"Gentlemen, General Martin," Alan called out as they entered the Security Council Chamber. John Gutenberg, NUS ambassador, sat behind the old United States place card. He waved at General Martin. They knew each other from the many dealings the NUS had with the Kentucky Regulars.

"Sorry to hear about President Brown passing on." Josh walked over and shook Gutenberg's hand. "I understand the illness came on suddenly." He leaned in close. "A secret service agent died from the same kind of embolism. I wonder if that's significant."

"Yeah, it's too bad for them." Gutenberg peered into General Martin's eyes, but saw no deceit. "The president's family is fine, as is the rest of the staff. I don't know what caused it but went quickly. He'd been under a lot of pressure. Anyhow, President Sandford's address to the people assured the public that there is no need for concern. Personally, I'm not so sure."

Ian Burns huddled with the Japanese Ambassador, Oshara Tdacki. They glanced up briefly and then resumed their hushed conversation. Lin Chow Tsing yelled into the communicator to the Chinese Embassy's security personnel about another attack conducted by the New Yorkers. John Wilson Smythe paced the room, puffing furiously on a pipe that reeked of rancid smoke.

Gutenberg blew out his moustache and leaned over to whisper to Josh, "You know who visited Bob the day he died?"

Smythe interrupted before he could continue. "General, what took you so long? We expected you earlier."

Tsing pointed at Josh with an accusatory finger. "I just found out that my protection force took seven casualties in the latest attack on my embassy," he spat. "This is your fault, General. The attacks have grown more frequent since you sent your people into the city. Perhaps you have reasons to get the UN out of the city? Is that why it took you so long to get here? Are you helping us or helping them?"

Allan Baum walked strategically between the two men. "Relax. The General had to take care of a few things to set up this mission. Why don't we listen to what he has to say before we start pointing fingers?"

Josh thought he could only suffer these fools so long before he would explode. Working with them for the past six months had been excruciatingly difficult. He had no expression on his face as he started his briefing. Years of practice in front of the mirror paid off. If his true feelings were known to these men, they would run screaming from the room.

"Twelve days ago, I sent a platoon-size element to New York. They were searching for the Whippettes, two American doctors who disappeared while working for the UN." Josh looked down at his notes before continuing. "The unit encountered a sizable force that attacked them with sticks and stones."

"Sticks against modern weapons? What a joke." Tsing laughed aloud.

"You of all people should know bare hands can kill." Josh looked at his notes. "Ninth Dan black belt in Karate. You don't need weapons to kill."

Bowing his head, Tsing apologized. "I am sorry I interrupted."

"The platoon broke contact with the enemy and were making their way here to establish a secure base from which to work." Josh's visage changed, his face clouding. "I bribed the appropriate guards, ensuring the unit would gain access to the United Nations compound. The unit did exactly what I instructed them to do. Then one of your agents, Carole Bean, acting under your orders, interfered by contacting my people." He glared at the assembled ambassadors. "Your meddling in my military affairs caused me to change to my plans."

Josh's voice never changed tone or inflection, but the Security Council could hear the disdain his words carried. He went on. "Allow me to do my job or pay me what you owe me and tell me to go home."

Secretary General Allan Baum banged the gavel on the table, trying to stop the noise that erupted immediately after Josh's last comment. The French and German ambassadors each were claiming emphatically that the other had gotten involved.

The Polish representative sat quietly, amused by the chaos and patiently waiting for his chance to speak. The only good thing about this meeting so far was that the Ukrainian ambassador was suffering from some illness and couldn't be here today. Once Juri got into his weekly shipment of vodka, things could get out of control.

The pounding finally got everyone's attention. "Enough of this bickering. It doesn't matter who sent the girl. The damage is done." Baum sat down with a sigh. "Good. Now let's focus less on what has already happened and more on the problem we must deal with now. General Martin, please continue."

Josh thought about how much more effectively he could run the world without the UN and then put the thought out of his mind. First, he needed to complete this part of his plan. He continued. "I took over the interrogation of the platoon leader. I made him think he had been captured by a Techno faction who has evidence that the leader of the Neo Luddite group is insane and planning to unleash a new terror on the world. The platoon leader now believes the leader of the Neo Luddites has been secretly developing a bio-weapon, one engineered to attack humans."

The Security Council Members shifted uncomfortably in their seats.

"The real Neo Luddites would never work with such technology, but the evidence we manufactured is pretty convincing," Josh continued. "The plans we've made will convince the platoon leader even more that our intelligence is good. Once the Neo Luddite faction is removed, we can blame them for the new plague and send in our medical teams to cure those people we want to be cured. We will establish control over New York and turn it into a space port that will rival any in the world."

Allen Baum gently corrected General Martin. "You meant to say, 'The United Nations can establish control over New York,' didn't you, General? 'We' could be construed as meaning your military organization, can it not? I would hate to have my friends here think you were planning something untoward."

Josh snorted in disgust. "I said 'we' and I meant 'we'. The arrangement is that my people will take over control of your armed forces - land, sea and air - and that I'll assume command of them all. That means I'm as much a part of this as anyone here and will suffer just as badly if this goes wrong."

Once again, the room erupted. Baum let it go this time. Josh could see that the members of the Security Council were united against any power grab he might consider making.

The noise increased until Josh could no longer stand it. He slammed his meaty palms down on the table with such force it sounded like a shot. Both the German and French ambassadors ducked under the table and were lying on the floor while the others visibly flinched and uncomfortably slumped down in their seats.

Baum almost laughed but controlled himself. "Karsten, Andre, please get up and retake your seats. The General appears to have something to say." He turned once again to Josh. "Yes?"

Josh slowly removed his hands from the table and sat down. He took a deep breath and spoke. "I have no desire to run the UN."

That much was true. "I have been given an opportunity to do something for the good of mankind, and I don't intend to let the bickering of the Security Council ruin that chance. I am confident that once I'm given control of the UN forces, things will change for the better. You just have to trust that I know what I'm doing and let me do my job without interference. I promise that I'm asking for nothing more."

"My dear General," Baum's voice took on a soothing quality. "We intend to let you do whatever it takes to rid us of these factions in New York." He looked around the room. The other members of the Security Council nodded, one by one, in response to his questioning eyes. "I believe, General Martin, we have an agreement."

Josh Martin believed only one thing. Once he had a free hand in controlling the military forces of the UN, he'd never have to worry about these idiotic meetings again. Besides, his personal spy would make sure that no one in the group being sent into the city would survive. He briefly thought about his son, then pushed that image from his mind and walked out of the room.

Chapter 37 - Traitor

The spy sat in the interrogation cell, waiting for further instructions. Bright light stabbed through the darkness and a voice rang out.

"You understand what you have to do?"

"I understand completely," the spy replied. "Infect the others as soon as we make contact. I have the vial, and I break it when I get the chance. The virus will kill all of them within a few days and spread throughout the city." The spy looked into the camera lens. "Are you sure the vaccination will keep me safe?"

The voice responded, "I took it myself. If it isn't safe, we'll all be dead in a few weeks. Trust me."

"I have no choice, do I?" The light faded out, and the spy sat in darkness.

Chapter 38 - Revelations

The guard pulled the hood from Paine's head. Paine blinked in the bright sunlight. There were piles of rubble all around him. He looked around and saw that Marcus, Elle and Carole were with him. All of them were dressed in rags, cast-off clothing like what New Yorkers would be wearing. He looked at the guard. "Where are the rest of my people?"

The guard shoved him to the ground and put his fingers to his lips. He motioned toward the buildings 80 yards away. "Gangs control everything on the other side of them buildings, so I would stay quiet." Drawing a combat knife from a leg sheath, he approached Paine.

"Take it easy."

"I said to shut up," he whispered. "I just want to get the hell out of here. Cross your legs, and I'll cut the cuffs off." Crouching behind Paine, he began to hack at the plasticuffs holding Paine's wrists together. He didn't care that he cut away flesh. "The last time I went this far outside the perimeter, my partner got shot in the eye with some kind of dart. I don't want to be hit."

Marcus grunted as the other guard cut his cuffs off, along with a few strips of flesh. He flexed his muscles to warm them up and tensed for possible hand-to-hand combat. Then he noticed the women. Carole and Elle had been freed first and were under the plasma weapons of the other two guards. One spoke in a stage whisper, "Try anything and the women die. We can always blame it on the gangs. No one would believe you two, no matter what you say."

Signing Marcus to wait, Paine thought *At least we're all alive.* He recalled the instructions the voice in the interrogation room had given him.

"I need you to find the leader of the Neo Luddites. Bring her in. We have intelligence that she is planning a biological attack on the citizens of New York and on the UN Compound. She must be stopped."

Paine didn't believe that lie for a minute. All his intelligence indicated that the Neo Luddites would use no technology. How were they supposed to develop bio-weapons? He didn't reply. He just nodded to indicate he understood his instructions. If he didn't agree, he assumed he and his entire platoon would be killed. At least this way, he and his companions had a fighting chance.

"We prefer you bring her in alive, but if you can't," he paused, "then kill her." The venomous emphasis on the word "kill" came through the filtering. Paine assumed, correctly, that they wanted her dead. He didn't care, but the way he had been treated irritated him. He wanted to find out why they wanted her eliminated.

The four guards slowly backed away, all the while keeping their weapons pointed at Paine and Marcus. They dropped a small duffle bag of equipment 20 feet away from the captives. Marcus moved toward the pile. The crack of a warning shot whistled by. He froze, hands over his head, as the guards retreated. His eyes on the retreating UN soldiers, Marcus spoke to Paine without turning.

"I bet they turn and start running when they get to that low wall over there," he nodded to his right front. "I can get three out of four before they can take cover."

"Marcus, don't miss," Paine responded. "You need to make it four out of four. I'll lead the women to safety. Meet us in the building at your five o'clock, third doorway from the left."

"That building is no good," Carole spoke up. "There are too many places for bad people to hide. Head for the brick house on the corner. It has good fields of fire from the windows and would be easy for the four of us to defend if we get attacked. Besides, there's an escape route that goes through the basement if we need to run."

Paine looked over at Carole in anger. "Why the hell should I believe you? You led us into a trap."

"Two week ago, soldiers from the UN came into the sewers. They had guns and sleeping gas. I woke up in handcuffs. My sisters were tied to rungs leading up to the surface. The water started to rise. You've seen how fast it comes up. They told me that a small military force would be trying to get to the compound. I'm guessing they meant you. My choice? Work for them or watch my sisters would drown right in front of my face. I would be next. They're all the family I got left." Carole wiped the tears from her eyes and continued. "They wanted me to lead you to the ambush point and then tell you to come up to the surface unarmed or you'd all be killed. I'm not the only one they coerced. They must have taken six other hostages. If I hadn't found you, someone else would have done this job."

Marcus coughed into his hand. "Time to shit or get off the pot."

Paine finally nodded. "All right, you know the terrain better than we do. We'll go to the corner building." He tensed himself for action as their guards neared the wall and told both women, "When I say go, run for your lives. Sprint to the building and don't look back, no matter what." The guards turned. "Go."

Marcus jumped at the pile as the guards turned and broke into a shambling run. He pulled parts for an old-style bolt-action rifle out of the bundle and eyeballed the bullets in the ammunition pouch. The bullets for all four weapons were mixed. Marcus made his choice and pulled out four identical rounds, then threw the duffle bag to Paine. Paine wrapped his arms around it and took off at a dead run. He soon caught up with Elle. Carole had almost reached the building as Marcus calmly put the rifle together, worked the action a few times, and quickly fed the four rounds into the tubular magazine.

Taking up a good prone supported firing position, Marcus wet his finger and held it up into the air. Then he adjusted the sights and fired four times, one for each guard. He looked for movement and saw none. Satisfied with his marksmanship, he leapt to his feet and followed the rapidly retreating trio.

With only the rifle to carry, Marcus gained on the others and ran into the doorway a few seconds behind them. Elle, out of breath, crouched in a corner. Carole and Paine were already tearing apart the packet and dividing up the load into piles. Marcus looked at Paine, held up four fingers, and then put the other three weapons together from the parts. He tossed Paine a submachinegun, a box of ammunition and two magazines.

"I got all four. I forgot how sweet one of these old rifles can shoot," Marcus grinned broadly as he picked up his rifle.

Loading one magazine, Paine inserted it into the well and charged the weapon. He watched the bolt chamber a bullet as it slid forward. "I'm glad you remembered how to use one of those. You sure you got all of them?"

Marcus just looked at Paine and sniffed. "So, what do we do now?"

"We do what we were told to do. Go find the leader of the Luds." Paine turned to Carole. "This is where you earn your keep. I promise I'll do everything in my power to save your sisters." He noticed the look of doubt in Carole's eyes. "What will it take for you to believe me?"

Carole shook her head. "I don't know. What if you're lying to me just to get what you want?"

"You're a fine one to talk," Marcus growled. "Paine, forget about her."

Paine's eyes took on a thousand-meter stare as he thought about how to convince Carole he could be trusted. When he spoke, his voice barely above a whisper. "You have sisters you want to save." He took a shuddering breath, "I had a brother, a year older than me. We used to fight each other all the time when we weren't fighting for our lives. Our father expected us to help defend the compound where we lived and to always be ready to fight. An even better shot than Marcus, my brother was damned good at fighting."

Marcus moved to Carole's side, checking the edge on the knife he'd taken from the bundle. "I didn't know you had a brother, Paine."

Carole didn't take her eyes off Paine, fearing she would miss something.

Looking intently at his hands, Paine went on as if he didn't hear. "I must've been 10 at the time. A group of marauders attacked the compound, and four of them managed to get inside the perimeter. My brother Adam and I were responsible for keeping anyone who broke into the compound from leaving. Anyway, these guys came running, shooting at anything that moved. Adam yelled for me to get down, but trying for a shot, I hit him in the shoulder. Two of the attackers were coming at me while the other two kept Adam pinned down. I must have been screaming. It's all kind of hazy to me. I remember hearing firing right next to me. One guy fell on top of me, his head missing."

Paine closed his eyes, remembering the horrors of that night.

"Shit, Paine." Marcus broke the silence. "What happened next?'

"Blood spraying everywhere, I couldn't see clearly. I still had my rifle. There were two guys right next to Adam, so I pulled the

151

trigger. I killed them both, but my bullets went through one of them and hit Adam right in the chest."

Carole reached out and touched Paine's hand. Her question came out in a barely audible whisper. "Did you kill him?"

He started, jerking it away. Taking a ragged breath, he wiped away a single tear. "No, he didn't die then. Luckily, I got him to the meditube in time to save his life. It really pissed off my father. He threw me into the meditube after Adam got out, and then he did something to the machine to make me suffer." Paine visibly shook as he thought about being inside the machine. "After I got out of the torture chamber, he stood us both at attention and yelled for nearly an hour."

Paine paused again. "Father split up Adam and me and told us we would never fight together again." Paine's eyes were shining as he continued. "During the next attack, we were on opposite sides of the compound. I couldn't save him that time." He drew a ragged breath. "He died."

Marcus looked at Paine in wonder. They'd been as close as any two men could be for the last 10 years and he'd never heard the story. The Regiment had a tradition of not talking about the dead, but this was his brother. "Jesus, Paine, I'm really sorry."

Paine refocused his attention on Carole, who had been listening intently the entire time. "Now will you believe me if I swear on the soul of my brother?"

Carole had tears in her eyes. Not trusting herself to speak, she simply nodded.

Paine shook his head and rechecked the weapons. He handed a carbine to Carole. "Do you know how to use this?"

Carole dried her eyes and drew a deep breath, then took the weapon in her hands. "I believe I do." Expertly pulling the bolt back, she looked into the chamber. She stuck her little finger into the weapon and rubbed it around. It came out black, and she snorted in disgust. "It will work as long as I don't have to shoot too much. There's enough carbon in there to jam the weapon if it builds up any more."

She put her thumb in the weapon to reflect the light off her nail and looked down the barrel. "Rifling is good, not too much gunk in the barrel." Then she turned the weapon over and looked at the sights. She wiggled the front sight. "Not too bad, but I maybe

I'll lower the front sight a little. My zero is just about flush with the rear sight centered." Carole slammed her hand on the butt of the weapon, causing the bolt to slam forward on the empty chamber. She handed it back to Paine "It'll do. What do you think?"

Both Marcus and Paine stared at the young girl. Paine took the carbine and loaded the magazine into the weapon. He chambered a round but didn't lift the weapon.

"Just who the hell are you?"

"You want me to trust you." Carole ignored the weapon in Paine's hands. "I do, so can you trust me just a bit longer? I've been living under a false identity for so long that I have a hard time getting out of character." She pulled her hair back and tied it with a band to keep it out of her face. "Just believe me when I tell you that all your questions will be answered shortly."

Marcus considered all that had happened. He slipped the knife back into the top of his boot and stretched out his ham-sized hand. "My name is Marcus, pleased to meetcha."

Carole took his hand and looked straight into his eyes. "My name really is Carole. My mother came to New York years ago. I grew up in this city." She lowered her voice and looked down at her feet for a moment. "I learned lots of things little girls shouldn't have to." Carole raised her eyes up and looked at Paine. "My boss sent me to work for the UN as an informant on the Neo Luddites. I've been feeding them false information for the past year, until I got caught by the Kentucky Regulars."

Paine broke in, "Why were you anywhere near the Regiment's area of operation? We don't have anybody in New York. At least we didn't until my platoon went in."

"Paine, there have been mercenaries here for the past two years, training the UN forces and sniping at the various groups trying to survive here in the city," Carole told him. "Where do you think the units General Martin banishes to the space colonies really go? They're here, doing something for the UN. We don't know what they're planning, but lately, more people have been disappearing. A man at the cell block instructed me on my mission. He only spoke via a speaker. I never saw his face. He did tell me he would kill my sisters if I didn't do what he told me to do. When

I talked to my mother, we agreed that I would lead you guys into a trap."

She paused when she saw the look on Paine's face, "Little sisters are also part of my cover story. They're really two younger agents who look a lot like me. They knew the risks when they agreed to pose as my family."

"I told you something no one else, not even my best friend here," Paine pointed to Marcus, "knew about. And you want me to trust you after you lied to me again?"

"I know, I would have told you sooner, but I had to be sure." Carole looked directly at Paine. "It is a part of my cover."

Paine glared back at her.

"When we were taken, I figured that all of us would be killed. We all accept the fact this is a risky venture." Carole sighed. "I just hope the girls are all right, and that he let them go like he promised. General Martin believes that I'll do what he wants and that you will, too."

Paine thought about his orders that came from the faceless voice. It could have been his father. This sounded like something he would do. "What makes you think it's the Regulars?"

"My mother has been in hiding most of her life, and her location is known by only a few people. She fears the UN and the Kentucky Regulars. I told her I'd bring you to her I believe I can trust you. I really trust you." She held out her hand. "May I please have my rifle back? We may need it later."

Paine handed over the carbine. He looked at Marcus, who winked. He then turned to Elle, surprised to find her slumped over, staring blankly at the floor.

"Elle, what's wrong?"

"I don't know. I just feel shaky inside. It's like I can't get my breath, and I'm not sure I can stand up. And it has nothing to do with running to get into this building." Trembling, she looked up at Paine. "I'm scared."

Paine moved to her side, touching her forehead. "She's burning up with fever." He looked at Carole. "How soon can we get to your boss?"

A voice came from behind Paine, "How about now? I've been waiting for you, son."

Chapter 39 - Reunion

Paine spun around. He stood in disbelief as his mother appeared to walk through the brick wall on the other side of the room. He dropped his machine pistol to the floor and ran to her, only to freeze when he reached her. He held her by the arms and looked deeply into her eyes.

Tears welled up as he tried to speak, "Momma." Then she took him in her arms. Another set of arms encircling him from behind. Paine heard Carole's muffled voice as she buried her head in the middle of his back.

"It's been so hard not to tell you, Paine. Mother was pregnant with me when she escaped from our father. I'm your sister. Welcome home."

Ashley gently pushed her son away. She reached out and brushed a tear from his eye. "We don't have time to do this now, Michael." She pointed at the girl, shivering in the corner of the room. "Elle must have been infected by the plague, and we have to get her to our medical facility quickly. I fear we all have been infected, and if we don't find a way to cure this thing, we'll all be dead within a few days."

Carole reached into her pocket. "It's all right, Mother. I have a vial of the virus right here. I guess father decided that I wouldn't get this to the right people." She held up a glass tube about 40 millimeters long, "He must have infected Elle."

"We have to leave now" Ashley turned to Marcus, and froze in place.

Marcus picked up Paine's submachinegun, pointing it in the general direction of the reunited family. "We're not going anywhere." Marcus gestured with the muzzle of the weapon. "Put your hands up. I have orders to contact General Martin as soon as we linked up with you, and I follow my orders."

Stepping in front of his mother and sister, Paine slowly moved toward Marcus. He kept his eyes on his friend, talking in a low voice. "This is a day full of surprises, isn't it Marcus? We've been exposed to a virus that may kill hundreds of thousands, if not millions, of people. Do you want to be responsible for all this?"

"He didn't give me a choice," Marcus responded robotically. "Your father told me that if I didn't turn you in once we found the leader of the resistance, the entire platoon would be killed. You know he'd do it, too."

"We all swore to follow orders, but the person we swore the oath to has not been faithful to us. You know how the old man is. If he planned on killing the entire platoon, he would have made us watch." Paine saw Marcus tilt his head to one side as if thinking about what Josh would do.

"Yeah, that would be just like him," Marcus whispered.

"We'll be the ones held responsible. I'm not going to die just because I've been given immoral and illegal orders. Marcus." Paine took a step, then froze as Marcus raised his weapon. "Listen to me. We've killed lots of people, not always for the right reasons, but ones we could live with. We've shared pain and suffering, shed blood together, and have always been there for each other. We didn't fight and bleed for the regiment or for the general. We bled for each other. I lost one brother, I can't lose another." Paine took a step forward. "You are my brother. Do you hear me?"

Marcus shook his massive head and stepped back, weapon at the ready. "Stay away. I swear I'll shoot." Marcus's eyes flashed, his conviction wavering even as he menaced Paine. Sweat popped out on his forehead and his hands began to shake.

Ashley slowly stepped around Paine and looked at the large man. "Marcus, we understand you have orders, but we have to get you and Elle to medical care. Can't you see that?"

Shivering, Marcus handed the weapon to Paine without making eye contact.

Ashley looked at Elle. Her condition had worsened during the dramatic confrontation. "We have to get her to my research facility. We need to save her."

Marcus slowly walked across the room and bent to pick up Elle. "All right. Where do we go from here?"

Ashley walked into the brick wall and disappeared. Paine shook his head in confusion as Carole led him by the hand through the projection. "This is just one of the benefits of having scientists on your side. Watch your step, big brother. Give me five seconds, and then just step off." Carole smiled at Paine. "Trust me..." She dropped out of sight.

Chapter 40 - Infection and Deception

Paine counted to five and stepped into the darkness. He went into free fall for a full 10 seconds, gritting his teeth to keep from crying out, only to be stopped by a wall of air blowing up from a giant fan leaving him suspended just above it. Carole reached out, pulled him from the slowing fan. Just as Paine stepped out of the swirling air, the fan revved up again and Marcus came to a violent stop, still cradling Elle. As the fan slowed down and lowered them to the floor, Ashley guided Marcus to the platform and then felt Elle's forehead.

"Michael, we have to hurry. She is burning up." Paine's mother herded the group up a wide stairway that led to a waiting subway car. Before they were strapped in, the car took off.

"Where are we going?"

"To the research center. Elle's parents are there, and I think they may be able to help us." Ashley glanced over at Marcus, noticing his symptoms were worsening. "Are you all right?"

"Son of a bitch, the general will kill us all," Marcus shivered, clenching his jaw. "If I live, the first thing I'm going to do is jam that damned flag of his, pole and all, right up his lying ass. He told me I'd been given the antidote."

Ashley looked over at Carole's flushed face. Carole grinned, confirming Ashley's diagnosis. "I've got it, too, Mom. We need a cure, and quick."

Paine reached over and grabbed Ashley's hand. "Mother, what about you? You look like you don't feel well, either. I can't believe how fast this thing spreads. I'm next, obviously, but right now I feel fine. Tell me what you want me to do."

Ashley opened her jacket to reveal an explosive vest. She pressed the detonator into his hand. "Son, if Elle dies before we get to the medical center, detonate the explosives. That will allow us to save the facility, for a while."

The speaker came alive with a crackle. "Do not blow up the car. This is Doctor Whippette," Elle's eyes flickered with recognition as soon as she heard her father's voice.

Delirious, she croaked out, "Dada, is that you? I'm so sorry."

"Yes, Baby. Just hang in there, you'll be fine. Michael, do you have any symptoms at all?"

"No, I feel good. I don't know why, but I don't think I've been infected." Paine felt his pulse. It beat normally and he still had no fever coming on.

"You must have been the only one immunized before the mission. I guess your father wanted you to survive. Now, I need you to do something for me. Open the compartment over the front seat and take out the medical kit."

Paine followed the instructions.

"Take out one of the syringes with the greenish fluid in it. Good. Find a vein in your arm."

Paine ripped off his sleeve and tied it around his arm, watching as the vein popped up.

"Don't depress the plunger. Put the needle in and then draw enough blood to fill the syringe all the way."

Once the blood had filled the syringe, Doctor Whippette continued with his instructions. "Shake the vial as hard as you can for ten seconds."

Paine counted out the time, then looked up anxiously. "Now what?"

Doctor Whippette's voice faltered momentarily, but he regained his composure and continued with the instructions. "I need you to inject the fluid into Elle. I hope it will prevent the virus from attacking her nervous system." Paine bared Elle's arm, hesitating as the car came to a stop.

"What's going on?"

"Michael, trust us, please. Elle is our only daughter, but we have to be concerned about the rest of the population of New York." Doctor Whippette's voice cracked. "If this does not work, you all must die. The car is under the East River and sitting on enough explosives to destroy it and all of you. Your deaths will be much quicker and less painful if this doesn't work. But we have to try."

Paine injected the solution into Elle's arm. "What about the others?"

"There are more syringes, repeat the process for each one of them," William's voice strained as he finished talking. "Then we wait."

He began to inoculate the others.

Incoherent and fighting demons in his delirium, Marcus slapped Paine as he stuck in the needle.

Rubbing his bruised face, Paine went to Carole. She lay on her side, sleeping fitfully, shivering. He smoothed her hair, then injected the potion directly into her neck. "Get well, lil' sister."

He approached Ashley next.

Still conscious, she looked at him through bloodshot eyes. "Michael, I wanted to come to get you. I just couldn't do it. I am so sorry. I wanted to get you both away from your father. I failed you."

Paine touched his mother's face and gently laid her down on the car seat. He watched as her eyes seemed to lose focus. She shivered, her teeth chattering.

Covering her with his jacket, Paine slumped down on the bench seat. He looked at the camera mounted on the ceiling. "What do we do now, Doctor?"

"We wait. God help us all." The speaker went silent as William cut the connection.

Chapter 41 - Paine the Savior

The stress of the last few days caught up with Paine. He drifted off to sleep. He woke with a start as the car started moving.

"This is Doctor Whippette." Paine heard a catch in his voice. "How are the patients doing?"

Sitting up, Paine saw Marcus hunched over a ration pack, shoveling food into his mouth.

"They all appear to be fine, Doctor."

"Thank God for that. I've been debating whether to press the detonator all night long."

"Don't do anything until I finish my meal," Marcus yelled. "Man, I thought for sure we were all going to die," He talked around a mouthful of food. "What the hell just happened?"

Paine filled everyone in on the events of the last few hours, Ashley, Carole, and Elle began eating ravenously.

Relief flowed over Paine. "I'm so glad you are all feeling better, but where's my meal?"

The women threw food all over him, then swarmed him, showering him with kisses. Marcus looked on in bemusement.

Paine made a half-hearted effort to fight them off, then gave in and let them smother him. In this moment, surrounded by more family than he had ever known, he never felt so good.

His reverie ended as Doctor Whippette's voice came over the speaker. "I need the vial Carole has. That will give us the most recent strain of the virus. I also need to get blood from each of you. We need to come up with the vaccine for this disease quickly. You'll be kept in isolation until we determine you're not contagious. Thank you for your help, Michael."

The car slowed to a stop. Paine could see figures in hazmat suits waiting at the station. The suited people led them to a glass-walled room.

*****

"I'm thin I'm going to go crazy."

"Calm down, Marcus. Doctor Whippette told us we have to wait." Paine took out a well-worn deck of cards. "Why don't I teach you guys to play hearts?"

Carole, Elle and Paine were involved in a spirited game, while Marcus and Ashley were talking in the corner.

The tiny tattoo on the inside of Ashley's wrist attracted his attention.

"What do you have on your arm?" Marcus reached out, taking Ashley's hand. He turned it over to reveal a black butterfly. "This tattoo, I know this tattoo. It's a bug, for good luck, right?"

Unexpected images from the past assaulted his memory like gunfire but being shot would have been less painful. Marcus remembered New Orleans, watching his mother swaying to the music coming from Bourbon Street, whispering things in his ears to drown out the occasional shot and shouts of people fighting.

He saw his mother standing over his bed, running her fingers through his coarse black hair and telling him to be quiet while she entertained one of the "gentlemen" who came to call. He recalled his mother climbing into the small bed with him, holding him tightly and crying in her sleep. He could hear her saying the same thing repeatedly. "My fault, through my own fault. I never should have gone into that room. I brought it out to the world." Marcus stood there, lost back in time.

Ashley nodded slowly. Her voice jarred him back into the present. "It's a butterfly, but it's not for luck. It's black. That signifies death. Why do you ask, Marcus?"

"It's nothing. My mother had a similar tattoo, on her left cheek," Marcus briskly explained.

She looked hard at Marcus. "Wait, this same tattoo?" Ashley thrust her wrist inches from Marcus's face, forcing him to study its intricate design and shading. Marcus noticed that the wings of Ashley's butterfly appeared as if they were two hands held together, just like his mother's.

Frustrated with the line of questioning and the unwelcome torrent of sentiment resurfacing in his mind, Marcus pushed Ashley's arm out of his face. "Yeah, whatever. You got the same tat as my mom." He nodded as he tried to maintain control of his emotions.

Ashley put both hands on his massive shoulders. She looked directly into his eyes and spoke slowly and deliberately. "Marcus, your last name is Pace. Your mother worked with me on the plague project, along with Elle's grandfather. Her name is Amy Pace. She left the project, disappeared about four months before I did."

"You knew my mom?" Marcus looked like he might start crying.

"Yes. She was a brave woman, much braver than me. She insisted we get matching black tattoos." Ashley rubbed the image, remembering that night long ago. "A black one signifies death. I didn't understand the significance of the color until much later. We got these tattoos while we were still working together, shortly before she disappeared. We both tried to stop the project from happening. We complained to Elle's grandfather, Dr. Amatto, once we found out what they were trying to do."

"But Mom left."

"She had guts enough to quit and walk away. I'm the coward. That's why my tattoo is on my wrist. She put hers on her cheek for everyone to see. I stayed until the very end, and it nearly cost me my life." Ashley stared intently into Marcus' eyes. "Be proud that your mother had such courage."

*****

"I win again."

"That's the last time I show you how to play a game." Paine's ego felt bruised by his third straight loss.

"Another game?" Carole smiled at her brother's discomfort.

"I think I'll sit this one out."

"Can't play with two people, so maybe I'll go rest for a while." Elle got up from the table. Stretching, she went to the couch and sat down.

Carole, with nothing else to do, busied herself by breaking down her weapon.

"What are you doing that for?" Paine paced the floor, agitated by the inactivity.

She just looked at him. "Are you mentally deficient? I'm cleaning my weapon."

"We're in a safe room at the hospital."

"So, what's your point?"

Paine smiled when he realized his little sister was right. He picked up his own weapon and field stripped it. As he reached for the cleaning kit, Elle touched his shoulder.

"Paine, can I please talk to you for a minute?"

"Sure, Elle. Just let me put this back together. I can't stand having a non-functioning weapon lying around." Turning to Carole, he grinned. "This one's mine. I'll clean it when Elle and I are done."

Elle took Paine's hand, guiding him to the corner of the room. She looked deeply into his eyes, opened her mouth to speak, but nothing came out. She laid her head on his shoulder, and her body shook as she cried.

Paine didn't know what to do. He awkwardly patted her shoulder and put an arm around her. "Elle, what's wrong? You're safe now."

She buried her face against his chest. She conjured up a muffled whisper. "I am so sorry. I almost killed us all. You, Marcus, your mother, and sister. Not to mention my parents."

"What on earth do you mean? You got sick. That's not your fault."

"I have this." Elle took a small vial from inside her bra. "He told me if I released this when we found the leader of the Luds that he would let my parents go free. I didn't want to take it, but I did to protect my mom and dad. What else could I do?"

"You did what Marcus and Carole were forced to do. My father gave all of you the virus." Paine gently removed it from Elle's hand. "Elle, you didn't know your parents were safe. And look," he held up the vial, "this hasn't been opened. You didn't give us the plague. It seems we were infected before the trip out here." He turned toward the others in the room. "Mother, I think you better have a look at this."

Ashley came over looking at the vial in Paine's hand. "Michael, is this what I think it is?"

Paine nodded.

Ashley walked over to the intercom and called for Doctor Whippette. "William, I think you need someone in an isolation suit to come pick this up. We have another sample of the virus."

Chapter 42 - Carly

The air lock cycled and the inner door opened. Everyone looked up in anticipation as a tall, attractive older woman walked in.

"Hello, Boss. How's it going, Carole?" She walked over to Ashley and peered into her eyes. "You look a lot better than I feel right now."

"Carley, what do you mean?"

"I guess I couldn't let you have all the fun, so I volunteered to be a lab rat. I got myself infected with the virus," she responded grimly. "The vaccine Doctor Whippette developed didn't work as well as we had hoped. I got sick and almost died, but I'm better now."

"Mother? Who is this?"

Ashley looked at her son "I'm sorry, Michael. This is my chief of staff, Carley. Carley, this is my son, Michael, who has told me about a hundred times in the last two days that he prefers to be called Paine. The big guy pretending to be asleep in the corner is Marcus. Take your finger off the trigger of your weapon and say 'Hello' Marcus."

A deep voice rumbled out as Marcus placed his machine pistol on the bed. "Hello, Marcus."

"The beautiful young woman making eyes at my son is Elle, the Whippette's daughter," Ashley laughed as both Paine and Elle blushed but beamed at the newcomer.

"So, what brings you here?".

"Elle, your father sent me here to keep you company and keep the rest of the city safe."

"What's the prognosis?"

"Your parents are working hard on the vaccine, and they managed to convince the Technos to send some scientists over to help." Carley saw the look on Ashley's face. "I know we don't have a good track record with the Technos, but they realized after looking at the film of you guys almost dying in the car that if they didn't help, we'd all be dead. They managed to find out one thing."

"What's that?"

"Your son, Michael," she stopped when she saw the look on Paine's face, "Sorry, Paine, had a lot of nanoprobes in his blood. It seems they were left over from a meditube procedure. They are what stopped the virus from infecting him."

She looked at the others. "When he injected his blood into you guys, he saved your lives. We thought he'd been given a vaccine, but we were wrong. I almost paid the ultimate price for that error. Luckily, the Technos had a meditube nearby. So, I'm still alive."

"Then we'll have to get people into a meditube if they're infected."

"It's not that easy, Marcus. Meditube technology is very expensive, and there are not nearly enough tubes to take care of everyone in New York." Ashley turned to the newcomer. "By the way, Carley, how did you get the Technos to help you? I thought they hated you."

Carley laughed. "It is amazing what people will do once they're faced with certain death. They helped, hoping to assist the Whippettes in finding a vaccine or at least identifying the virus or whatever it is that's making us sick. That way, the Technos can produce nanoprobes that can fight this thing and save all our asses." She suppressed a yawn. "Anyway, I'm bushed. Fighting off that virus wiped me out. Do you mind if I sit for a while?" Carley pointed at the bed in the corner.

Ashley smiled, "Go ahead, you've earned some rest."

"Mother, why do the Technos hate you and your people?" Paine asked, curious to find out more about his mother's past.

"It has to do with the Times Square Massacre."

"What about the Times Square Massacre? Were you involved in the killing of the police?" Elle shocked at the revelation, stared at Ashley.

"I arrived in New York before it happened but didn't participate in the fight. I do know what happened, though. NUS and the UN continue to misinform people about what really occurred." Ashley began the tale of the Times Square Massacre.

"The NUS sent a political appointee to New York to take back the city. The police he commanded were armed with the latest hypervelocity weapons. He made the mistake of encircling the square, then meeting with the various factions within the city." Ashley grimaced as she remembered the carnage she'd seen.

"When the faction leaders basically told him to go to hell, he had his force open fire."

"You've got to be kidding," Marcus sat open mouthed thinking about what happened. "The casualties must've been horrific."

"Five thousand hypervelocity weapons fired at the same time. I lost some colleagues in the cross fire. We know what happened because the idiot had it filmed. The live stream ended as he dropped his hand and the police opened up on the crowd." Ashley sighed. "All sixty-six people in Times Square disintegrated as the five thousand hypervelocity darts, meeting no resistance, continued their flights. The police, who'd been armed with chemical weapons, didn't know what their new weapons could do. At least two-thirds of the police were killed or wounded in the initial volley by their own people. In the ensuing confusion, they thought they were being attacked by the gangs and continued to fire, adding to the casualties."

"The real casualties occurred when the fighting ended." Carley took up the narrative. "City residents came to Times Square hoping to get food, clothing, or modern weapons. A pitched battle began between the factions, and casualties soon passed twenty thousand."

"New Yorkers now had thousands of state-of-the-art weapons, and the NUS president's hope of retaking the city evaporated." Shaking her head, Ashley looked at Paine. "That's why your weapons had to be keyed every day. Rather than risk losing more technology to lawless hands, the NUS produced a new generation of hand grips equipped with a self-destruct mechanism. The user put in a simple eight-digit code, which needed to be re-entered every 24 hours. If the code is wrong, the grip fuses to the weapon, rendering both inert."

Ashley drew in a deep breath as she came to the end of her narration. "Naturally, the NUS public relations people blamed everything on the gangs. The story spread and became the accepted truth."

"How come you know so much about the battle?" Marcus wanted to hear more about the story.

"I got it from the most reliable source. The Technos captured her shortly after the massacre. They held her responsible for the carnage although I don't see how she could have done much from her jail cell." Ashley looked at Paine. "You know how much I hate being locked up. The Technos are reasonable if they have all the facts presented to them. When I found out they were holding her for something she tried to stop, I negotiated her release from the Techno prison about 10 years ago." She pointed at her chief of staff, sitting on the bed. "Ladies and gentlemen, I present to you Miss Carley Squires, the deputy chief of police involved in the Times Square Massacre."

Everyone stared open-mouthed at Carley, deep in their own thoughts. They were startled by the sound of Dr. Whippette's voice coming over the intercom.

"We've found something. There is no plague. The infection you all have is a simple flu virus. It makes you sick but won't kill you. Clever bastards, they use the virus to mask specially engineered nanoprobes. Those get into the blood stream and attack the vital organs and nervous system on command. I am sorry, Paine, but it looks as though your father didn't want you to survive. The old nanoprobes we found in your blood detected, attacked, and destroyed the dangerous ones. We've isolated some of them. The Technos say they'll be able to mass produce their own probes within the next few days. They'll be programmed to destroy Corvis probes. The only issue we have is how to get them out to the general population."

"How is this being spread?" Ashley asked.

"The plague nanoprobes jump from body to body like fleas. Once they have done their work, they can move up to two meters to find their next host. If we don't stop the probes from jumping, they'll spread through New York." He paused. "Deaths will be in the tens of thousands. Maybe more."

Ashley spoke up, "Is there anything we can do to help stop the process?"

"All I can tell you is to get better," William answered. "There really isn't anything you can do right now, unless you want to pray."

It took two more days for the Whippettes, working with the Technos, to produce enough nanoprobes just to protect themselves against the plague. Once the immediate population were inoculated against the flu bug, they let Ashley and the others out of isolation. They were quickly taken to the waiting med tech and put into meditubes to purge their bodies of any remaining plague nanoprobes.

Stepping out of the laboratory building, Paine looked up at the clear, blue sky.

Marcus deeply inhaled the spring air and then let out a bellow.

"General Martin, you son of a bitch, I can't wait to get my hands around your throat." He turned to Paine. "Sorry, buddy. He's your father, but he's absolutely no good."

Momentarily comforted by the sun on his skin, Paine looked back at Marcus. He couldn't think of an appropriate remark.

Chapter 43 - Katrina

Katrina looked up at the large red cross on the side of the lifter. She and her older brother Carl with about 100 other people, had been rounded up by the UN security forces.

"Damn it all," Carl whispered. "If we hadn't gone into the shop to steal some food, we'd have been in the clear."

Shrugging, Katrina patted her brother on the shoulder. "There's nothing else we can do. I'm faster than you are, but I can't outrun a plasma blast, let alone hypervelocity rounds they'd throw at us."

An amplified voice addressed the crowd. "The United Nations is providing free inoculations to protect you from the plague infecting the city."

She'd seen the bodies and knew lots of people were dying. However, Katrina didn't trust the UN to do anything that would benefit the people of New York.

The troopers guarding the crowd didn't look or act like the UN soldiers she dealt with before. Most of those had been stumbling drunks or drugged-out junkies. These guys moved with an efficiency that the UN had never displayed, and that worried her.

As Carl shuffled forward, she started devising a plan to get away. Noticing the man in front of her had a cockroach on his sleeve. she gently picked it off and popped it in her mouth.

He turned, yelling, "Are you crazy or what? Leave me alone." He swung at her.

Katrina easily avoided the blow, jumping back out of the way, hissing through her teeth.

"I've had worse." She grinned, thinking back to a meal she and Carl had shared ten years ago. "Carl, you can let him go."

The man shrugged out of Carl's grip. "Watta ya mean, you had worse?" He said as he rubbed his damaged arm.

"I remember. Our mother left to find our father after the entire block chased after him, out for his head. With both our parents away, they came after us. We had had to fight them off." Carl grinned at the man who'd tried to hit his sister. "We had to beat up, what? Thirty irate people?"

"You two did that? I don't believe it."

Reaching past her brother, Katrina grabbed the man by the belt buckle with one hand, lifting him two feet off the ground.

"What makes you think I can't fight off thirty on my own?" She smiled sweetly at the quivering man dangling in front of her.

"I believe," he stuttered. "I believe you can. Please put me down."

Dropping him, Katrina turned to Carl. "Mom came home and stashed Dad's body in a closet. You said she's upset and told me to leave her alone. I remember you kicked me when I complained about being hungry."

"And Mom said, 'I'm not upset, just tired. I found your father. He's dead. He did bring us some food, but you have to be patient. Go back to sleep.' She didn't even shed a tear."

"The wound in her arm got infected. She was dying from sepsis and had just found Dad with two holes in his body. What did you expect her to do?" Katrina remembered her mother's face. "She passed three days later."

Carl and Katrina looked at each other and shrugged. They had seen so much death they felt their parents were in a better place - no longer in the hell where they still lived.

"At least we got a good meal out of it." Carl smiled at the bittersweet memory.

"You ate your parents?" The man gagged. "How could you?"

"Oh. We didn't eat them." Carl laughed at the expression on the man's face. "We aren't cannibals."

"Two days later, Mom went back Dad's body." Katrina picked up the narrative. "Maggots were all over the corpse. She carefully picked them off one by one, then brought the pail of wriggling worms inside our hiding place."

"Then what happened?" the man asked.

Katrina and Carl spoke in unison. "Dinner."

The man threw up what little he had in his stomach.

"Gets 'em every time." Shaking her head, Katrina eyed the vigilant guards watching the crowd.

"Something's not right, Carl. This whole setup stinks. I don't like it but can't really see a way out."

Chapter 44 – Inoculation

The guards prodded the frightened people forward, closer to the fence.

"Not much we can do right now. These guys are really good at their jobs." Carl nodded toward the soldiers guarding them. "Maybe when we get nearer, we can try something."

As the line moved slowly toward a white-coated doctor, Carl and Katrina watched silently, waiting for an opportunity.

"Doctor Engle, your next patient is ready." The guard took the person at the front of the line by the arm and led her to the small table set up right outside the barbed-wire fence.

Herman Engle had a degree in micro-programming. In his stiffly starched white coat, with longish hair slightly graying at the temples, chiseled features, penetrating blue eyes and a charming smile, he looked the part of a medical specialist.

"Hello, how are we feeling today? Any fever, chills, pain in the joints, stiff neck? No? That is a good sign. You do not seem to be infected yet, so I'm going to give you a small injection to protect you against the new plague. Please roll up your sleeve." Engle repeated the same scripted litany for each patient.

His warm hands gently took the newest patient's arm, and he picked up a syringe from the box on the table. "You may feel a slight prick. You can look away if you want to."

Gently removing the needle from the woman's arm, Engle placed a small Band-Aid on the injection sight. "You'll be better in no time at all. You may go to the holding area. Please wait there for at least one hour to make sure you don't have an allergic reaction. Then you are free to go." He motioned for the next person in line to be brought forward.

They were getting closer to the front of the queue. When there were three people in front of her, she gave Carl the sign.

"You son of a bitch." Carl kicked the man behind him squarely between the legs, causing him to collapse to the ground. Guards came running as Carl kept kicking him, yelling, "He touched my ass. The guy's a pervert. I'm going to kill him."

Katrina jumped over the barrier dividing those who had been given shots from the waiting crowd. She hid behind the largest person she could find. Her fellow New Yorkers closed in around her, happy to do anything to disrupt the UN's plans.

The guards pulled Carl away from the prostrate man and pushed him to the front of the line. He couldn't avoid getting the injection. Carl went through the ritual, all the while mumbling, and then joined Katrina on the other side.

"Now what?" Carl whispered.

Katrina shook her head. "I don't know. I guess we have to wait."

Herman Engle looked up. "And you're the final one." He watched as the last patient arrived at his table. He went through the same perfectly rehearsed drill as before and administered his last injection. Carefully washing his hands, he dried them on a towel, throwing it into a receptacle marked biohazard.

"Lieutenant Curtis." Engle waved for him to come over.

"Yes, Doctor?" Chris Curtis felt uncomfortable in the uniform of the UN, but orders were orders. He knew what would happen if he disobeyed General Martin.

"It is time to pack up your troops and leave." Engle folded the table, picked up his box of syringes and walked into the lifter. He did a quick mental calculation and figured he had inoculated about three thousand people this week alone. A job well done.

A chime caused Chris to jump. He clicked over to the command net. General Martin's voice echoed in his ears. "Captain Sanders, gather the troops and move them out. Lieutenant Curtis, I want you and four of our troopers to stay until the end. Inform me when you are ready to return to base. Use route three bravo."

The double click Chris heard in his ear bug told him they heard and understood their orders.

Chris looked at Trisha. "Man, I didn't sign up for this and I'm sure you didn't. If you want go back with the UN troops, I'll deal with the people here."

"Come on, I'm stronger than you are about this kind of thing." Trisha punched him on the arm. "If you can't take it, why don't you go, and I'll cover for you."

"You know I can't do that." Chris smiled at Trisha. "Then stay here with me. I won't mind the company on the trip home."

The waiting soldiers backed away from the restless crowd and moved to the lifter. Four soldiers stayed with Chris and Trisha. They kept their weapons ready as the lifter took off.

Engle ordered the pilot to hover above the crowd. He opened his briefcase and looked carefully at the panel inside. The new nanoprobes were modified to activate when they received the transmission. If no signal reached them in twelve hours, the nanoprobes would activate themselves, then transmit the plague slowly to spread it to others.

Time to test the new system.

Shivering with anticipation, Engle looked over the upturned faces below, savoring the moment. He pushed the numbers that activated the signal to the nanoprobes he'd injected into the mass of bodies below. He motioned the pilot to go lower so he could watch their death dance.

*****

The hair stood up on the back of Katrina's neck as people dropped around her. She looked at Carl. Turning blue, she watched him trying to breathe. A little girl with a tattered toy pulled it to her chest, then fell to the ground, clutching the doll in a death grip. An older couple died in each other's arms, face-to-face on the tarmac. Everyone in the enclosure dropped to the ground or gasped for air. Within a minute, only she still lived.

Katrina went limp, lying on the hard asphalt with her eyes half closed. She heard footsteps behind her.

"Trisha, come here. I think this one is still alive."

It took all of Katrina's efforts to not move as a hand touch her shoulder. It slowly turned her over. A young blond woman looked directly into her eyes. Katrina stayed stock still, hoping she would just leave.

Trisha picked up the drooping body. It felt like a rag doll.

"Chris," she yelled over her shoulder, "I think I have a live one here. She seems paralyzed. I'll put her out of her misery." A flash of something in Katrina's eyes reminded her of another time, when she'd been scheduled for execution in the San Francisco brothel, sure she would die but refusing to give up.

Trisha dropped the limp body on the ground and waved Chris away with one hand while taking her pistol out with the other.

"Why don't you go check out some more bodies? I'll take care of this one."

As Chris walked away, Trisha whispered, "I'm pretty sure we're being watched so you better make this look good. Lie still until we've been gone for 10 minutes, then you can go." Trisha dropped Katrina's limp body on the ground, slowly raised her silenced pistol, and pointed it at Katrina's head. The muzzle moved slightly to the left as she squeezed the trigger and the bullet passed close to Katrina's ear. Fragments of asphalt hitting Katrina in the side of the head caused her to flinch, and Katrina made her body jerk convulsively and then go still.

As Trisha turned away from Katrina, she found Chris standing right behind her. "I heard what you said. We can't let her go."

Trisha smiled and took his arm, walking him away from the girl. "Chris, come on. They have cameras on us, and I did what needed to be done. What are you going to do, report me?" She kept pulling Chris farther from the girl. "I thought you told me you didn't sign up for this shit, so why don't we just leave it at that? What do you think that creep Engle will do if he thinks we let one of them live?"

When Chris didn't respond, Trisha shook her head and continued, "He is some piece of work. I don't ever want to talk to him again, so forget what we saw and did here. Got it?" Chris stared at her as Trisha continued. "Besides, that one doesn't have long to live. They all got the injection. She's been exposed to the disease and is a walking corpse. Let her go and she'll spread the disease on her own."

Trisha kicked the nearest body on the ground. "Then we won't have to do this kind of work anymore." She bent to look at it, then quickly pulled out her pistol and put a bullet in the dead man's head. "That'll make whoever might be watching think we had more than one we had to finish off." As Trisha walked away toward the rendezvous point, she shook her head. "Give me a nice shooting war and I'll be happy, I'm not made for this kind of killing."

Katrina heard every word. Anguish consumed her, she could no longer hold in her tears. Her mother and father meant everything to her, but she'd held it together after they were dead, for Carl's sake. She'd always been emotionally stronger than him.

He'd been her partner in crime, a great brother who looked out for her every step of the way. She didn't need his help when they were fighting for their lives, but always let him think he'd saved her from the many situations they'd gotten into.

Tears streamed down her face. *He's gone.* Now all alone in the world, she cried for herself, for her brother and the others lying dead around her. She cried for her dead father and mother. She knew they were in a better place, safe from the horrors to come. Try as she might, she couldn't stop weeping. She cried for the living.

Anger welled up inside her, burning like a lava flow. She didn't know how long she stayed there, but she once again heard footsteps.

"There has to be at least a hundred here. Check them all," a deep voice echoed in the empty silence. "See if anyone survived."

She thought they were returning to finish her. Katrina's mind told her to be patient, but her body exploded into action. She became a hissing, tearing animal.

"You're going to pay for this," she screamed. She attacked like a rabid Tasmanian devil.

It took all Marcus efforts to grab the wild thing that scratched at his face like a crazed bobcat. Marcus went down, twisting his body so he fell on top of the woman. He put his two hundred pounds on top of her.

"We're here to help you."

She kicked him off as if he were a kitten.

Springing to her feet, she leapt at Marcus. Her long hair, wild and clinging to her tear-soaked face, obscured her vision.

He caught her chin with a well-timed punch. The feral girl went down in a heap. Marcus quickly scooped her up and tied her wrists together.

"Marcus, did I really see that happen?" Paine walked over and looked at the bruise beginning to show on his friend's cheek. "You just got your ass kicked by a little child?"

"Child, my foot. She's the toughest person I've ever met. She coulda killed me." Marcus rubbed his face. "This is some woman."

"Okay, lover boy. Cut it out. We've got to figure out how all these people died. Maybe this one can tell us what happened. Let's get her back to HQ so I can question her." Paine called out to the team. "Check the other bodies."

"Make sure she's secured before you go into the room. This little one is strong, and fast." Marcus carried her to the waiting lifter.

They found no one else alive.

Chapter 45 - Promises

Katrina woke to find herself zip-tied to a chair. Looking around the stark room, she could see bare, grey walls and a steel door. The chair, bolted to the floor, sat close to the lone table. Feeling like a trapped animal, she wanted to scream, but she controlled the outburst. *Calm yourself.* She began to move her arms and legs against the zip-ties that secured her.

The door squeaked as it opened, causing Katrina to sit still. A clean-cut young man, wearing black coveralls, entered. *He doesn't look like a murderous bastard. But neither did Engle.* Pulling out the other chair, he sat across from her.

"My name is Paine Martin. I'd like to ask you a few questions." He put a device in front of her. "I'm recording this. We found you at the scene of a mass-murder that occurred yesterday. You were the only survivor. We need to find out how you managed to live."

Katrina stared at the table.

"Why were you in that part of the city?"

Silence.

"Were you caught in a random sweep?"

Silence.

"Did they target specific groups of people?"

Silence.

"Did you notice anything about the soldiers who were part of the security force?" Paine looked at his notes.

Katrina hissed at him through clenched teeth.

"At least that's something. You need to tell us exactly what happened."

She stared at Paine. Katrina felt rage building up inside. "I won't help the UN, or anyone associated with it."

"We aren't with the UN." Paine protested. "We're trying to stop what they're doing. We need your help."

"I don't believe you."

"If you don't tell us what happened, more people will die." Paine sounded exasperated. He tried a different tack. "Do you want to be responsible for the deaths of others?"

Katrina's eyes narrowed, as if focusing on a target. "Only one."

"Who is it?"

Closing her eyes, she sat motionless, refusing to speak further.

After five more minutes of unanswered questions, Paine stood up, turned off the recorder and walked out of the room.

When the door closed, Katrina continued her efforts to loosen her bonds. The bolted-down chair gave her some leverage. She could feel the zip ties on her arms giving slightly. The events of the last day caught up with her. Visions of what happened flashed through her mind.

Her enhanced hearing allowed her to eavesdrop on the conversation happening in the hall.

"I got nothing, other than she wants to kill someone. I hope it isn't you."

"She tied up. What can she do?"

"Just be careful."

She could smell someone coming to the room. She recognized the large person she'd attacked by his strong, earthy scent. It almost overwhelmed her senses, surprising Katrina by how much that aroma affected her. She felt anxious and aroused at the same time. She looked up as the door opened once more. *It is him.*

The chair scraped against the floor as he pulled it out. It creaked when he sat down. He looked at her with dark eyes.

Sitting still, Katrina waited in silence.

The man's voice rumbled out of scarred, twisted lips. "Glad to see you're awake. I didn't mean to hit you that hard, but you gave me no choice."

A shiver ran down Katrina's spine. His deep voice, its timbre somehow soothing, echoed in the small room. She detected no malice. Sitting straighter in the chair, she studied him.

"You're a lot younger than I thought."

"And you are a lot older."

"What?"

"I don't mean it that way. It's just you're so small. At first, I thought you were a child." She could see his eyes scan her body. "I can see now you aren't."

"Don't get any ideas." Katrina glared at him. He had an aura about him, one of strength and self-assurance. *Despite the scarring, he's an attractive man*

"This conversation isn't going very well, is it?" He rubbed the bruise on his face.

Shifting slightly in her bonds, she turned her head to one side. Her hair fell across the left side of her face. Responding with a silky, smooth voice, she almost purred her words. "Why don't you cut me loose, so we can start again."

"I think we know how that would turn out," Marcus chuckled. He reacted as she hoped he would, reaching across the table to move the hair away from her eyes. "Sorry for the restraints. I don't think I'll take them off just yet. You aren't a prisoner, but I can't spend my time fighting you."

"What makes you think I'd fight you?" *Lull him into submission.*

"How did you get so strong?"

"Why can't you let me go?" *Softly, make him want to remove the restraints.* She leaned backward, arching against the chair. *His eyes should be shifting. Here they come. Ha! I thought he might be attracted to me. Play the coy lady.* "Please?"

"There are rules…"

Shit. So, he's one of those guys. Different tack.

"Screw them." Katrina's eyes flashed.

"I can't set you free yet."

"Then I can't talk to you." She closed her mouth once more, refusing to speak.

"Answer my questions. Then I'll release you." Marcus turned the device on the tabletop back on. "We seem to have gotten off to a rough start. Let's start over. My name is Marcus Pace. I'm part of a coalition trying to stop the plague from killing the people of New York. And you are?"

He'd been the only man to get the better of her in a fight, except for her brother. She ached inside as she thought of living without having him watch her back. *Carl.* She couldn't believe he died like that. The voice cut into her thoughts.

"Listen, we want to help you. Can't you tell me your name?" His approach differed from the other man's. It made her want to speak to this one. "I go by Katrina…" When Marcus snorted,

Katrina stopped talking and glared at him. "If you call me Kat, I'll break free of these bonds and scratch your eyes out."

His eyes twinkled as he replied, "I can respect that." He looked past her at the wall, pressing his lips together. "We need you. Paine told you we aren't with the UN. We'd like your help, Katrina."

"Why the hell should I help you? I don't care what group you're with. You're all the same, pushing people around and butchering anyone who doesn't do what you want." Her eyes flashed with anger. "You attacked me. You killed my brother." Katrina screamed.

"As I recall, you jumped me." Marcus stayed calm. He pointed a finger at his bruise. "I just defended myself. I had nothing to do with your brother's death."

Katrina slumped in her seat. She felt defeated. "All I want to do is get free and find the man who murdered him. He called himself Doctor Engle. I'll make him pay, I can promise you that." She could feel her hair bristling as she spoke. "You have no idea what I went through."

Marcus leaned forward, his hands gripping the edge of the table. "Like you're the only one who's in pain?"

She couldn't control herself anymore. A primal scream exploded from her lips. Tears of anger and frustration flowed down her face.

Marcus jumped to his feet. He leaned over the table.

Katrina tried to withdraw. Her head pressed against the back of the chair. She watched as his hand went into his pocket. Expecting the worst, he surprised her by taking out a tissue.

"We've all lost people close to us."

She tried to avoid his hand.

"Hold still." He gently wiped the tears away.

Katrina noticed a glistening in his eyes. *He's trying to control himself.*

He talked as he dried her face. "You won't find your brother's killer without our help. But first I need your cooperation." He sat back, smiling. "You look better now. Have you calmed down enough to tell me what happened?"

Katrina could feel his sincerity. It seemed like he hid a pain of his own. She sensed it went as deeply as her own. She had another thought. She could use his obvious attraction to her advantage. "Since I can't get away, I might as well talk. But if you lie to me, I'll kill you."

"Fair enough. I don't lie, so I've nothing to fear."

She talked through the events of the day, up to her feigned death.

Marcus interrupted her narrative. "That fits with what we discovered when we got to the scene. You were infected by the same nanoprobes that killed your brother." He sighed. "They jump hosts."

Fear coursed through her body. She had no idea how long she'd been unconscious. "How much time do I have?"

"The incubation period is about twenty-four hours."

Katrina jerked forward, struggling to get free of her restraints. "Don't hurt yourself."

"I'm going to die, and you tell me to relax?" Katrina strained even harder, feeling the bonds loosening.

"You don't have to worry."

"That's easy for you to say." She continued her struggle.

The computer beeped twice. Marcus tapped a few times on the screen. He looked up from the display. "We put you into a meditube. Extracted the nanoprobes. Proved our theory. The rats that got them died a few minutes ago." He looked up from the computer, meeting Katrina's gaze. "Look. You may have lost your brother, but your actions saved thousands of lives. Thanks to you, we know how the infection spreads."

Her stomach churned at the thought of Carl. Katrina fought to stop the tears from cascading down her face once more. "Son of a…"

Marcus interrupted her. "Anything else you can tell me?"

"The soldiers who came up to make sure everyone died were not like UN soldiers." Katrina remembered their efficiency. "They knew what they were doing."

"Can you describe them for me? What about their uniforms, any special equipment, maybe some identifiers?"

Katrina continued to flex her muscles against the bonds that held her arms. They were loosening. She kept her attention on Marcus, to make sure he didn't notice her exertion. She found herself wanting to get to know this man.

"Their boots. They were clean and new. Most of the UN soldiers sell their boots or trade them for drugs." She furrowed her brow.

"Tell me more about the soldiers."

"There were four of them outside the fence. Two of them were checking bodies. They came up to me." She could feel her heart racing as she recalled the events.

"What did you notice about them?"

"The man's not as tall as you. Skinny. About five-foot eleven, maybe six feet. Red hair. His accent told me he's not from around here. The female soldier shot at me." She relived the fear of being killed.

"At you?"

"She intentionally missed. I don't know why she let me live."

"What did she look like?"

"Blondish, short, well-muscled. Blue eyes." Katrina shivered as she realized how close she had been to dying. She brought her focus back to Marcus.

"Did you get a good look at her?" Marcus pressed on. "What else did you notice?"

"She had a small scar over her left eye. It looked like someone bit her there."

"A bite mark? You're sure about that?" Marcus shook his head. "I think I know who these two are. But what would Trisha and Chris be doing here in New York?"

"That's what she called him. Chris." Katrina strained at her bonds. "You liar! You know these people, the ones who killed my brother." She wanted to tear his heart out with her bare hands.

"See? This is why I kept you tied up. I'm not lying to you. Calm down, Katrina. Let me explain." He crossed his arms, waiting until she stopped squirming.

Realizing the futility of fighting the bonds, she immediately stopped struggling. "I'm calm now. Tell me."

"We were in the same unit before all this stuff started happening. I came to New York to assassinate the leader of an underground movement. The man who sent me almost killed me and Paine when he infected us with the plague. The same plague that killed your brother. Instead of killing the leader, we joined the resistance." Marcus leaned on his elbows, clasped his hands together and put his chin on his interlaced fingers. "General Martin must be somehow involved with the UN. I don't understand what he's up to, but I've got to find out. That bastard is definitely up to no good."

Slowly slipping her arms out of the loosened bonds, Katrina thought about attacking Marcus. She had no doubt she could beat him. *My legs are still tied. Even if I get them loose, I won't be able to get out of the room. That Paine guy is probably waiting outside with a gun. I'll have to use him as a hostage. You get to live, for now.*

Katrina moved so quickly Marcus had no time to react. Her small hands grasped his, holding his interlocked fingers. Her legs, still bound to the anchored chair, gave her an advantage.

Startled, Marcus jerked his head back and tried to pull his hands away. He couldn't. "That's quite a grip you have there." Their eyes locked.

"I told you if you lied to me, I'd kill you. Maybe you didn't lie, but you left out some critical information. I need to get out of here and find that bastard Engle." She tightened her hold. "I can crush your fingers. I'll do it if you don't release me."

Hearing the exterior bolt sliding, Marcus yelled, "Don't come in. I've got this under control. We aren't done yet." Straining as hard as he could, Marcus could not escape Katrina's vise-like grasp. "I'm not going to let you go."

"Then I won't let you go, either." Katrina watched as he began to sweat.

He surprised her with a laugh. "Hell, girl, I've been hurt much worse than this. Look at these scars. They show what I've been through. You think broken fingers scare me?" His look challenged Katrina to go ahead and do her worst.

She squeezed harder. "My scars don't show like yours do."

"I'm sorry you've suffered, but who hasn't?" Marcus tried to escape her grip once more. He failed.

"I'm an orphan. Carl is dead. Now I have no one." The tears were beginning to form once more.

A bitter snort escaped Marcus. "Welcome to my world. I've been alone since I turned five. The authorities killed my mother. I never knew my father. We are much alike, you and I."

"Except in size," Katrina's laugh rang out.

J. B. Durbin

"And strength." Marcus didn't try to fight against her. "I told you before, but you obviously weren't listening. You aren't a prisoner here. We need information from you, then we'll let you go."

"I've told you everything. What more do you want?"

"I want you to trust me. Join us. Maybe we can stop the murders. Let's work together. It'll keep both of us from being scarred more than we already are. You can't do it alone."

She looked at Marcus with a fresh perspective. Her grip lightened. She noticed he didn't try to pull away. Cocking her head to one side, she tried to determine his sincerity.

He quit fighting against her grip. "I'm literally leaving myself in your hands."

Katrina traced the scars on Marcus' forearms. "You have very strong hands, big hands. I like them." It sent a thrill through her body. "I'll help you however I can. You have my word."

Marcus took a deep breath. "I swear I'll help you find whoever killed your brother. I won't stand in your way when you take your revenge."

Katrina didn't flinch when Marcus stood up and pulled out a knife. She waited as he gently cut through the ties that secured her legs to the chair. He banged on the door, turning to her as it opened. He held his hand out to Katrina.

She hesitated for a moment. Walking to him, she slid her hand into his. The touch electrified her. Katrina smiled. "Okay, let's roll."

Marcus waved at Paine as he passed by.

"Really, Marcus?" Paine hid his smile. "Cozying up to the girl who kicked your ass?"

"Let it go, Paine. I like this one. She's given us some great information."

184

Chapter 46 – Making Contact

Paine reacted to the news about Trisha and Chris with anger. Marcus stayed out of his way as he exploded into a fit, swearing, and punching the wall. As Paine shook his damaged hand, he realized the futility of his outburst. Marcus simply held out a Quickheal patch for Paine's skinned knuckles.

"I can't believe it. This means the general is up to his eyeballs in this mess. We must tell my mother." Paine turned to the door as it opened. Ashley walked in. Marcus quickly briefed her on the information Katrina had provided.

"I heard that mercenaries were involved in this, but I didn't think Josh would incorporate Regulars into the UN forces." Ashley mused, "I wonder what's going on."

"There's only one way to find out. I have to see Trisha."

Ashley looked at her son and shook her head. "There's no way you'll get to her without being recognized," she warned.

"I have a plan. Take me to the Technos medical facility." As much as he hated the meditube, Paine would need several trips to make his plan work.

*****

"Sergeant Jones." Trisha listened to the radio call coming through from the guard commander. "There's a UN officer walking around checking on the troops. Can you see what he's up to?"

Trisha turned away from the soldiers she'd been dressing down for sleeping on guard duty and moved to the front of the UN building. As she walked around the corner, she came to the position of attention. She felt the hair standing up on her neck, but she couldn't figure out why. Hesitating slightly, she saluted with a flourish.

The colonel, average height and black as coal, moved closer. Something about him made her think she'd seen him before, but she couldn't put her finger on it. His accent, thick with a hint of French, grated on her ears as he spoke to her.

The colonel whispered, "I need to speak to you somewhere private, if that is a possibility,"

Trisha shook her head as she saw what appeared to be her old patrol sign language flashed at her, the sign of danger. Training took over. She moved her hand to the pistol grip of her weapon, scanning the area for possible threats. Perceiving none, she looked at the face of the colonel. His eyes were a deep blue. Alarm bells ringing in her head, she nonetheless kept her composure. "What can I do for you, sir?"

The colonel whispered, "You can start by taking your finger off the trigger and hear me out."

The colonel then backed up a few feet and yelled at Trisha. As a stream of undecipherable French flowed from his mouth, getting louder every moment and accentuated by wild arm movements, the colonel's right eye drooped in a wink. Paine flashed, "We are being listened to," in patrol sign language. "Reports of my death were greatly exaggerated. Marcus and I are alive and well and need your help. Snap back to attention, salute and wait for fifteen minutes. You can find us in the last place we were together."

Trisha stiffened and saluted the rapidly retreating officer, who gestured and cursed in French as he stormed away. Her communicator chimed.

"Trisha, this is Chris. What the hell is that all about?"

"I have no idea, but I can't wait until we get done with this mission," Trisha replied. "These UN types give me the creeps. I think he said, 'la mort,' several times. That means death in French. He may have been threatening me or talking about all the bodies we've been finding. He scared the heck out of me." She paused for a moment. "Can I take a short break to compose myself?"

"You've never feared anything," Chris shook his head "If you need a break, go ahead. Take as much time as you want."

The last time she'd seen Paine, they'd been taken by the UN Forces from the sewers. Trisha walked down First Avenue toward 42d Street. She scanned the road, looking for some clue as to where to go, and then spotted a small ear bug lying on top of a manhole cover. She continued walking down the street, the blank windows staring down at her. She knew where the UN guards were posted. If she learned anything in the past month, it was that the guards would be asleep or high about this time of day.

Stopping her forward progress, Trisha turned smartly on her heel, and purposefully moved back toward the UN compound. She intentionally looked up, pretending not to see the break in the pavement directly in her path. Her foot caught the edge of the buckled asphalt and she stumbled forward, landing on one knee and keeping herself from falling with her left hand. Cursing loudly, she straightened up and rubbed her hand on her side, slipping the ear bug into her pocket. Hoping Paine could see her, she signed "Got it. 0400 hours." She went back to her post.

Trisha made it through the rest of the day without incident. She avoided Chris as much as possible. She believed he would sense her agitation and start asking questions. She skipped the usual drinking games many of the Regulars participated in to wash away the carnage they were inflicting upon the people of New York and went to bed early. Just before going to sleep, she put the ear bug in, but got no sounds.

Her wrist alarm vibrated at 0250. Trisha lay there for a few minutes until Chris began to snore again. She pulled on her phototrophic camouflage and slipped out of the building. Most of the guards were staring blankly into space, afraid one of the crazy NUS soldiers would show up and chew their asses. She passed through without incident and walked to the manhole cover where she'd found the ear bug. *Only 0340, too early.*

Rather than wait for the designated time, she slipped inside. Memories flooded her mind.

"Trisha?" She jumped as the ear bug came alive. She stayed silent, not wanting to make her presence known.

"I can see you. Don't start shooting. Don't get your knife out, either."

Lights flooded the tunnel. Paine appeared with Marcus, Carole and Elle. He lifted off the special goggles that canceled the invisibility effect of the phototrophic uniforms.

"Look who I brought along," Paine pointed at the three figures behind him. "The last time we were all together, we were standing right here. Lots of things have changed since then, but I don't think we have time to go through all the particulars."

"I thought you guys were dead."

"Not yet." Marcus held out his hand to Trisha. "Go ahead, touch me. I'm really here."

"I believe you."

187

"I just wanted you to see we're alive. Some really bad things are happening to the people of New York. We want to stop it. We need your help."

Trisha removed the hood and faceguard of her uniform, exposing her head. She looked at Paine. "May I at least ask a few questions? I think I have a right to know what is going on."

"We only have 10 minutes, and then you have to leave." Paine started the countdown feature on his chronometer. "You can ask three questions. Then we have to get answers from you."

"I'll be brief, then. Did you find the leader of the resistance?"

Taking a deep breath, Paine replied, "Yes, she's my mother, the general's ex-wife. She's also friends with Elle's parents, who are here fighting the plague that the general is spreading throughout the city. I found out I have a sister who happens to be an old friend of yours." He pointed at Carole, who stuck her tongue out at Trisha, then smiled. "I'll explain that later. Next question?"

"How did you change your appearance so much? I almost didn't recognize you."

"My mother has access to a meditube that used by supermodels before the coca plague hit."

"He wanted to get all beatified for you," Marcus chimed in.

Paine chuckled. "It can do all kinds of things to change one's appearance. Question three."

"What can I do to help?" Trisha wiped away a tear. "I hate what we're doing here. I want to stop, but I can't. This is not what I signed up for, killing innocent people." She looked down, remembering when her brother died in the bordello. "The children are the worst."

"Tell us what you remember about the plans."

"I really don't know that much about what the overall plan is, but we're supposed to provide body counts after each infection. I don't understand why that's so important."

They jumped, turning their weapons toward the sound of a loud splash. Everyone pointed them into the darkness.

Katrina's voice rang out. "Hey, Marcus, do you want me to kill this guy or let him breathe?"

"I told you to stay out of sight." Marcus shined his light at the slight girl.

Katrina, hanging from a pipe with one hand, had other curved as if she held something.

"I am out of sight," she laughed. "I'm just doing what you want. You've been begging me to show Paine how strong I am, so he'd stop teasing you about being kicked around by a little girl." She swung around, as if something invisible struggled in her grip. Katrina whispered, "If I can keep you from escaping, what makes you think I can't snap your neck? Hold still."

Pulling his goggles down, Paine saw a soldier in phototrophic camouflage struggling in Katrina's iron grip. Stepping toward the figure, he pulled off the mask and hood.

"Chris. What are you doing here?"

Turning blue, Chris tried to choke out an answer.

Paine touched Katrina's arm. "Katrina, let him breathe."

It took a few moments for Chris to get his breath back. His voice came out raspy as he looked at Trisha. "Give me some credit. I know you better than you know yourself. When you went to bed early, I knew enough to watch you. I thought you were going to off yourself after all the crap you've been through."

"I wouldn't do that without telling you first."

He coughed to cover the catch in his voice. "I couldn't bear the thought of losing you. I never dreamed you'd go over to the enemy."

"We aren't the enemy, Chris." Paine said.

"And how in the hell do you know my name?"

"Look at me."

Chris could see the blue eyes staring out of the black face and recognized his former commander.

"Jesus Christ, am I dreaming or seeing the dead? Paine?" Chris looked down the tunnel. "Marcus?"

"Elle and Carole are here, too."

"I saw you guys die. I could smell the burning flesh. What the hell is going on?"

"Everyone shut up and let me talk. We only have four minutes left." Paine looked at Chris. "I'm putting my life in your hands. You guys need to get back to the UN compound and find out what's going on. Trisha can fill you in on what little she knows."

"I'm not so sure about this."

"Listen to me. We need you to work with us. I trust you, just like you always trusted me." Paine patted Katrina on the arm. "Let him go."

Chris rubbed his neck. He looked at Trisha and shook his head. "Well, you said you didn't sign up for this shit, so I guess we'd better head back."

"You got that right." Trisha turned to leave.

"Communicate through the ear bug tomorrow at 0400. Keep us informed about what's happening and we will try our best to stop this madness." Paine held up his hand. "Wait. Before you go, I need your phototrophic camouflage."

As they were stripping off their clothing, Chris looked at Katrina. "How did you see me? These things are impossible to defeat without the proper equipment."

"I could smell you coming a mile away. You really do have to stop smoking."

"I told you cigarettes would kill you." Trisha punched him on the shoulder. "Let's get out of here."

"Keep the ear bug, but don't turn it on unless you have good intelligence for us. The battery life is not very long." Paine waved goodbye to his friends. "Please don't waste it."

*****

Trisha watched Chris turned away from the manhole cover. She saw him stop and stare at her in the ambient light.

"What?"

"You are so beautiful. I never noticed that before."

Glad the darkness hid her blushing face, Trisha folded her arms across her chest to keep her hands from shaking. "I'm scarred, outside and inside." She fought to keep her voice calm.

"I know, Trish."

"Then let's forget about this and get back to the compound." Trisha turned to go, shivering in the cool night air.

Chris held out his hand. "Why don't we run? It'll keep us from freezing."

She took it, noticing how warm it felt. She felt a thrill run through her body. Trying not to show emotion, she pulled Chris down the street. "You better keep up. I'm sure your smoking will slow you down."

They sprinted toward the compound.

The UN Guard saw a rather strange sight coming his way. He recognized the lieutenant and the sergeant who ran the guard mount dancing down the street, arm-in-arm, singing at the top of their lungs. Chris barked, "Attention." He casually returned the salute of the stunned guard as they passed by. They laughed as they heard the guard mutter, "Look at them idiots, wandering around drunk and naked in the middle of the night."

Chapter 47 - War Council

The smell of ersatz coffee permeated the meeting room. Powered-down computer notebooks littered the table. No one had slept for more than a few hours, each trying to work on a course of action for the defense of the people of New York.

"Let's listen to what Paine has learned so far," Ashley reconvened the meeting to discuss their options.

He briefed the others on what he discovered. "They made it back without incident. Trisha went into the headquarters to check the guards on duty there. She overheard one of the staff officers talking about the tipping point on the body count."

"Do we know what that is?"

"When the body count is more than three hundred thousand, the troops will move in and clear the city of whoever is left. They'll have to step up the infection rates or this could take forever to accomplish." Paine looked at his notes. "Something new is going happen, and soon."

Raising her hand, Carley asked, "How can we keep them from killing more people? We can barely make enough nanoprobes to keep our own people alive, much less come up with more."

William Whippette shook his head and looked down at his hands. "We're doing all we can, but it just isn't enough. We need a better plan."

"What about a surgical raid?" Everyone looked at Marcus. "We go in and take out the general and the top brass. We have the phototrophic uniforms and can get close enough to make it happen."

"It's a suicide mission," Paine replied. "We could take the general out, but we'd never make it ourselves. His security is very good. They are ready to die protecting him."

"So we kill them first."

"Marcus, they could be using the same goggles I used to spot Trisha. If they find out there are two uniforms missing, we could be compromised. Whoever tried it would die." Paine looked around the table. "I won't send anyone else. I'll lead the mission if that's our only option. I don't think we're that desperate yet. There has to be another way."

Looking up from the console, Carley suggested a different plan. "We disguise a group of our own people as UN soldiers. Once we are inside, we shoot everything in sight. If that doesn't work, then we take the two phototrophic uniforms, wrap one around a tactical nuke and I carry it into the UN compound. Problem solved."

"If anyone is going to go on a suicide mission, it will be me," Paine looked across the table at Carley. "Let's just pray it doesn't come to that."

Ashley had been staring off in the distance. "We're brainstorming, right?" She looked at her staff. "Let's consider this. They want the body count to go over three hundred thousand, so why don't we get it there? If we do, they'll think the virus is finally working and stop developing more. They'll also think our forces will be so weak they can just walk in and take out those still standing." She looked at her staff. "What we have to do is figure out how to make them think they're killing more of us than they really are, then set up an ambush. We take out the Regulars and the UN soldiers will run away."

"I don't like the idea of killing Regulars," Marcus snorted.

Ashley made a come-on motion with her hand.

His face darkened. "Trisha and Chris could die, along with some good friends."

"Trisha still has the ear bug and Chris could try to convince the Regulars to separate themselves from the UN troops." Paine worried about them, too. "Right before the attack begins, we could have him tell those he thinks he can trust what's going on."

"Right now, we need to figure out how to save New Yorkers," Ashley sighed. "The Regulars can come later."

"Can we have the factions get the word out to all their people not to go pick up the dead?" Betty chimed in. "That way, we can have our own crews go and collect the bodies. Trisha can send us the locations of the inoculation sites. The plague nanoprobes will be destroyed as they jump to protected people. We'll at least stop the spread of the nanoprobes by infestation." Betty paused. "Unfortunately, that means more people have to die until we can convince the UN that their plan is working."

"That's a good idea." Everyone looked at William in shock. "It has to look like more people are being killed by the virus. If we can get the bodies to a morgue, we can slow the decomposition process just like we do for medical school cadavers. The bodies won't decompose for several days. We get our crews inoculated and functioning. They go collect the dead from the streets. Then we can scatter them throughout the city, close to the inoculation sites. That will increase the body count by at least five times."

"If they think we're dying in droves, maybe they'll stop the inoculations." Ashley looked around the table. "Then they'll launch an all-out attack to destroy us. We must be prepared to fight."

Chapter 48 - Yenissei

"He's been a medical examiner and a loyal worker for almost fifteen years. Yenissei will do whatever he's told." The coroner led Paine into the morgue. "He's handled a few delicate disposals, mostly involving young women who died under mysterious circumstances while visiting some of the less reputable members of the UN."

They entered the crematorium to see a slight man standing in the middle of the room near a gurney ready to go into the oven. Paine rushed over as the man leapt on it, kicking himself toward to open door.

"What the hell?" Paine yelled as he stopped the man. He could feel the intense heat of the furnace on his face and hands.

"Let me alone," the man screamed. "I want to die." Striking Paine with balled-up hands, he tried to get back on the stretcher. "Let me go."

The coroner grabbed one of the man's arms. "Yenissei, what happened?"

Freeing himself, Yenissei pulled back the sheet covering the body. He looked down at his dead wife and cried. Her lifeless body would be one of the first to be cremated that day. He'd prepared her body lovingly, cutting the tendons in her legs so her body wouldn't sit up as it burned.

"She'd been out giving food to the poor. You stopped me from joining my wife, you bastards." He picked up a scalpel and waved it at Paine. "Get away or I'll cut you."

"Yenissei, my name is Paine." He backed away from the enraged man, hands held wide. "We need to talk to you before you go in there."

The coroner came over, pulling the scalpel out of Yenissei's grip then put an arm around his quaking shoulders. "Your wife died at the hands of the UN. She must have been caught up in a UN sweep."

"How do you know these things?" Yenissei had tears streaming down his face.

"The people of New York are being systematically killed, through inoculations provided by the UN. The shots contain nanoprobes that are activated remotely, killing those injected almost instantaneously." Paine waved at the body bags lining the hallway. "She died along with all those others waiting to be cremated."

Yenissei looked up through tear-stained eyes. Paine could see the rage consuming him.

The coroner tightened his grip and went on. "The UN is using us to dispose of the bodies. They rely on us to give them a count of the dead each day. What Paine needs us to do is inflate the count and only burn the bodies that are badly decomposing." The boss pushed Yenissei to arm's length. "We need you to continue to prepare the bodies."

"Some of my friends will be arriving shortly. They need as many corpses as possible. Let them take the cadavers out after the morgue is closed and the guards leave." Paine felt empathy for the distraught man in front of him. He wanted to give him a reason to live. "I'm violating security by telling you this. You want to know why we want you to help? We're setting a trap for those bastards. If they think more people are dead, they won't expect us to be able to fight against them. When the battle does start, we'll have sufficient force to defeat them. Will you help us?"

Yenissei shook off his boss' grip, blinked back his tears and wiped his cheeks with his sleeve.

"I have a new purpose in life." He looked down at his dead wife's face. Pushing her into the chamber, he closed the door. When he turned around, he spoke to Paine in a cold, hard voice. "My wife, my love, is dead. I want to join her now, but I'll help. I only ask for one thing."

"Whatever you want."

"When the time comes to kill them, I want to be there. I want to punish those who did this to her. I will avenge my wife with as many lives as possible."

Paine simply nodded. He followed the coroner out of the crematorium. They didn't hear Yenissei whisper to himself, "Before I join her in death."

Chapter 49 - Engle

"He's a sneaky weasel, but he has been useful," Josh sat down at the table. The room still reeked with the smell tobacco from Ambassador Smythe's pipe. He thought to himself, once all this is over, there will be no smoking in any UN buildings. Josh spoke into the intercom, "Make sure he doesn't bring in the suitcase."

The aid ushered the doctor into the conference room.

"Doctor Engle, please come in."

"You asked to see me, gentlemen?"

Baum pulled out a chair and joined Josh at the conference table.

"Have a seat." Baum waved Engle to a chair. "We have been going over the casualty figures and are pleased to note that the deaths by infection are increasing exponentially. Bodies are being found all over the city. The body count will exceed the target numbers within the week. That is indicative of your fine work, Doctor. However, I must ask if you have modified the protocol in any way. My staff and the delegates to the UN need to be assured that we are all well-protected from the virus."

Josh coughed into his hand.

Baum glanced in his direction and added, "And that our brave forces fighting for us have also been properly protected."

Josh carefully watched as Doctor Engle leaned back in his chair. He could see sweat forming on Engle's brow. *He must feel like he's walking on a razor's edge, trapped.* Josh had a hard time keeping a smile from his face.

His lizard-like eyes darted from one to the other. "We've been very careful, making sure the deaths are slowly increasing. You don't want the people to be afraid. That might cause them to fight against our program." Licking his dry lips, Engle continued. "I believe the deaths may be a bit exaggerated." Engle leaned forward in his seat. "I'll do an immediate field study on some of the recent findings to determine the actual cause of death."

"My dear doctor, it appears that you've managed to perfect the virus and protect us as well. Well done." Baum stood up and put his hands on the table. "I think it is time to terminate our partnership."

"I am sure that you understand you must remain quiet about all this, don't you?" Josh looked at the nervous man sitting across from him.

Engle had to force his dry lips open. They were stuck together. "But of course. I expect nothing more than what you promised me. I'll be on my way, with my mouth shut forever."

"Your money is in the Swiss account you designated, and your new identity is already in place." Baum smiled as he slid the bank book and a passport over the table. "Your old life will end. You begin your new life today, just as promised. Goodbye, my friend."

After a slight hesitation, Engle scooped up the documents and stood. He extended his hand, but neither man took it. He turned and walked out the door.

"What an evil little man. Now what?"

Josh snorted in disgust. "He will keep his mouth shut, I promise you that. People who are no longer needed tend to disappear." He looked at his watch and counted down, "Five, four, three, two, one…" A muffled shot rang out, followed by two more.

A smile appeared on Josh's lips.

Chapter 50 - Training for Revenge

The soldier dragged another body off the lifter. Sweating from the exertion, he complained aloud, "Why do we have to keep dumping bodies?"

"So we don't lose even more people." Paine wiped his hands on his coveralls. "Help me with the next one, and let's make sure his body is visible. Maybe over there, on the sidewalk next to the lamp post?"

"I have the latest report from Trisha and Chris," Marcus called out as he walked over to Paine's lifter.

"You take it from here," Paine told the soldier. "Try to make him look natural."

"The body count is going up. UN and Regular forces are preparing for the final clearing action." Marcus looked at his hand-written notes. "The bastards are discussing how to eliminate the rest of the city's population. According to Chris, the city's been divided into sectors, with the least populated areas being given to UN forces. The areas where the most action could take place are assigned to the Regulars. Staff officers in both units are trying to devise the most efficient systems for eliminating the remaining New Yorkers."

"Just how do they think they can do that? Don't they know we're going to put up a fight?"

"I guess they think we're too weak to do much against them." Flipping pages in his notebook, Marcus read the information Chris sent. "One commander wants to herd the people in his area of operations into a local church and then set the church on fire. An engineer got several subway cars running on the Red Line. She wants to fill the cars with refugees, then send them under the East River and flood the tunnel." Marcus growled at the next entry. "This SOB is planning a 'decontamination' prior to shipping people out of the city. He ordered a half a ton of insecticides, which will be lethal to humans if released in confined spaces."

"I can't believe this," Paine, amazed at the callousness of the plans, looked for the sources. "Is any of this coming from our guys?"

"The staff officers Chris mentioned by name weren't Regulars. I would hope our people wouldn't come up with ideas like these." Marcus looked down at the tablet again. "You know damn well your father would order them to do things like this."

"You're right, he would." Paine shook his head. "I think he's recruiting other mercenary groups to help."

"Chris said something about Corvis security guys showing up a few weeks ago. I think that's where the Engle character Katrina told us about comes from."

"Who else would have the technology to build these nanoprobes?" Paine shook his head in wonder. "This is truly despicable. Did Chris say when all this is going to happen?"

"You aren't going to believe this." Marcus paused for dramatic effect. "The target date is June 26."

"What's so special about that?"

"It's the anniversary of the charter that established the United Nations in 1945."

"How ironic."

Carley and Ashley also had a plan in place. As victims were brought from the morgues to designated areas in the city, the living were evacuated and replaced by the dead. Bodies were placed in homes, common areas and on the streets. Ashley's irregular troops worked to get people out of harm's way. Evacuees were hidden in areas the UN forces had already cleared. Many of the old and very young residents of New York were sent to refugee camps outside the city limits. They received medical care and were provided with food and shelter. Carley estimated that sixty thousand were out of harm's way, at least for now.

The able bodied were given a different task.

Yenissei rinsed his hands and placed them under the dryer. Six hundred bodies cremated this week alone, with another five thousand returned to the resistance. He checked a body that came in. Much too bloated to look like a recent death, he put it in the crematorium. This last one, he thought, and I can go for the day.

Waving the guards out of the building, Yenissei cackled, "Go home, boys and girls. You don't want to spend your time with the dead." He grinned at them and waved a finger in the air, "You'll be joining them someday. Go now and enjoy life."

The UN guards left in a hurry, happy to be away from the crazy old man. Some took his advice and were already snorting scarf as they walked to their waiting transports. Yenissei waited until the streets were completely empty, then unlocked the door.

"Sorry to say, we have more bodies that are decomposing." Paine waved his soldiers into the room. Each of them carried a long, black bag containing a corpse. "You can burn these tomorrow. Any fresh bodies for us?"

"I have three dozen," Yenisei waved the soldiers into the morgue. "They're over by the wall. Put the bad bodies on the gurneys and take the fresh ones out. I hope those who are doing this will be rotting soon." He stopped Paine by grabbing his arm. "When can I send those killers to hell?" He had his own personal vendetta. Nothing Paine would do could stop him.

"Come with me after we finish here." Paine knew the look in Yenissei's eyes.

The streets were dark and deserted when Paine and Yenissei left the morgue. They walked with their heads down, shuffling as they walked along 42d Street to the Hell's Kitchen area.

"Follow me." A ragged man came out of the alley and waved Yenisei over. "We have to get off the street."

"I think I'll come see the class," Paine followed Yenisei up a small stairway that led to an apartment on the third floor. There were seventeen men and women sitting in a circle listening to a tall, well-built man with horrible scars on his face and arms.

"I see we are all here, now, so let's begin." Several empty bottles and a gallon jug of a flammable liquid were on the floor. Marcus poured gasoline into one of the bottles, and stuffed a rag in the mouth. "This is how we make what is called the Molotov cocktail."

Paine left to visit other training sites. Classes were going on all over the city. He figured there were thirty-eight hundred half-trained soldiers available for the coming fight. The combined UN and Regular force numbered 15,000. The odds were not good. Ashley's plan had better work.

Chapter 51 - Getting In

Since returning to the compound, they'd kept up the masquerade of being lovers by sleeping in the same room. They both suspected there were listening devices in the room and they were being monitored.

After two days of being close to Chris, Trisha could finally hold him without shaking. She cuddled up to Chris in the narrow bunk bed.

Biting him on his ear lobe, she slid the ear bug she had hidden in her mouth into his ear, whispering, "Just turn it on when you get into the meeting and the good guys will hear everything." She paused and took in a deep breath. "I always knew you were my soul mate."

Chris looked at her in shock. Trisha and he had been team members for a long time, and she had been on his mind a lot lately, especially after the drunken naked act they'd put on for the UN guards. But he knew her history better than anyone else and had always been afraid to touch her for fear she would shrink back into her shell.

"I'm scared," Trisha's tears fell on Chris' chest. "I want to be with you, be a part of you, but I'm afraid you'll hate me for what I've been through."

Pushing her up, so he could look into her eyes, Chris brushed away her tears. "I overheard Paine and Marcus talking about the mission to San Francisco. I know where they found you, and I only wish I'd been on that raid. I would have killed all those bastards myself." He pulled her back to his chest, squeezing her tightly. "I don't care what happened, I just know I really care about you. I want to make you happy."

Wriggling free of his arms, Trisha turned her back to Chris. She closed her eyes, reliving the horror of the bordello. His gentle hands rubbed her shoulders, soothing the tension. She felt something other than fear when he touched her. *The doctor said I would find someone. I hope I'm making the right choice.* For the first time in a long time, she felt something in her heart. "I love you for doing this." Pulling her tee shirt over her head, she rolled on top of him. "And I really meant that last part."

Chris arrived two minutes late to the planning meeting the next morning. He put the ear bug in his front uniform pocket, so it could pick up the briefer's comments. He had a hard time staying awake. He kept dreaming about getting the ear bug back to Trisha.

*****

"The big kill-off will occur on the 26th." Carley sat back and rubbed her red eyes. "That means we have two days to make this happen."

Carley turned to the two men seated at the table. "Michael, Marcus. Are you ready to go in?"

They both answered in unison, "Yes, Ma'am"

Ashley got up from her seat and moved to her son. "Michael, please don't do anything stupid. Get the information and get out. People who try to be heroes usually end up dead. I can't lose you again."

Paine couldn't trust himself to speak. He just gave her a hug and followed Marcus out the door.

Marcus and Paine pulled on their equipment harnesses. Each carried a short-range shielded communication device with video capability, two days' rations, a water bottle, a combat knife, and a pistol. Any other weapons would be of no use. The pistols were for self-defense only.

"This could be useful." Carley handed Paine a strange looking weapon. "It's non-lethal. Just point and pull the trigger. It shoots out a web that wraps around the subject, immobilizing them. Push this button, and it acts like a taser, shocking the body."

"Why should we carry anything that won't kill?" Marcus picked up the pistol. "I thought if all else fails, we kill the general."

"I understand Carley's thinking. We may need to show the world how evil he is, and that we are compassionate people. It might be better to take him prisoner and put him on trial, instead of making him disappear." Paine took the weapon and attached it to his equipment vest. "But if I get the chance, father is a dead man."

*****

Elle and Katrina were there to see them off. Paine gave Elle a big hug and turned away quickly, not trusting himself. Marcus held out his arms and Katrina jumped into them, snuggling up to his chest, her head under his chin.

"If you don't come back to me soon, you ugly man, I'll find you and make your life a living hell." Katrina gave him a bone crushing squeeze and backed away.

Marcus and Paine put on the phototrophic uniforms and disappeared. The girls saw the door open and close, and their men were gone.

Jogging down the street toward the UN compound, Marcus asked, "Can we go over the plan again?"

"How many times do we have to do this?" Paine snapped. He glanced over at Marcus, sorry for the outburst. The smile Marcus had on his face reminded him of the faces of the dead they'd been bringing out of the morgue for the last two weeks. "Sorry, I know this is a long shot. But what else can we do?"

"We go over the plan again, and execute it to perfection." The macabre smile left Marcus' face, replaced by a concerned frown. "Either that, or we all die. You and me, we'll go quick. But Elle and Katrina…"

"Focus. We go to the east side entrance." Paine recited. "Trisha is sergeant of the guard there. Once we contact her, she'll get us through the barriers. We get inside, make our way to the translator booths, find an empty one and plug into the system. Then we wait until the meeting starts." Paine wasn't even panting as he ran down the avenue.

"What do we do if someone comes into the booth?"

"We unplug, wait until they get settled in and move to another empty one." Paine paused. "No killing, it would compromise our mission." Paine pointed to the left. He and Marcus ran by a parked UN vehicle. The soldiers inside couldn't hear their boots on pavement above the hum of the engine.

"Coming up on check point Tango, time to go slow."

They pulled the hoods over their faces and began to breathe deeply to slow down their heart rates. They could see Trisha walking near the guard post, just inside the perimeter set up to keep the press out of the building. Paine watched for her to show them a way to get through the barricade. He hoped Trisha would get them inside soon.

Chapter 52 – Newsworthy

The video announcer looked directly at the camera. He began on cue. "Here we are at the General Assembly of the United Nations, waiting for what we have been told will be a major policy announcement. All the member nations are gathered here today to hear an address by Secretary General Baum. The press has been instructed to stay outside the meeting hall for the time being, due to the possibility of the new virus getting into the sterile chambers, but we have been assured we will get video feed from the hall after the meeting has closed. This is Brian Watters, CNB News."

The light went off on the camera. Watters walked up to his cameraman. "Now what? Does Baum just expect us to stand around and wait for something to happen?" He moved toward the barriers the UN soldiers had set up. He noticed a female soldier staring at him. "Hey. You over there. Come here and let me talk to you for a minute."

Paine watched as Trisha turned and glared at the reporter.

"Sir, you have to step away or I'll be forced to move you." She walked to the laser line marking the electronic barrier. "Back off, now." she barked. Her hands flashed a sign to Paine.

"Just a quote from you," Watters flashed her a smile. "You'll be on the nightly news."

Tapping Marcus on the arm, Paine moved up to the line marking the perimeter.

"Fine, I'll make a comment," Trisha moved to within inches of the laser line. She waved Watters forward.

Watters thrust the microphone at her, causing the barrier to activate. The shock wave that coursed through the microphone and into Watters sent him flying backward. Screaming at the top of his lungs, he lay on the ground, twitching from the burst of electricity that coursed through his body. Alarms were sounding all over the perimeter. Trisha activated her communicator.

"Shut down sector 1516, ASAP." She shouted. "I'm going out of the wire. I need 10 seconds. Now." As Trisha walked from the green zone into the street, Marcus and Paine slipped through. The laser appeared again just as they passed through.

Trisha ran to the reporter and cradled his head as the effects of the shock wore off. He mumbled incoherently as she whispered, "Thanks, you just made my day a lot easier."

Cameras and reporters surrounded her, all sticking microphones into her face, so she hit the panic button, calling for reinforcements.

Marcus and Paine ran into the building as troops poured out from the front door to respond to the breach of the wire. Pushing Marcus against the wall, Paine flattened himself to the opposite one. They waited until the reaction platoon passed, then made their way to the UN General Assembly chambers.

Paine, sweating in his phototrophic uniform, continued down the now-empty hall. "If one of those guys had bumped into your fat ass, we'd be toast."

The chuckle from Marcus broke the tension both were feeling. "Hey, we're inside. That's more than I thought we'd accomplish. Now let's take my 'fat ass' to the translator room and set up for the next phase of this brilliant plan."

They were overlooking the assembly room. Paine turned on the console and plugged in the headset to see what he could hear. "Test time," he whispered to Marcus.

Stepping into the hallway, Marcus made his way to the entry of the chamber. He stopped. Taking out a small metal rod about two inches long, he threw the rod into the chamber.

Through the headset, Paine heard the ping of the rod hitting the floor. He removed his glove and gave Marcus a thumbs up sign. Once Marcus returned, they settled in to wait for the chamber to fill up.

Chapter 53 - Power Play

"Monica, I'd like for you to watch the proceedings. I want you to be there to see history being made." Secretary General Baum turned to his assistant. "I just hope everything goes according to plan."

She looked at her boss with a mix of admiration and concern. "I can't see how it could go wrong. We've done everything possible to make this plan work. The other delegates are on board with the plan. We just need them to conduct a public vote and all your dreams will come true. You'll have total control of the world and will get the space colonies to join with minimal effort. Within a few days, you'll control everything." Walking behind Baum, Monica reached out to stroke his hair, but stopped herself from showing any affection. "You've done a great thing for mankind."

"Just stay away from the meeting room. You can listen in from one of the translator booths." Baum rubbed his hands together and stood up. "It is time to go." He walked out of the office without looking back and headed for the assembly floor.

The chamber seemed almost empty, with only a quarter of the seats occupied. The ambassador from the Ukraine hadn't shown up yet, but his delegation sat at their places. Ambassador Smythe of Australia, suffering from a bad chest cold, stayed away.

"This meeting will come to order," Alan Baum stood at the podium, hands tightly grasping the edge. "Many of you are aware that a plague has ravaged New York for the last few months. Deaths have been in the hundreds of thousands. Even though we here at the UN offered a massive amount of aid and medical support to the people of the city, we were rebuffed. The people of New York attacked our humanitarian efforts and as a result, UN Forces suffered casualties in the hundreds. The time has come to take sterner action." Baum took a sip of water. He looked over the delegates and continued.

"With the consent of the delegates and the nations represented here, I plan to ask that the United Nations be granted sovereignty over all the peace-loving peoples of the world." A murmur ran through the crowded room. Baum waited for silence. "We will conduct a coordinated campaign to stop the plague from spreading beyond the borders of New York. We will establish a world government that will coordinate all humanitarian, military and social programs worldwide. Once they hear what we have done, Luna Colony and New Germany will join us. It will be a giant leap forward for mankind. There will be no more war, no more famine, no more plagues to ravage humankind. How say you?"

The chamber erupted, with most delegates calling for the election of Alan Baum as the first president of the world. The NUS delegation sat silently, the ambassador not knowing what to do.

"Let's have a vote, shall we?" Baum took a deep breath. "All in favor of the new government please say Aye." Baum waited as the chamber echoed with a thunderous, "Aye."

"All those opposed?" Baum shouted.

Several ambassadors were trying to contact their leaders and didn't respond.

"The 'ayes' have it. The inaugural meeting of the Earth Government will now come to order. The first order of business is to deal with the problems here in New York." Baum continued. "I have requested that General Martin of the Kentucky Regulars mount a humanitarian operation, in conjunction with UN – sorry - Earth's military forces, to save the remaining people of New York. The operations will begin in 24 hours. All forces are to be under the tactical control of General Martin and his staff. At this time, I would like to turn the meeting over to General Martin."

Smiling broadly, he welcomed Josh to the stage with a warm handshake. As Baum walked to his seat, he rubbed his hand. It hurt from the force of Josh's grip.

*****

Josh looked over the faces in the crowd, some of whom were still trying to figure out what had just happened. He thought about how they would look after his speech.

"Ladies and Gentlemen, thank you for your welcome. I have come here not to inform you of Mister Baum's plan, but of his deception and lies. I have a plan of my own."

A buzz ran through the chamber.

"I need your support and compliance to make this plan work and am prepared to ask for a General Assembly vote on the matter." He motioned toward the back of the chamber. Soldiers dressed in UN uniforms filed quietly into the room, lining the back walls.

"Mister Secretary General, before we begin, I would like to inform the delegates of your actions." Josh pointed an accusatory finger at Baum. "I hereby charge you with genocide."

Baum tried to get up but found himself held in place by the strong hands of the two soldiers standing behind him.

"Assembled ambassadors, this man says he wants to unite the people of the world, but what he really wants is to control you all through fear and intimidation." Josh faced the delegates. "He has conspired to kill all of you with a bio-engineered plague of his making. He has also placed agents throughout the world with this virus, ready at his command to infect your good people and kill them all. The proof of this is simple. I have his chief developer here in this room with us now."

Doctor Engle walked on stage with his briefcase. He opened the briefcase and dialed in numbers. Looking at Josh, he waited for the signal to begin.

Baum stared at the doctor. "How can you be here? You're supposed to be dead."

"Your Secretary General would have you all die in agony, if he had his way." Josh nodded to Doctor Engle. "Doctor Engle will demonstrate the effect of the plague now."

Engle pushed one button and looked directly at Baum. He smiled and mouthed, "Goodbye, my friend." Baum, wracked by spasms, collapsed in his chair. The soldiers who had been holding him carried the lifeless body from the dais.

The delegates all spoke at once. Josh let them panic for a while and then banged the gavel for two full minutes before he regained quiet.

"My good people, as you can see, the Secretary General is an evil man doing evil things. He isn't the only one, but we have an opportunity to set things on a new path, a path to greatness." Josh paused for effect. "Who would you have lead you in this time of great trouble? Who would you have unify the world in a way that has never been done before? Who would you give the power to restore order and bring stability to the chaos of this world?"

A voice from the back of the assembly hall yelled out, "We need you."

Pandemonium reigned as delegates pulled out communicators to contact their governments, only to find that all transmissions were blocked.

Josh sat down in the chair recently occupied by Secretary Baum. He leaned back and crossed his legs, waiting for order to return. Doctor Engle took a seat to Josh's right.

After a few more minutes of panic, the noise level dropped low enough for Josh to speak. From his seated position, he held up his right hand. The room became silent.

"Once again, I ask you, who do you want to lead the world into the future?" Josh consulted his tablet. "Let us begin with a roll call vote. Australia is absent, so I call on Argentina. How do you say?"

Adelmo Garcia, the ambassador to Argentina stood up, closed his briefcase and walked out, yelling, "I'll never let you control this organization, you filthy pig. I would rather die."

"So be it." Josh signaled Doctor Engle.

Garcia collapsed on the top step. The guards took the body away.

"Chile, I believe you are next on the list."

Fortunato Soto stood up.

"Perhaps we could have the assembly discuss the matter for a short while before we vote? There is no reason to rush...."

He collapsed back into his seat.

The room erupted with frantic cries of "We need you, we need you," as two more soldiers carried out another body.

Josh basked in the flood of acceptance. The vote was unanimous.

*****

Ashley and Carley were watching the video feed from Paine. After the death of the Chilean Ambassador, it went blank. Ashley looked at her communications expert who shook her head. "Signal is completely blocked, Ma'am. I can't keep up with the frequency skips and I don't think we have anything that could cut through it."

"Carley, what do we do now?" Ashley hoped to get outside help, but now that didn't seem possible.

Turning to the communications specialist, Carley ordered, "Send out the following message." She paused and took a deep breath. "Code blue is in effect."

"The battle for New York begins." Ashley stood up and looked around the command post. "I can't order my people to do what I won't do myself." She picked up the carbine slung on the back of her chair. "I think George S. Patton said no good decision was ever made from a swivel chair." Ashley pulled back the bolt and chambered a round. "It's time to get out there and lead some troops. The plans are made, now all we can do is fight for our lives."

*****

When Allan Baum died, Monica ran from the observation room toward her office.

"Why did you trust that evil man?" she cried as she ran down the empty hallway. She jumped into her chair, slamming her hand down on the console in the center of the desk. The desktop slid back revealing a sophisticated electronics suite. Monica tapped in her personal code. A burst message went out to the NUS White House. She wiped her eyes. "I'll be with you soon, my love." She swung the desktop back into position and stood up just as the preset explosive went off.

Chapter 54 - Sandford

President Sandford's head of White House communications came into the office without knocking. He interrupted the president's putting stroke, causing the ball to miss the cup by a foot.

"What is so damned important that you have to ruin my practice?"

The secret service agents following the officer grabbed the president under the arms and carried him, putter and all, out of the office and into a waiting meditube.

President Sandford knew this was no drill as the meditube went through the decontamination process and injected him with several types of nanoprobes. His staff waited for the machine to finish. As the door to the meditube opened, his valet held out a robe for him. His clothing lay shredded on the floor of the tube.

"Would someone tell me what the hell is going on?" President Sandford pulled on his robe and walked back to his desk.

"Sir, you have to see this. You are in grave danger."

The communications officer pushed a button and the Oval Office appeared on the screen. Sanford watched as Alan Baum walked behind President Brown and put his hand on his shoulder. The death of Bob Brown played out, then the medical staff rushed into the room. The screen flickered.

The face of Monica Wheatley, Alan Baum's assistant, filled the lens.

"Mister President. If you are seeing this message, Allan Baum is dead, killed by a citizen of your country, one Joshua Martin. General Martin has enlisted the aid of several rogue scientists to develop a plague that can be activated upon command, utilizing nanotechnology." Her voice caught for a moment, then she continued. "He infected Alan with it and forced him to murder President Brown. You must be decontaminated. You have been infected with nanoprobes that carry the plague. General Martin is at this very moment taking control of all UN forces and utilizing the plague to blackmail other world leaders, such as yourself, to support his leadership. I would recommend a strike against the UN compound by any means possible to stop this madman."

President Sandford sat down just as the phone on his desk beeped. He pushed a button. "Who is it, Mary?"

His secretary answered, "It is General Martin, Kentucky Regulars. He says it's urgent."

"Tell him I'll be with him in a moment." President Sandford turned to his aide. "Get the vice president in here now. We don't have much time. And get me a new suit."

*****

Josh waited impatiently for the call light to come on. Looking at the screen in the Secretary General's office, he noticed a message waiting icon in the top left corner. He tapped it.

Good luck on the vote today. It will go well. SC

Your speech is good. Now we can go to work. SC

What the hell just happened? Why is Josh Martin there? SC

Smiling, Josh typed, *We'll talk later. JM*

Admiring the artwork, he wondered how the desk would look moved to the other side of the room. The incoming call light blinked, and he waved the staff outside the room. Only Doctor Engle remained.

President Sandford's face appeared on the screen.

"Hello, Josh. What can I do for you today?"

"Mister President, we have a situation you may be interested in. I have secured the United Nations Building and am prepared to take control of the city. My forces, which include the UN military in and out of the city, will clear out the last of the insurgents. I plan to establish a spaceport here in the harbor area. I have already gotten a verbal commitment for eight thousand workers from Poland and 5,000 from Australia and I'm asking you for ten thousand from Atlanta. I'm sure you can spare them."

"What makes you think I'll help you?" President Sandford sat back in his chair and rubbed his chin. "What about Secretary General Baum? Where is he and why am I not talking to him?"

"Mister President, the secretary general no longer has anything to do with the UN." Josh paused and then continued in a commanding voice. "I speak for the UN. I control the air defense systems around New York. I have the UN nuclear launch codes. I know what you're thinking, that I only have 10 nuclear devices and they're all targeting the major capitals of the world." Josh paused

213

for effect. "Just remember one of those capitals is Austin. I would rather not have to use them."

"You are an egomaniac and I'll not put up with any kind of blackmail."

Josh made a quick hand gesture to Doctor Engle.

Sandford saw the movement. He stood up and grasped his throat. Secret service agents swarmed him, blocking the cameras. One of them turned in profile. "The president is dead. Someone please get the vice president in here now."

Meghan Driver, who became vice president only a short while after President Brown's murder, stood in front of the camera.

"Madame President, did you hear my request, or must I repeat it?" Josh smiled at the distraught woman.

"When do you need your workers? I can have the advanced party of five hundred there in under twenty-four hours."

"That will be just fine. Thank you very much, Madame President. If I need anything else, be sure you respond to my call immediately."

Meghan nodded her head.

"Good. I'm glad you understand your position." The screen went blank.

*****

Sandford sat up, throwing off the blanket they had covered him with. "That bastard!" He shook his fist at the screen. "How many troops does he have in New York?"

The Chairman of the Joint Chiefs Adam Fogle flashed a schematic of the units in New York on the screen. "He has no more than six thousand Regulars and another twenty thousand UN troops. He has a very sophisticated air defense network, but we can jam it for a short while. Our intelligence also reports five thousand irregulars in the city, mostly using antiquated weapons, who have been resisting the UN takeover for some time. We aren't sure how many of them are left after the plague, but we think about three thousand may have survived."

"Do we have soldiers we can send in to deal with this maniac or do we have to send that advanced party?" President Sandford asked.

The Chairman looked at his tablet and checked NUS troop status. "We have Colonel Flagehty's regiment down at Fort Benning. He's been testing a new drop system for mass tactical use. Maybe we can fly his unit up there?"

"Make it happen. I want Martin dead."

General Fogle saluted and walked out. "Alert the press that the president is dead, then clamp down on any additional coverage. We need that information to get to Martin. Get everyone on the national security team into meditubes within the hour." General Fogle pointed at Vice President Driver. "You first, Meghan. I need everyone focused on this crisis and not worrying about dying from the plague."

Chapter 55 - Orders

"Colonel Flagehty," Ryan answered the incoming call.

"Ryan, General Fogle. I hate to ruin your day, but I have a mission for you straight from the president. Go secure now."

Ryan activated the encryption feature of the communication station and waited for the telltales to light up. He had already heard the news report that the president had suffered a heart attack and wondered if this had anything to do with his upcoming mission.

A voice came on the net, "White House communication, you are cleared for presidential communication."

Ryan spoke first. "Madame President, I offer my condolences on the loss of President Sanford."

The male voice that answered him surprised Ryan.

"Colonel, I am happy to inform you that rumors of my death are premature. We have a situation of national importance here. I need you to tell me if you can do what General Fogle has planned." President Sandford continued, "You're on conference call with the National Security Council."

"Yes, sir. Glad to hear you're all right. Do you want me to get my staff in to listen, or wait until the discussion is finished?"

"Ryan, let's wait until we know we can accomplish the mission before we involve anyone else," General Fogle interjected. "This is Top Secret Black level four."

If word leaked out, Ryan would be tried for treason and possibly executed. "I understand. What is the mission?"

General Fogle briefed Colonel Flagehty on the intelligence they had on General Martin and New York. Ryan soaked it all in, thinking about how he would attack the forces in the city.

"I have it, now what do you want me to do?"

"Tell us if your new delivery system is operational."

Ryan responded, "We are ready and able to conduct the mission." Ryan thought back on the last few days…

Chapter 56 - Airborne

"NUSAF one four niner niner on final approach." Ryan heard the voice of the pilot crackling over the command net. Troopers sat in eight rows of fifty in the cavernous bay of the C-181 Super Lifter. The bay, bathed in a blue light, signified normal flight operations. Ryan sat in the command seat at the front of the aircraft next to his newly promoted Command Sergeant Major Benjamin Neel.

Ryan leaned over and yelled in Neel's ear, "We've come a long way from chasing bandits and escorting humanitarian missions, haven't we, Ben?"

Ben, grinning from ear to ear, simply nodded. Young for this position, he'd proven himself many times in the past fifteen years and deserved the promotion. "Sir, we need to be ready to drop soon."

The light changed to red and blinked slowly.

The training for the troops took over. All four hundred stood up as soon as the red light came on. Their seats folded down as yellow outlines appeared on the floor. The troopers positioned themselves in the center of the outlines. They adjusted their weapons, so the muzzles pointed downward and the assault carbines they all carried were vertical. No heavy weapons teams were involved in the first test drop. That would be worked out in later tests.

"NUSAF one four niner niner, three minutes," the ground controller told the pilot.

Neel called out over the all-hands net, "Check equipment."

Four hundred pairs of hands moved almost as one as the troopers made sure all their equipment was in the right place, secured and ready for the drop.

"Sound off for equipment check." rang out over the net.

The heads-up display in Ryan's helmet lit up with all green lights, signifying all the troopers were ready to go.

"At least that part went right. So far, so good. Let's hope the rest of the drop goes smoothly."

The voice of the pilot crackled "One minute."

The red light bathed the compartment in an eerie glow.

Ryan hoped this worked. He and Ben would be the first to drop, followed by his 1st Battalion. Ryan never had his troops to do anything he wouldn't do. He would be first out of the aircraft.

The Corvis Corporation worked with the NUS to develop a delivery system for airborne soldiers to replace the T-30 parachute. Military planners determined that the chute no longer served as the best method for delivering soldiers to the battlefield due to the effectiveness of modern weapons. Soldiers were too exposed because it took 15 seconds to get to the ground.

The delivery system consisted of a single-use platform each soldier stood on. It provided a one-second burst of lift when a meter off the ground, allowing the soldier to step off, ready to fight.

The troopers had new boots designed with a metal plate in the heel and toe. These plates would keep the soldiers secured to the platforms through electromagnets which would release when the power cell burned out on landing. It eliminated the landing roll and possibility of being dragged by the parachute or caught up in the shroud lines. Small stabilizing thrusters were supposed to keep the platform and soldier upright during the drop, and a proximity sensor fired the retarding burst at the appropriate time.

Although the platforms performed flawlessly in simulations conducted by Corvis scientists, they hadn't been used in the field. Ryan protested dropping an entire planeload on the first test, asking for a smaller operation. The chain-of-command denied his request.

The C-181 had been modified. The entire belly of the aircraft had been replaced with a honeycombed structure. The drop platforms fit into each chamber and were programmed to release at half-second intervals. The electromagnets were turned on and the platforms, soldiers attached, were lowered into launch position.

In the simulation, the system worked flawlessly. Four hundred platforms landed exactly fifteen meters apart from one hundred feet. The entire drop took three seconds.

The troopers all had been told to prepare for the drop by flexing their knees and keeping their weapons and arms tight to their bodies. The three weeks of training they had gone through replaced standard parachute training. Most troopers were young. Some of the older ones with numerous parachute jumps couldn't adjust to the changes in procedure. Ryan hoped he wouldn't revert to his old habits. He had more than four hundred jumps. He kept telling himself to focus as the light turned green and the platform lowered into the chamber. Ten seconds later, he exploded out of the plane.

The aircraft, moving at one hundred twenty-five miles an hour, flew a hundred meters above ground level to minimize time over the drop zone. When the turbulence from the engines hit Ryan, he flipped over, but the platform righted itself before impact.

Feeling the magnets releasing, he stepped forward as he'd been trained. The inertia of the flip caused him to fall forward on his face. The front sight post of the weapon caught him under the chin, cutting a four-inch gash in his face. Blood spurted on his uniform jacket. Jumping to his feet, he looked down the drop zone.

Most of his troopers were moving away from the drop zone toward the designated assembly areas. Ryan could see that at least 30 troopers were down, some motionless, others waving for medics.

Sergeant Major Neel walked up to Ryan, apparently unhurt, and slapped a Quickheal patch on his commander's face. Ben's voice strained as he reported to his commander.

"We have seventy-two injured, mostly minor, like yours." He paused and took a deep breath as he looked over the heads-up display. "We have four dead and 15 who will need meditubes. Most of the initial reports say that the platforms are unstable in the initial second of flight, but right themselves prior to impact. The dead were among the last to drop. I think the aircraft accelerated too early, trying to get out of the drop zone area. That exacerbated the turbulence effect." Ben unsuccessfully tried to keep his emotions out of his report.

Ryan opened his mouth to reply when a Corvis technician ran up to him.

"Wow this is great. I can't believe how great it is. All of you were on the ground in less than five seconds. Not a single platform malfunctioned. This is a great success. Colonel..."

He never finished the sentence as Ryan Flagehty's fist caught him just below his left eye and fractured his cheekbone. The tech crumpled to the ground.

"Sir, I think you better calm down, the head of R&D is coming over now." Ben took his commander's arm and led him nearer to the approaching vehicle.

Danny Corvis, grandson of the CEO of the foundation, stayed in the H5 hummer and motioned Colonel Flagehty over. His gaze never moved from the computer screen in his hand as he scanned the data from the jump.

"Sorry for the loss of your soldiers, Colonel. I didn't anticipate the turbulence effect and for that I am very sorry." Corvis pointed to the screen. "I've already plugged in the data from the test and have determined that if we drop at one hundred twelve meters and decrease speed to one hundred five miles per hour, the effect will be minimized. That will solve the flipping problem and reduce incidents to no more than ten. With a full load of soldiers, there's no way to eliminate all casualties."

Ryan took a deep breath and slowly let it out. "Thank you for your condolences. I just wish you'd let me conduct a practice drop with a few troopers first. I might have saved those boys from dying." His hand reflexively clenched as he imagined Corvis' neck between them. Ben touched his sleeve and Ryan let the thought go, at least for now.

"We need to clear the drop zone and get our injured taken care of, and then we'll be ready for another try. Next time, only myself and the command sergeant major will be dropped, me first and him last. You can drop all the platforms you like between us, but I won't put my troopers in harm's way again. And if you don't want to do it that way, then you can just take the whole program and stuff it right...." Ryan caught himself, turned on his heel and walked toward the nearest ambulance to see about his troops.

Ben looked at Corvis. "Call when you're ready to test again." He hurried to catch up with his commander.

The second test went perfectly, followed by another mass tactical drop. As promised, injuries were minimal and required no more than the applications of a few Quickheal patches. After the fifth jump, the troopers were awarded their new jump wings which comprised a bar suspended from their old wings with PLATFORM written on it.

Chapter 57 - Attack plans

"And so, Mister President, we are ready to go." Ryan sent a troop list to General Fogle via secure network. "I can have my entire regiment in the air in 12 hours, but I can't promise you any more than light infantry weapons. We haven't started the heavy drop testing yet, and I don't want a repeat of the casualties we suffered in the first test. My plan would be to fly in three planes, identifying themselves as the lift for the workers requested by Martin."

Ryan couldn't bring himself to use the military rank Josh gave himself.

"That's twelve hundred soldiers on the ground inside one minute." Ryan continued. "We take and secure the airfield, and you can bring in the rest of the division with heavy-lift aircraft. They can be ready to go forty-eight hours after alert, so we will be on the ground for two days on our own. I just need you to take out the air defense batteries around the airport and keep the enemy forces out. I promise they won't get through us. Once the division has landed their heavy weapons, we'll be able to take the city."

"Colonel Flagehty, as your commander-in-chief, I order you to load your troops and launch your attack within the next six hours. You are further directed to take a company of your best soldiers and make your way into the city. I need you to contact the resistance and provide them with any support you can to disrupt the defense of New York." President Sandford paused and added, "I'll not order the rest of the division to mobilize for action until you're on the ground, due to the secrecy of the mission and the likelihood of a leak to the enemy. You'll be on your own for more than two days, I'm afraid. I trust you to do your best."

General Fogle chimed in, "Only let your immediate staff know what's going on, and keep them from communicating with anyone, including family."

Ryan thought for a second. "I planned on informing the troopers we are going home and conducting a mass tactical demonstration jump at Fort Bragg. The drop will be with full equipment, followed by a live-fire exercise and then we will all be going on leave for ten days. That'll keep the plan from leaking out and allow us to gear up for the attack on the airfield."

"It is now 1800 hours, plan on wheels up by 2100." General Fogle issued the order. "Colonel, you are the mission commander. Inform the pilots of the change in mission once you are airborne. Have them drop to tree-top level and divert course to Atlanta. They will then fly over the spaceport and move to cruising altitude. That way, if radar picks up the incoming aircraft, it will show departure from the Atlanta spaceport. Our new president will inform General Martin of the deployment of workers from Atlanta when you pass through ten thousand feet. Make the drop at precisely 0030 hours tomorrow morning. Good luck and God speed." The secure link went silent.

Chapter 58 - First strike

The four American Airlines' passenger planes carrying the Atlanta Space Port workers took off one after another in the darkness. As they passed through five thousand feet, fighter aircraft flanked them, and tight beam communications were established.

Colonel Flagehty's voice came through the headphones. "Flight 424. Continue to fly your designated route. You'll receive instructions later in the flight. You other three aircraft need to stay below eight thousand and change heading to 180 degrees. You're being diverted to an alternate airfield where you'll land and maintain radio silence until further notification. Failure to comply with instruction will result in you being fired upon and destroyed. Flash your landing lights to acknowledge the message."

All four aircraft quickly flashed their lights. The civilian pilots saw three large military transports flying in proximity to them. As three of the civilian planes turned on their new vector, the military transports took up positions behind American Airlines flight 424.

The Air Defense battery commander looked at the radar screen. There were four blips coming in over the ocean. Each of his missile positions picked up an incoming aircraft. He flashed the identification beacon at the lead plane and it came back as civilian aircraft inbound from Atlanta. He called the tower to confirm the incoming flights were the American Airlines planes from Atlanta.

The lead transport pilot, NUSAF Lieutenant Colonel Charles Kemper had his communications paired with the American Airlines jet. He accelerated to move to the front of the formation. The other military aircraft passed the civilian jet.

"Roger, Kennedy Air traffic control, this is American 424, lead ship, arriving with five hundred souls aboard, plus a crew of sixteen. Coming to heading 270, descending to two hundred fifty feet, preparing for landing." The light switched to red in the cargo hold as the lead elements of the airborne brigade prepared to drop.

Kemper radioed the tower, "One minute to wheels down."

Five NUS cruise missiles, flying at six hundred miles per hour, swept in on the air defense battery and the tower. They hit their targets within a second of each other, destroying all heavy opposition to the landing. The UN soldiers guarding the airport reported that the lead airplane blew up attempting to land, scattering bodies across the tarmac. Before the debris from the destroyed air defense launchers settled, four hundred armed troopers were moving to assigned positions, engaging the few soldiers who stayed to fight.

The airfield fell to the attackers in less than three minutes. The remainder of the force landed on the ground and moved into defensive positions.

The communications sergeant sent a secure message to the NUS White House. Ben Neel went to the parking lot to see what kind of vehicles they could commandeer for the ride into New York.

Ryan split his force into two parts. The bulk of the brigade, assigned to secure the airfield, had instructions to stop anyone from entering or leaving. Ryan left his executive officer in command.

A Company, 1st of the 504th Infantry, began scouring the local parking lots for functional vehicles. They were told to have enough transportation for the company and be ready to depart for Manhattan in ten minutes.

"Move in platoon strength to the three intact bridges connecting Long Island to Manhattan. Attempt crossing only after reconnoitering the other side. If the crossing is too dangerous, hold position and keep anyone from entering or leaving the island." Ryan checked his message board as the platoon leaders responded that they'd received the message. "All three platoons report either successful crossing or blocking position by 0400 hrs."

At 0358, 1st platoon reported they'd found a crossing site at the Brooklyn Bridge. The plague hit before the new bridge opened, and the old bridge had been blocked off due to safety reasons. The platoon leader drove her stolen car around the barriers, crossing the bridge. She established a hasty defense on the other side.

Despite the danger of being shot down by UN air defense batteries, Ryan and Ben commandeered a light lifter. They flew toward the Brooklyn Bridge, ordering the other platoons to hold position. They were lucky. The defenders, spread thin, were too disoriented to cover the waterfront area. Ryan entered Manhattan.

Chapter 59 - Ruined Plans

One of the staff officers called out, "General Martin, Kennedy airport called to report a crash of the airliner carrying the Atlanta workers. There are reports of numerous casualties, and we've lost communications with the defense forces there. We don't know why."

"Sir." Major Miller reported, "There are reports of small units attacking the perimeter throughout the defensive position. They're armed with modern weapons and are fighting in well-coordinated groups. UN and Regular forces suffered some initial casualties, but we are holding them off."

Josh slammed his fist onto the table top. "Who would be stupid enough to attack me? I want to find out what forces are at the airport. I'm guessing either the Irish or NUS, since they have forces nearby." He ordered, "Get me Doctor Engle."

The intelligence officer broke in, "General, I just received a message from one of our operatives that the 82d Airborne has been alerted and will be deployed within the next forty-eight hours."

The General fumed. "That answers my question. President Driver is a dead woman."

*****

"Marcus, you need to go find out whatever you can about what the Regulars are planning." Paine looked perplexed as he continued his attempt to contact his mother. "Get back here as soon as possible. If I don't make contact in twenty minutes, I'm going after my father."

"Buddy, if you do that, your chances of survival are going to be pretty slim," Marcus sounded worried to Paine.

"Don't worry, we've been in worse situations than this and managed to make it out."

"Cover up," Marcus whispered. "I hear someone coming."

Both pulled out their pistols and put the phototrophic hoods over their heads. Paine opened the door and they both went out.

Standing in the hallway, invisible in his phototrophic uniform, Paine heard footsteps and flattened himself against the wall. He recognized Doctor Engle from Katrina's description.

Engle ran down the hall with two guards trying to catch up to him. He had his briefcase clutched to his chest. "Hurry, you fools. The general needs us now."

Marcus stepped out from the wall, blocking his path. Engle never saw the fist coming.

Standing over the unconscious Engle, Marcus fired his silenced pistol into the advancing guards from a range of three meters. He and Paine dragged the bodies to an empty room and closed the door. As Marcus returned, Engle began waking up. "You bastard, you've killed so many innocent people. I ought to kill you now," he hissed. "But I made a promise and I plan to keep."

"What are we going to do with him?" Paine looked down at the frightened man.

"He made lots of people suffer. I plan to let one of them get her revenge." Marcus punched Engle in the face again, knocking him out. He threw the doctor over one shoulder.

"We've got to find another place to hide," Paine grabbed the suitcase and ran down the hall searching for another empty room, far from the bodies of the slain guards.

*****

Ashley slapped a fresh magazine in her weapon as she took stock of her position. She and the headquarters platoon had defeated a much larger UN force trying to storm the insurgent bunker. Her defense force had mostly modern weapons. They were more than a match for the less well-trained UN forces.

Her heads-up display flashed with an incoming message from her command center. One of the Techno drone operators appeared on the screen.

"I'm flying my drone between the islands, looking for enemy troop locations. I spotted a lifter crossing the water, flying low under the old George Washington Bridge. When it landed, two men in uniforms I don't recognize got out." The screen changed. The magnified video showed two men walking into an abandoned building. "I scanned it into the computer database. The AA symbol on their shoulders shows they are from the NUS 82d Airborne Division. The tall man is wearing an eagle with spread wings. He's a colonel, either a brigade commander or general staff officer."

She stared at the colonel on the screen. "I think I know this guy. Betty, come over here and tell me what you think."

Betty Whippette took the helmet from Ashley and looked at the screen. She exclaimed, "Oh, my God! That's Ryan. I can't believe that he's here."

"This couldn't be better," Ashley turned to her communications chief. "Get Carole on the net for me, I need to speak to her right now."

*****

Resting behind a wrecked car, Carole reloaded her carbine. Grateful the UN troops were terrible shots, she still took casualties. Her squad of fifteen already suffered six KIA. She estimated at least 30 casualties for the other side, but knew from the intelligence briefing that the other side was winning. The resistance couldn't continue to take these losses and hope to stay in the fight.

Carole looked for her second in command. Yenissei fired at some UN troops moving across the street. He took down two before he had to shift position due to return fire. She could see him scratching grooves into the stock of his weapon, then looking for more targets. She knew he would die rather than give ground, but she had no choice.

"Yenissei." He looked over in annoyance and then recognized his commander. "You need to move your section to the upper floors and make them come to us."

He waved while firing one-handed at an exposed soldier. He scratched in another notch and ran for the open door of the nearest building. Four members of the squad made it to the building. The rest lay dead in the street.

Her communicator bleeped in her ear. She actuated the microphone just as hypervelocity bullets crashed through her hiding place. Rolling from behind the car, she sprayed the facade with automatic fire from her carbine. She ran to the building. Putting in a fresh magazine, she spoke into the microphone.

"Carole one, go ahead."

"Carole, it's Mom. Can you give me a quick SITREP?"

"The situation is not good." Carole wiped the sweat from her eyes and looked over her part of the battlefield. "We're managing to hold our position, but the UN Forces are pushing our other units farther away from the complex. We've got to move soon or be surrounded. My team is down to three effectives, and we aren't the hardest hit element out here. I'm guessing we can keep this up for another few hours, then we'll have to fall back or call it off. There are just too many of them." She fired at a UN soldier who appeared in her area, sighing as he dropped.

UN soldiers, sneaking through the alley, threatened to cut off her troops. "Yenissei, do something to stop them."

Carole watched him moving to the window. She could tell by his volume of fire that he was running low on ammunition. His weapon ran out of power.

Picking up a bag of Molotov Cocktails, Yenissei slung it over his shoulder. He lit the first one, waiting until the enemy moved under his position. Return fire from the defenders stopped the group from advancing further.

Carole watched in horror as Yenissei climbed on the ledge outside the window.

"For my wife, you bastards," Yenissei screamed as he jumped from the window. Yenissei's falling body killed four instantly. The remaining seven soldiers, engulfed in flames from the exploding Molotov Cocktails, ran into the open and were cut down.

The insurgents were losing. Most squads were down to one or two people. UN and Regular forces were driving the New Yorkers away from the UN compound.

"Carole, can you hear me?" Her mother's voice cut through the fog. "Can you leave someone in charge of your squad? I need you for a special mission right now."

"I'm all that's left of my squad, mother."

After a moment of silence, Ashley issued Carole instructions.

Running out the back of the building, Carole sprinted through rifle fire toward the subway entrance and ducked inside. She dropped her weapon and ammunition vest, untied her hair, and ran through the tunnel.

Chapter 60 - Thanks to My Mother

The soldier on guard at the west window called out, "Colonel, I think you'd better come here."

Ryan picked up his weapon and moved to the window, careful not to expose himself.

"What have you got?" Ryan put his finger on the trigger.

"Looks like a young girl running down the street. Should I engage?" Ryan could see the soldier tracking his target.

"Wait. See what happens, but be ready."

Carole stopped running, bent over for a moment with her hands on her hips, trying to catch her breath. She could feel eyes upon her, she prayed the NUS soldiers would want to find out why she came there instead of taking out a perceived threat. She straightened up and spread her arms wide, slowly turning in a complete circle, and then looked directly at the squad's position.

"Colonel Ryan Flagehty. I bring you a message from the Whippettes, William and Betty. You were with them in Kentucky fifteen years ago." She stood completely still, waiting for a response. "Please let me talk to you."

"Could be a trap, sir." Ben Neel sighted in on the girl.

Ryan raised his weapon and looked at the girl through the scope. "She looks vaguely familiar, but doesn't resemble the Whippettes. She can't be more than 15 years old. No weapons are visible, and her clothing can't hide any explosives. She looks harmless." He lowered the weapon. "Private Schmidt, go secure the girl and bring her to me. The rest of you stay alert. You may be right, Ben. This could be a trap."

Carole came into the room and walked up to Colonel Flagehty. She noticed that even though he did not have his weapon ready, three others were pointing at her. Trying not to show any fear, she took a deep breath to calm her nerves and saluted sharply.

"The insurgency needs your help as soon as possible. We're suffering heavy casualties, but are inflicting damage on the UN and Regular forces. Our weapons are mostly old, but old weapons can kill you just as dead as the new ones." Carole paused for a second then continued, "They have us outnumbered five to one, and we can't keep up the fight much longer. I have instructions to give you access to our communications, courtesy of the Techno faction in the city, so that your men can link up with our fighters."

Holding out her communications device, Carole continued. "All of our secure communication can be accessed through this. My commander will relinquish command of all insurgent forces to you, so the efforts are coordinated. We know the city, your people don't. With our help we can minimize casualties for both of our forces." She noticed Ryan's expression changed when she mentioned saving soldier's lives, and a thrill of hope surged thorough her. "All you have to do is say the word and we can take these bastards down."

Ryan took the device and turned it over to his sergeant major. He never took his eyes off the girl who stood waiting, arms at her side.

"Sergeant Major Neel, get the S-3 on the horn. Send the communication information to him and have our units make contact. Get as much tactical information as possible and come up with three courses of action on how to move our troops onto the island and link up with the locals. Tell him I need to conference with the staff in five minutes. I want our troopers moving into the city as soon as possible." Ryan turned to Carole. "Is there anything else I need to know? We don't have much time."

"Actually, there is." As her adrenaline wore off, Carole began shaking. She had tears in her eyes and fought down the lump in her throat. "I worried about this mission. You could have ordered me killed."

"I'm not in the habit of shooting down unarmed people, especially young girls."

"That's what my mother thought. She wants me to thank you for saving a woman running for her life, keeping her from being killed on that road in Kentucky. You knew my mother as Ashley Smith, a doctor friend of the Whippettes. You'll be happy to know she survived, had me, and is now trying to save New York." Carole put her arms around Ryan and buried her head into his shoulder, "Thank you."

Sergeant Major Neel coughed into his hand. Ryan gently pushed Carole away. "What is it, Sergeant Major?"

"We have contact with the resistance headquarters."

"May I introduce another of your saviors? This is Command Sergeant Major Benjamin Neel, a buck private back when we rescued your mother."

Carole shook his hand.

"She's right about one thing. We don't know the battlefield. Our units are trying to find secure routes into the city, and are being blocked by UN forces. Casualties are mounting. Any help would be greatly appreciated." His communicator pinged. "The staff is ready for you, sir."

Ryan turned back to Carole. "Would you like to sit in? You may be able to help with the situation report."

"I'd be happy to," Tears formed in her eyes once more. "We've lost far too many people and need to end this as soon as possible."

They moved to the temporary communications screen and began the meeting.

Chapter 61 - Communications

Communications near the UN were disrupted. The Technos couldn't break through the static to contact those units closest to the building. The best technicians feverishly searched for a solution.

Returning from the battlefield, dirty and tired, Ashley entered the communications center. "We'll be getting a message from the NUS force commander soon." She did her best to sound confident. "I still need to get through to my son. Any progress on restoring contact?"

"We're working on it."

Ashley looked at the Techno who answered her. He had his eyes closed. "Are you sleeping? We're in the middle of a battle here."

"Just thinking." Twenty-one-year-old Walter Biddle, the youngest and most reclusive of the Techno drone operators, had been flying his drone ever closer to the building. He refused to be relieved and had been at his station for eighteen hours.

He tried to sneak the drone into range of the UN building, determined to contact the men inside. Every time his drone lost contact, Biddle managed to reprogram the sensors to break through the static. He flew the drone in a circle above the UN building, about five hundred feet from the top.

"I noticed something odd. There's a new antenna array that hadn't been present two weeks ago." Biddle opened his eyes and stared at the monitor. He changed to a multiscreen view, ran a few quick calculations, and backed the drone off.

Biddle sent a command to the drone and then shut down the command feed.

"Are you crazy? We need that drone." The shift leader tried to reestablish contact. When he found himself locked out, he moved toward Biddle's console. "Just what in the hell are you doing?"

Ashley grabbed his arm to stop him.

"Wait for it." Biddle sat back, putting his hands behind his head and his feet up on the desk.

The drone dove for ground level, pulling up at the last second. It flew through a hail of fire down the street at its maximum speed of two hundred miles per hour. Ten feet from the building, it pulled up and flew straight to top of the building. The surprised guards kept shooting at it, to no avail. The retro rockets in the nose brought it to a complete stop and the drone self-destructed. The explosion shredded the guards on the rooftop, along with the dish antennas of the mysterious array.

The shift leader yelled, "You dumb SOB, we just lost one of our last drones."

"You can contact our forces now."

The communications panel had gone from mostly red telltales, indicating no communications, to a green board.

Biddle got up, and stretched. "I think I'll go take a nap now. Good night."

Ashley's hands were shaking as she pressed the talk button on her communicator.

Paine's device vibrated slightly. He activated the ear bug.

"Paine, can you read me?" came loud and clear.

"Five by five."

Ashley's heart raced as she heard her son's voice.

"We have all our communications back. NUS forces landed a day ago and are coming into the city to help with the fight. Right now, what we need is intel. Have you planted the listening device yet?"

"No, I wasn't sure if we were going to have contact with you. The longer it's there, the greater the risk of discovery."

"Go to the command center. Plant the device as close as you can without being caught. Then I want you to get out." Ashley gave her son his orders, but didn't expect them to be followed.

"Mother, I'll plant the bug, but I'm staying here until the end. What happens if it's discovered, or communications fail again?" Ashley's hopes died as she listened to her son's logic. "If we don't win this battle, I won't have a choice. I'll wait as long as I can, but if it looks like we're going to lose, I'm going to take father out. Do you copy?"

"Five by five." Ashley sighed, saying a silent prayer for her son. "Stay in contact. Out."

Chapter 62 - Military Necessity

President Sandford looked up from the National Security Agency briefing paper.

"This says reports suggests we let the Regulars and the UN destroy the insurgent forces in the city."

General Fogle replied, "Our analysis shows the insurgents will continue to fight against outside intervention in their internal affairs. Even though NUS forces are currently supporting them, the New Yorkers will preserve their independence."

"So, if we help them win, we lose?"

"They'll resist any effort to force them to join the NUS. We failed when we tried to take over before. Remember the Times Square Massacre?"

"I was a congressman then. We failed miserably. New York became even stronger after capturing all those weapons. But what does that have to do with the battle going on now?"

"If we let the Regulars and UN destroy the opposition, the problem of New York and the spaceport will be solved. They'll be weakened by the effort, and it will be easy for us to move in to help stabilize the situation." Fogle sounded like a history professor as he continued. "The Soviet Union did that in 1944, outside of Warsaw. They defeated the Poles in 1939, helping Hitler divide the country. When the Polish Resistance rose against the Germans near the end of the war, Stalin stopped his army. The Nazis and Poles killed each other, making it easier for Stalin to take over once he 'liberated' Warsaw from the Germans."

"Perfect. Let's hold in place, but be ready to continue our attack once we know the factions have been neutralized." Sanford rubbed his jaw. "Screw helping save the UN delegates. They haven't done us any favors. I want New York back under NUS control, and I want Martin dead." He pushed the intercom button. "Get me the Chief of Staff."

*****

"Colonel Flagehty, go black level four secure now."

Ryan cut out of the command net and walked away from the display. "You are to stand down your troops," General Maxwell ordered. "This is coming from the president himself."

Ryan couldn't believe his orders. "My staff has done a great job of identifying rendezvous points for our units to link up with the insurgents. Coordination between the insurgent headquarters and the subordinate commands had been established. The advanced parties of most units are already on the move."

"You have to stop them, Ryan."

Ryan shook his head. "General, I believe that we have a chance to end this conflict now. With the help of the New Yorkers, who know the terrain and have a tactical advantage, I'm thinking we can defeat the UN forces and secure the city."

"Your orders are to wait for further instructions. The factions and Martin's forces will just have to bleed each other dry." Maxwell paused. "It's for the good of the nation."

"What about the people here who are trying to save their homes and their families?" Ryan looked over at the situation console. Carole stood there, pointing out routes into the city to the brigade operations officer. "We came here to save them and the world from a madman. Now we're just supposed to let them die?"

Angrily, Maxwell shouted, "Colonel, your orders are to hold in place. Go to hasty defensive positions and engage only in if fired upon."

"Sir, I protest this order. The other brigades will be here in less than twenty-four hours. We can end this if we act now." Ryan, shocked at being ordered to stop his attack, protested once more. "Victory is within our reach."

"The division has been taken off alert." Maxwell replied, "Stand down, or be relieved of command."

Ryan cut the link. He walked back to the communications station, pulling the plug on the display. "Sergeant Major, send this message to all units, voice only. Move into New York with all haste. Link up with your insurgent counterparts." Ryan took a deep breath and continued. "Our communications have been compromised. Any messages countermanding these orders will be ignored for the next twenty-four hours. Tell them I want the city secured ASAP."

Ben Neel and the rest of the staff looked confused. Ryan yelled, "Now!" He motioned Carole into the hallway.

"Go back to your mother. Tell her that she only has our support until tomorrow." Ryan saw the shocked look on Carole's face. "I don't understand why, but I've been ordered not to assist you. My troopers will do what they can to help right now. Tell her it's like the road to Lexington. I think she'll understand. I bought you some time, and me a court martial." Ryan pushed her toward the door. "Go."

It took less than two hours to deploy the brigade into Manhattan. Airborne troopers were scattered across the city in small units, each with a handful of locals to help guide them to targets. The UN Forces, used to police work and fighting against poorly equipped and partially trained troops were no match for the airborne soldiers. Many deserted, dropping their weapons, stripping off their uniforms and changing into civilian clothes.

Technos broke into the UN command net. They began giving false orders to surviving units. They placed functional UN forces in indefensible positions where the insurgent-directed NUS soldiers decimated them.

*****

"Biddle, can you do something for me?" Ashley looked over at the slightly built Techno. "There's no reason for more people to be killed. If you can break into the UN Command network, send this message – 'Flee for your lives. The end is near. Don't die for nothing. Save yourselves'."

Ashley smiled as Biddle's fingers flashed over his keyboard.

"It will delete every other message from the command center and play continuously." He looked over at his shift leader. "Another job well done. Can I go back to my video game now?"

The UN forces melted away in front of the 1st Brigade's assault. However, NUS casualties rose when they ran into the Kentucky Regular blocking positions around the UN Building.

Ashley increased the tempo of the attack.

Chapter 63 - Hard Choices

Slipping through the door to the Regular's Tactical Operations Center, Paine planted the bug behind the coffee pot. He stood motionless against the wall, invisible in his phototrophic uniform. Chatter from several Regular units indicated they were in combat with the 1st Brigade.

Josh watched the casualty reports flowing in. "It's only one brigade. We should be able to defeat them handily."

"They have help from the locals, about three thousand of them. The UN troops aren't standing and fighting. They're deserting in droves."

Staring at the operations officer, Josh thought, *I can't believe I'm going to lose to a ragtag bunch of civilians. How can they be beating us?*

Suddenly, the communications nets went silent.

"This is Colonel Flagehty, commander, 1st Brigade, 82d Airborne Division. Kentucky Regulars. I order you all to lay down your arms or be destroyed. You have five minutes to comply, and then the full force of the division will be brought down on you."

"How did NUS get the division here that fast?" Josh screamed at his intelligence officer. "You told me they couldn't be here for another forty-eight hours."

"Sir, our analysis showed ..."

Josh shot the major in the head.

If they captured him, he'd be tried and executed by either the UN or NUS. He considered his options carefully. Stepping over the dead staff officer, he went to the nuclear control panel. He considered launching missiles at the capitals of the world. His finger caressed the launch key. Then he formulated a new plan.

"Rachel, you and the rest get as far away from here as you can. I'm staying with my guards until the bitter end. Tell Colonel Daniels that command of the Regulars is his, and I want all units to fight to the death. Remind them of their oath." Josh shook his head. "Make sure he knows to get everyone at least one kilometer from ground zero." He pushed the key into the slot and turned it. "A tactical nuclear device has been activated. It will go off in," Josh consulted his watch, "exactly fifteen minutes. Make sure the doors to the General Assembly hall are locked. I want all those UN idiots to go with me."

Rachel saluted Josh and turned to go.

"Thank you for your service, good luck against the enemy." Josh watched them walk away, then hurried to the elevator. He thought to himself, *Idiots, they failed me. At least the nuke will destroy all evidence of my involvement in this fiasco. Now I'll have to find another way to take control.*

Shadowing his father down the hall, Paine typed out a message for Marcus. He slipped into the elevator as the doors opened, plastering himself to the back wall.

Josh told his personal body guards, "Stay here. No one gets in." They nodded and turned, pointing their weapons down the hallway. The doors hissed shut and the elevator began its descent.

"At least I'm still alive" Josh took a deep breath as the elevator doors closed. He felt a hard object pushing into his spine.

"Maybe not for long. I've been waiting for you, father."

Exploding into action, Josh swung his left elbow around at head height, connecting with Paine's ear. Paine fell back. He dropped to the floor, sweeping his father's legs out from under him. They both tried to get a killing hold on the other. Paine got behind Josh. He put a choke hold on his father's neck while wrapping his legs around his squirming torso.

"Not this time," Paine yelled as he fought to maintain his hold on Josh. "I'm not going to let you win."

Josh had kept up his fighting skills but couldn't escape his son. He gasped for air until darkness overcame him.

As the elevator slowed to a stop, Paine put plasticuffs on his father's wrists. Dragging him into the shelter deep in the basement, Paine closed and sealed the door.

Chapter 64 – Decisions

Marcus read the cut-off message. "Have target in sight. Evacuate building before..." He stared at the message, left the room, and headed for the operations center. He had to get to Paine. He heard footsteps pounding down the corridor. There were a lot of people coming his way, so he knew it couldn't be Paine. Pulling out his pistol, he waited. He saw Major Miller and her staff running down the hall. Marcus yelled, "Halt!"

The staff skidded to a stop, most hitting the floor with weapons at the ready. Rachel stood with open hands in the middle of the hall and spoke.

"I don't know who you are, but we have exactly thirteen minutes to vacate the building before it's destroyed." She consulted her watch. "A tactical nuke is ready to go off and we are running out of time. Show yourself."

That's the rest of the message Paine sent, Marcus thought. *Shit, now what?* "Everyone drop your weapons and stand up. Three assault rifles are covering you. In this hallway, no one will survive if you don't do as I say, now."

Rachel placed her carbine on the floor and stood up. "Drop them, and put your hands over your heads." One of Rachel's lieutenants stayed on the floor until she nudged him in the side with her foot. "Do you really want to die this way? Get up."

The lieutenant sheepishly put the weapon on the floor.

"All right, show yourselves." Rachel called out.

"Major Miller, I want you to think back to your early days in the Regulars. You were a good field soldier back then, when you hunted me down in the mountains of Utah." Marcus pulled the phototrophic hood back, revealing his scarred face. "You signed my death warrant after the mock trial General Martin held, and you watched while I died. Only I didn't die, and neither did the others. Paine is going after the general as we speak."

Rachel shook her head as if to clear the fog. "Where are the rest of your men?"

"It's just me." Marcus shifted his aim at the young officer looking at the weapon on the floor. "Don't think I won't shoot.

Major Miller, the general's wife is leading the resistance. She isn't dead, either."

"So, he's been lying to us all along. I wonder if he's really planning to die here."

"I kinda fucking doubt it!" Marcus exclaimed. "We need your help to stop the bloodshed. Come with me now, all of you. There's a lifter waiting outside the window. Major, I want you to send an all-hands message asking the Regulars to lay down their arms and wait to be contacted by the resistance or the 82d troopers. Tell them they'll be treated fairly."

"Marcus, first we need to warn every one of a nuclear blast that is less than ten minutes away." Rachel, visibly shaking, turned to her staff. "And we have to get the UN delegates out of the building."

"Let's move." Marcus began to sweat as he started a mental countdown in his head. He didn't have much time. He deactivated the phototrophs as he led the sprint to the bank of windows. When they neared the end of the hall, Marcus waved for everyone to stop. He pulled a detonator out of his pocket, pressing the trigger. The center window blew out and crashed down into the street. A heavy lifter appeared at the opening, and the staff jumped across the four-foot gap into the cargo bed.

"If I'm not back in two minutes, get the delegates out," Marcus ran back to the viewing room and picked up the large bag lying on the floor. He made it back to the window with twenty seconds to spare. Throwing the bag into the lifter, he jumped in after it.

Marcus and Rachel sent commands out over their command nets, ordering both sides to stop fighting and clear the area around the UN building. The lifter dropped to street level.

"Unlock the doors," Rachel yelled as she ran into the hallway. The UN delegates stepped back as she threw the doors open. The staff herded the delegates to the rescue vehicles landing outside the building.

Marcus waited until the last of the ambassadors and their support personnel were evacuated from the complex. He gave the signal to his pilot to leave. As they flew north, he saw people running away from the UN building.

"Paine, come in," he called over the network. "You've got to get out of there. Your father is going to destroy the building."

Nothing but static came through his earbud.

"Come on, brother. Answer me." His internal clock told him he only had a few minutes until the bomb went off. "Before it's too late," he whispered.

Broadcast over every network in New York and over all the military channels, the countdown to detonation continued. Vehicles landed, and everyone within five miles of the UN building took cover as the countdown reached zero.

Josh's guards were vaporized as the nuclear blast destroyed the headquarters of the United Nations.

"Dammit, Paine." Marcus couldn't stop the tears from running down his face.

Chapter 65 - Payback

Emergency lights flickered in the room. Paine coughed as dust settled to the floor. His ears rang as he got to his feet. Standing at the door to the bomb shelter, courtesy of the old Cold War, he looked at his unconscious father. He pulled Josh into a chair, attached restraints to his arms and dragged the chair to a storage closet. Slamming the door, Paine allowed himself a scream of triumph.

"Now what?" Walking to the red box near the door, he opened it to revel an old-style telephone. Surprised that he had a tone, he dialed the emergency number listed on the wall. 9-1-1.

It rang for what seemed like a lifetime. Paine, moving to hang up stopped when a voice answered. "May I ask who is using this antiquated communications device?"

"Paine Martin. I survived the blast. I need to contact Ashley Miller, ASAP. Tell her it's her son." Paine kept the phone to his ear, impatiently waiting for the call to be put through. It took more than five minutes before heard his mother's voice.

"Michael, thank God you're all right." Paine could hear the relief in his mother's voice. "Where are you?"

"In the basement bomb shelter of the UN main building," he replied. "I have father in custody. What do you want me to do with him?"

*****

Walking into the storage closet, Paine heard Josh groan. "It's going to take some time before they can dig us out, so we might as well talk. Be advised, I'm recording this conversation as evidence for your trial." Paine placed his communicator down on the table and stared at Josh. "Why did you do this? This is genocide. What in the world could you hope to gain from this?"

"The world itself. There are so many things wrong with the world. We don't learn from our mistakes, we keep creating the same kinds of ineffective and inefficient forms of government." Josh glared at his son. "I would have changed all that. The best thing for the future of our race is one man, making all the decisions, maintaining peace and order for everyone. I could have brought unity to the whole world and to the colonies. Don't you see that?"

Paine shook his head as if to clear it. "And to do that, you would kill anyone who doesn't think like you do. That's insane."

"No, it makes sense." Josh replied. "Eliminate the doubters and only the believers remain. You've seen this. You killed hundreds who were not following the rules laid out by the proper authorities. I sent you into multiple situations where you eliminated those who were not following the current government's directives."

"You're right. I did do those things."

"What makes you any different than me?"

"I never murdered people." Paine looked at his father with disgust. "Those I killed had a chance. They fought for what they believed in. I could have died as easily as they did. You murdered innocent people, people just trying to live out their lives. You gave them no choice. They had no means to fight back. War is one thing, murder is another. I admit I'm a killer, but you are a murderer."

"That man you ordered shot when you came to New York didn't stand a chance," Josh sneered at his son. "You are worse than I am. At least I admit I murder people. You hide behind your self-righteous attitude."

Paine stared at his father in silence.

"So now what's going to happen?"

"Mother and I have been speaking..."

"Ashley is still alive? I knew I should have killed her after Adam was born. Then none of this would be happening now." Josh launched himself out of the chair, slamming his shoulder into Paine's chest and attacked him with his feet.

Hitting the wall, Paine tried to catch his breath and protect himself from his father's kicks. His vest absorbed some of the blows, but he saw stars. Pulling the weapon Carley had given him, Paine pulled the trigger.

A web encased Josh. He dropped to the floor.

Pushing the second trigger, Paine watched his father writhing as fifty thousand volts pulsed through his body. He held the trigger down for longer than he should. He only stopped when the low-battery indicator flashed.

"I should kill you now. I won't do it."

"I always knew you were weak," Josh spat out though gritted teeth.

Picking up his father, Paine slammed him into a chair. He dragged him back to the table. Taking out his sidearm, he ejected the magazine and removed the bullets. Putting one round in the chamber, he let the slide go forward.

"You have two choices, choices you never gave those innocents." Paine contemptuously looked at his prisoner. "You can go on trial for the murders of thousands here in New York. You'll be turned over to the UN for the deaths of the delegates you killed and for the murders of President Brown and Secretary General Baum. My guess is you'll be convicted and executed after the humiliation of public trials." He placed the pistol on the table, then pulled a knife and cut the plasticuffs. "Or you can end it all now. There's one round. You have five minutes to decide."

Turning on his heel, Paine walked to the door. He gave Josh one more jolt of electricity. Out of power, the net fell off as the door hissed shut.

Josh picked up the pistol without hesitation, placed it under his chin and pulled the trigger.

*****

The efforts to get to Paine were painstakingly slow. A tunnel had to be bored from a nearby subway station. The teams operating the machinery were hindered by bulky radiation suits. When the rescuers broke through to the basement where the UN building once stood, Ashley waved everyone back, drew her pistol and turned the wheel that opened the vault. Paine met her at the door and whispered something in her ear. She waved the medical team forward, and they put a body bag on the stretcher. Paine quickly donned a radiation suit and followed the gurney to the waiting vehicle.

*****

Marcus carefully entered the sleeping chamber. He knew better than to disturb Katrina and rubbed his jaw as he thought about their first meeting. That thought caused him to chuckle, and he almost didn't stop the blow Katrina reflexively swung at the sound.

"Marcus, what the hell are you doing here?" He watched her smooth back her wild hair, thinking how beautiful she looked in the darkened room. "I thought you were still working on getting Paine out of the bunker at the UN."

"I'm glad to see you, too, my sweet." Marcus had to duck fast, but Katrina pulled the punch right before impact, so it didn't hurt too much. "Paine is fine. They'll be getting to him any moment now. I was just in the way over there, so I thought I would come see you."

She put her arms around his bull neck and gave him a sloppy kiss. "There, is that a better welcome?"

Marcus returned the kiss and then pushed Katrina to arm's length. "Do you remember my promise?"

Marcus saw a hunger for revenge come into those beautiful, almond-shaped eyes. "You brought me a gift, didn't you? Where is that bastard?"

Stepping out into the hall, Marcus dragged the whimpering Doctor Engle into the room. He felt no remorse as he dropped Engle on the floor at Katrina's feet.

Chapter 66 - A New New York

Colonel Flagehty stood in front of the communications screen in the resistance command center. He listened to his commander yell at him for a full five minutes.

Impatiently tapping her foot, Ashley kept making cutting signs to Ryan from beyond the pickup range of the camera. She got angrier by the moment. Finally, she'd had enough. Stepping into the camera's field of view, she put her put her arm around Ryan's shoulders.

"General, I appreciate your efforts to convey to my good friend here your displeasure. I think we've heard enough. I'm not going to release Colonel Flagehty to your military police. He has been granted political asylum here in the city of New York. We have the backing of the United Nations. They've recognized us as a sovereign state. If you like, I can send over the roll call vote taken just over an hour ago. It included a 'Yea' vote by the ambassador for the NUS. They really are thankful that we saved them from certain death."

"I insist that Colonel Flagehty be returned to NUS control at once." Maxwell shouted. "He's a traitor and will be punished. If you don't…"

Ashley cut him off once more. "By the way, Germany, Ukraine and Poland are sending volunteer soldiers to fill the vacant positions in the UN forces. They'll be here by the end of the week. They will provide us with protection until such time as we establish our own defense forces. So, unless you want to create an international incident, I suggest you leave my new military commander alone, he has a lot to do right now." She turned and put out her hand, "That is, if you want the job, General Flagehty."

Ryan saluted and then shook her hand. "It will be my great honor to serve you, Madame."

Chapter 67 - Changing Colors

Get General Martin's son out of New York, somewhere out of his mother's protection. SC

Not sure how I can do that. AC

Don't care. Do it or I expose you as a co-conspirator in the UN takeover. SC

It will be done. AC

*****

Paine looked out over the formation. He saw his A Company commander, Captain Chris Curtis, finishing his smoke as he waited for the unit to fall in.

Chris looked at his watch, snuffed out his cigarette and went to the rear of the formation.

Lieutenant Trisha Jones, the newly appointed adjutant of the battalion, marched quickly from the assembled blue-helmeted companies to the center of the parade ground. She passed Captain Curtis' A Company. Paine could see Chris had his eyes on her as she reached the center of the field. "Bring your units to attention and present arms."

Major Yuri Kompaniyets, a Cossack from the Ukraine and the battalion executive officer, took over the formation and ordered, "Colors, forward, march."

The staff and colors of the United Nations moved forward to the reviewing stand.

"Colonel Martin. Post."

Paine cringed as he imagined his father being hailed by a subordinate, then realized the voice called out his name. Reaching up, he fingered the silver oak leaf centered on his chest. Taking a deep breath, he marched forward to take over his unit.

Andre Chevalier, the newly appointed Secretary General of the United Nations, read the commissioning orders. "Today, we are activating a new United Nations Unit, the First Special Forces Battalion. Its mission is to protect the sovereignty the members of the United Nations any time peace and stability are threatened. Colonel Michael Paine Martin is hereby authorized to command the battalion."

The assumption of command went almost flawlessly, except when one of the UN soldiers passed out and fell on his face. The rest of the unit ignored him until the end of the ceremony. As medics carried the soldier from the field, Paine dismissed the unit.

Marcus grinned at his battalion commander. "We did it, Paine. We managed to live."

"Yeah, we managed to do just that," Paine looked for his mother. "I just hope things get better. I'm getting too old for this shit."

Snorting loudly, Marcus looked at the young man beside him. "You're only twenty-four, and a battalion commander. That has to be some kind of record."

"A guy named Pennypacker became a brigadier general at nineteen during the US Civil War. He's got the record." Paine saw the look on his friend's face. "I looked it up. I feel old, Marcus. I've been through a lot."

"Well, at least you got your father. I wish I'd been the one to do it. I really wanted it to be just me, him, and the guidon. I really would've like that."

Paine grinned, thinking about what damage could be inflicted by the long, pointy pole. "It doesn't matter now. He's gone." He walked toward the crowd waiting to congratulate him.

"Listen 'old man', I feel great. I don't want to squander what time I got left feeling sorry for myself. Let's shake a few hands, then find the girls and celebrate." Marcus laughed as they left the field. "Here's to life."

*****

In Radio City Music Hall, Miley Pickers stood on the stage in front of a growing crowd. When her mother fell ill, the Neo Luddites unanimously elected her their next leader. Slowly rocking back and forth, she used the ache in her injured leg to center her focus. Finally, she raised one hand to quiet the crowd.

She planned to fulfill her dying mother's wish.

"The mercenary leader Paine Martin cold-bloodedly ordered the death of Walter Chavez." Walter had been her mother's friend, one-time lover, and Miley's father. She took a deep breath to steady her voice. "You have all seen the transcripts of the communications between Martin and his ground forces. You know he ordered a defenseless man to be killed."

The cries of the people rolled over her like a wave.

"Now he works for the very same organization that killed many of our own people. We lost thousands of innocent men, women, and children to a plague the UN inflicted upon us. They hate us." Miley had to wait for the curses and shouts of anger to abate before continuing. "They would see us wiped from the face of the earth. Paine Martin is a part of this." She looked out over the large crowd. "You've heard all the evidence." Pulling a double-edged dagger out of its sheath, Miley raised it to the ceiling. "How say you?"

"Death," the crowd yelled as one.

Turning the dagger in her hand until it pointed toward the floor, she then held it out at arm's length. "From this day forward, Paine Martin is a convicted murderer, awaiting execution of his sentence. Any Neo Luddite who encounters him must, by lawful order, kill him. It is our way." Miley listened to the roar of approval. She whispered, "I will see justice done, father."

Chapter 68 – The Screw Turns

The chime kept ringing, even though the man slapped the off switch several times. He looked around his room. A small treadmill and a weight bench were in the center of the room. A monitor hung from the wall in front of a desk with a single chair. When he got up from the bed, it automatically closed into the wall, providing a little more space for him to move around. The alarm rang again. The monitor blinked off and on, signaling an incoming message. He toyed with the ides of destroying the alarm, but he slowly pushed the off button. Moving to the monitor, he touched the screen to activate the program.

A disembodied voice rang out in the close confines of the capsule. "Turn on exterior sensors."

The man touched the blinking icon. The screen came alive. He saw a piece of space junk not far from the capsule. Instructions appeared on the screen directing him to capture the disabled satellite and pull it close to the capsule. The object closed to within two meters.

An image appeared on the screen. The man's heart raced as he recognized the face.

"You disappointed me, General. I had great plans for you, but you had to ruin them. Didn't I tell you to do what I asked?" Corvis shook his head and glanced down at his notes for a moment. "I wanted you to control of the UN forces, not take over the UN. I would have made you famous, rich, and powerful. Now you're going to be doing nugg work for me."

Josh interrupted Corvis, "What exactly is a nugg?"

"Not unusually gifted guy." he yelled at Josh, "You acted like a complete idiot. You ruined what I set in motion."

"What do you want, Mister Corvis?"

"I want you to suffer, much like I am suffering now. You spoiled my plans. I have spoiled yours."

"I should be dead," Josh spat at the screen.

"I decided you wouldn't die. Not yet. I took it upon myself to put experimental nanoprobes in your system before you went on your little personal escapade. The only good thing that came from that is I now know they work."

"Glad to be of service." Josh could feel his frustration and anger getting out of control.

"I considered letting them have you, but I have to see how this plays out. You have no idea how hard it's been to keep from ending your miserable life. But that would have been too good for you."

"Thanks for nothing." Josh fought his rage, keeping his face impassive.

"Officially, you are dead. I confirmed your death with the UN. You'll be happy to know that they believe in your demise. Your son and wife identified the body at the bunker. They took you directly to the morgue, where you were cremated. They scattered your ashes over New York Harbor."

"If they burned my body, how can I be here?"

"The new nanoprobes kept you from dying. They're designed to repair extensive damage. I had them shut down most of your bodily functions until I could remove you from your family's loving embrace. I paid a lot to have the ambulance driver exchange your body with one of the honored dead from the Battle of New York." He bowed his head, placing his hands together as if in prayer. "The service, just a dust-to-dust, ashes-to-ashes verse or two then your children dumped the urn out. A touching, very short funeral."

"Why did you keep me alive?"

"Because I might find some use for you in the future." Corvis' face contorted with anger. Spittle flew onto the lens of the video camera. "You stupid fool! I had everything set up. The plan was perfect. The world would have one leader. Me."

"I understand now." Josh sneered at the screen. "You were using all of us to achieve your ends."

"Of course. You were just too stupid to see it."

"So now what do you have in store for me?" He imagined a bullet hole appearing in the center of Corvis' forehead.

"You'll be happy to know that Paine volunteered to join the UN military, to save the world from people like you. Many of your former soldiers went with him." Corvis laughed. "They actually like him. You'll be proud to know he's a good leader, despite your efforts to corrupt him. I plan to use him like I used you."

"He'll never do what you want."

"There are others who will make sure he's guided into the wrong place at the wrong time." Corvis opened his arms with a flourish, palms up. "His principles make him vulnerable. See what yours did for you?"

"I have no principles."

"That's correct, you don't." Corvis leaned back and folded his arms. "You have something worse, ambition. That made your actions predictable."

"If I'm so predictable, then why are we both in this situation?"

"I made one mistake." A grimace appeared on Corvis' face. "I won't make another one."

Josh silently stared at the screen.

"I have to go now. Remember, you are my personal dog. You'll remain chained until I decide to release you, and you'll do what I want when I call upon you."

"I'd rather die."

"Then push the red button above your sleeping cocoon. It will release the airlock. I promise you won't feel a thing." Corvis leaned forward. The screen went blank.

The thought of being controlled by Steven Corvis irritated him. He tried to kill himself once before, he could do it again. Josh caressed the red button that opened the airlock. He almost pushed it.

Death isn't the way. He'll have to release me to do whatever he wants me to do. When I'm free, I'll get even with everyone who blocked my path.

Taking his hand away, he began plotting his revenge.

New World Order
Book Two - World of Paine Series.

The plague that killed billions of people is over, but a more insidious plot is hatched, one that threatens the privacy of everyone on the planet. Michael Paine Martin joins the United Nations Military Force. His mission is to stop a potential war between Serbian guerrillas and the rest of Europe. Things go wrong. Steven Corvis, founder and CEO of the Corvis Foundation, attempts to establish control over the world. He enlists the aid of the sinister and vengeful General Josh Martin, Paine's father. Josh works with Corvis to destroy the United Nations and the recently established government of New York. Personal and political intrigue abounds in the fight between two conflicting ideas of the future of Earth – and who will ultimately rule.

J. B. Durbin

J. B. Durbin served in a variety of positions during his 23 years in the US Army, including mortar and infantry platoon leader, infantry company commander (twice), and battalion executive officer (twice) and Chief of War Plans for U.S. Army Europe. After retiring, he became a certified teacher and taught history and coached football at his local high school. Retired in Connecticut with his wife and three dogs, he spends his time playing golf, learning guitar and writing.